COMING BACK

By Tabitha J Arment

COPYRIGHT

DEDICATION

*This book is dedicated to my family and
friends who believed in me even when
I wasn't able to believe in myself.*

CONTENTS

PROLOGUE

I love this cafe. What with the fantastic coffee and the internet connection, nobody thinks twice about the amount of time that I spend here. Of course...I'm not here for the coffee. My interest in this cafe has more to do with its location than anything else. The apartment building across the street has been an obsession of mine for a year now. As the waitress walks by I wink to make her think I am here for her. Maybe she'll be next. First I need to take care of the inhabitant of that apartment. There is a sort of poetry in making her wait a year to end it all.

Her window is empty right now, but I know that she's in there. I can imagine her sound asleep in her bed thinking she is so safe. For a year I have let her believe this little myth. Every day I have watched her working to create a new life for herself. She has changed so much it's almost difficult to recognize her. She thinks she's created a safe little world for herself. I cannot wait to blow it up just like I did the *last one. It won't end there either. I will not rest until she is begging me to end her life for her. That'll be the best revenge. She thought she could take my world from me and I will make her pay.*

Crap! Damn car accidents! Why did it have to be here? It looks like nothing more than an inexperienced driver who lost control, but the police will be called anyway. Ah, yes. Here they come. I can already hear them. I'm sure the sound of sirens will wake her up. I hope it reminds her of what I did. Yup, there she is! She's already at her window watching and I can see her panicking. I love seeing that terrified look on her face.

Damn! The responding officer is someone I know. I love this cafe, but the giant window is leaving me too exposed. I should go. It doesn't matter...I know where she will be next and she's not going to be alone. Time to pay my bill and head home.

DAY 1

Veronica woke to the sound of sirens, and desperately tried to quell the panic attack that she could feel tightening her chest and stop the cold sweat that had started to permeate through her skin. She rolled over, seeking the warmth of Nick's arms only to be painfully reminded that he would not be there. He was taken from her on the same terrible night that left her home in ruins and soul traumatized. She forced the memories of that explosion to return behind the wall she had constructed in the back of her mind. Desperately working to regain control over her lungs, she took a moment to breathe. Then she climbed out of bed and went to the window.

The walls of her room were already splashed with flashing blue and red lights. She could tell by the pattern of lights that there was more than one squad car in the street, but she could not hear any ambulances approaching. She knew what she was going to see when she looked outside, but she peeked through the blinds anyway. If for no other reason than to give herself some peace of mind. She saw the accident in the street outside and was reassured that this had nothing to do with her past. With this knowledge firmly held in the front of her mind, bracing that wall that she had so carefully built, Veronica tried to go back to sleep.

Five minutes later she was back up and pacing the room, trying futilely to clear her mind. Veronica decided that this was a fruitless mission and changed into her running clothes. Rather than sitting in bed terrified she was going to try using some of her nervous energy. Veronica slipped on her well-worn running shoes. Feeling how they seemed to mold to her feet, she remembered her favorite running partner.

"Ace, come here boy!"

Her German Shepherd plodded around the corner ready to accompany her. This was not an unusual occurrence. All of Veronica's colleagues wondered how she stayed in shape, but none of them knew about the midnight runs that she had started taking once her leg could support her again. How they managed to miss the gray circles that spread out under her eyes was beyond her, but she liked that they did not ask any awkward questions. She took her usual route to the park near her apartment, and ran a few laps around it. She could easily run this on her own, but having been a police officer, she knew not to go out alone that late at night. Not wanting to bother any of her friends, Ace became her salvation.

As Veronica ran around the park, she relived some of her favorite memories of Nick. Falling deep into thought, her stride evened out and her breath came easily. The one that always came to mind first was how they met...

"Okay, I can do this. This is what the Academy was training me for, right? How bad could it be?" Veronica repeated this to herself, almost like a mantra while she changed into her uniform.

As she quickly threw on her utility belt she checked to make sure that she had everything on it and attached her radio. When she finished, Veronica joined her fellow rookies, Cheyenne, Jennifer, Andrew, and Tyler in the hall outside the locker room.

They all turned to walk to the briefing room together so they could receive their assignments for the day. They were joking and talking as they walked down the hall so none of them noticed when another man in uniform came around a corner, also headed to the briefing room.

Veronica had turned her head to say something to Tyler, so she accidentally bumped into the officer. She dropped her eyes and began apologizing profusely. When she finally managed to pull her focus back up, she was met with a wide smile and unnerving dimples. Ripping her attention away from his mouth, she was trapped by brilliant blue eyes. As her stammering came to a halt, she jolted free and dropped her gaze back to her shoes.

He spoke to the whole group, but his eyes were busy taking her in. "So...you must be the new rookies. Well, I guess you'll do."

His words finally managed to bring Veronica back to herself. She stood to her full height and gave him the most unabashed smile she could manage while looking straight into his eyes.

"Thanks for the assessment. I'm sure we'll meet your standards."

As she spun to leave, he leaned in and said, "You know you've got that on the wrong side, right?" He took one look at her mystified expression and knew she did not understand. He let his gaze drop to her radio and then fastened it on her eyes as understanding hit her.

She tried to quickly switch it, but became flustered and it fumbled from her grasp.

He smirked at her and bent down to pick it up. While fastening it to her belt he said, "Oh, yeah...I can already tell you guys are awesome." With that he turned and strode into the briefing room.

Veronica turned to her friends and asked, "Is it too soon to transfer?"

Ten minutes later, Veronica was sure that she had done something to piss off God. That, or she had the worst luck on the face of the planet. When it had been announced that her Training Officer would be Officer Nick Randle, she had looked around the room to see if she could identify him. She had been met once again by brilliant blue eyes and that dimpled grin that told her she was being laughed at.

This is going to be a very long day.

When Nick stood and beckoned her to follow him out to the car, she became aware of how handsome he was. Standing at just over six feet with strong arms and thick, dark brown hair, Nick Randle could make any woman melt.

Strike that... This is going to be a very long year.

It did not take long for Nick to warm up to Veronica. Within a few months the entire precinct was watching them.

After their shift ended one night, Veronica and the rest of the rookies were at a local bar having a beer. Then Nick walked through the door. Their eyes met and held as he walked across the room to sit with his best friend, Ben and their buddies.

"Earth to Veronica." Cheyenne's voice cut through her reverie.

Blushing, Veronica turned to her friend. "Sorry, what was it you were saying?"

Cheyenne shook her head, causing strands of blond hair to fall in her face. "Never mind that, we need to talk. I get what you see in him, but you know you can't go after Randle, right? He's your TO. TO's and rookies cannot date. It's against all the rules."

Veronica smiled and rolled her eyes. "It's not like that. He is my partner and my friend. That's all."

Cheyenne blew her hair out of her eyes and gave Veronica a knowing look. "Yeah, well, make sure it stays that way. At least until our probation is over. After that, you can do whatever you want, as long as you give me all of the details so I can live vicariously through you."

Veronica snorted, "Whatever."

Almost a year after they started, the rookies were deemed fit to perform their duties without a training officer. There was a short ceremony at the station. A moment for their staff sergeant to be able to discuss with them how much they have grown into their jobs, and formally acknowledge the end of their probation. The real party took place at Tim Finnegan's, the bar they all frequented after shift. Surrounded by the now familiar sounds of their colleagues' voices and the dim lights of the bar, the rookies partied well into the night. There were drinks all around and for once they were not the ones paying.

Amidst the festivities, Nick quietly pulled Veronica out of the fray and backed her up until she felt the wall behind her. "So, I've been thinking. You aren't my rookie anymore. So according to the rule book that Andrew seems to love quoting...we're free to do whatever we like." He had subtly shifted closer to her while he was talking, so that they were nearly touching.

Veronica's eyes darkened as she responded, "You know...I've been thinking the same thing." Having said that, she wound her fingers into the hair at the back of his neck, pulled him in and hungrily pressed her lips to his.

It only took a moment for Nick to respond and deepen the kiss. Pushing her more forcefully into the wall, he dragged his hands up her sides to tangle in her hair. It was only when both of them had become desperate for air that they finally pulled apart. The sound of their gasps was nowhere near loud enough to drown out the uproar of their colleagues behind them. Cringing, they separated and turned to face their friends.

Expecting to be told off by the other men and women in the bar, they were pleasantly surprised to see smiling faces and hear cheering.

Nick's best friend, Ben Becker, pushed through the crowd, "It's about damn time!"

The rest of the bar started laughing as Ben patted Nick on the shoulder.

Ben spun around and put his hand out. Barring his impeccably straight teeth, he yelled, "Alright! Pay up bitches!"

More laughter engulfed them, this time Nick and Veronica joined in.

As more and more money was grudgingly thrust into Ben's hands, Veronica stepped forward. "Did you have the entire station betting on us?"

"Yeah, pretty much." When he saw the ire enter her eyes he began to laugh. "Any idiot who bet against you two getting together tonight deserves to be fleeced."

Veronica began to laugh, but was quickly silenced when one of her friends, Mark, arrived in front of her.

His dopey face was being forcibly held in a disappointed frown. "Seriously, you couldn't have waited one more day? One more day and I would have been a rich man!"

Veronica was going to respond, but was interrupted when Nick pulled her aside and said, "Let's get out of here."

While their friends were distracted by Ben's antics, the two of them managed to sneak out the side door and into the night.

As she walked out, Veronica received a text from Cheyenne. "Details. First thing tomorrow."

Three years after her probation ended, Nick and Veronica were living in a home that he had inherited from his grandmother. He had put the property in both their names when she moved in.

But now she was worried. He had been acting strangely the last couple weeks. She knew that he was hiding something, but she could not fathom what it might be. In their entire relationship, they had never kept things from each other. Even when she was his rookie, he had always been honest with her.

The anger she felt, knowing he was keeping secrets, helped her to focus during her re-certification at the firing range. She had always been a good shot. Today she was exceptionally good. After earning top marks on the range and securing her certification for another year, she decided that it was time to go to Nick and demand to know exactly what was going on. She knew that he would never do something to intentionally hurt her, but she also knew that he was over-protective enough to try to hide bad news.

When she pushed into the hallway he

greeted her with his warmest smile. As always, his dimples managed to etch away at the worst of her annoyance. "You really know how to use those don't you."

Nick gave her his best "who, me?" look and shrugged his shoulders. "I don't know what you're talking about." Then he flashed the dimples one more time. "So...how was your shoot? Do I get to keep my partner or are you going to be strapped to a desk?"

She could not help but laugh at the question. "Do you even need to ask? My TO would expect a perfect shoot, and I wouldn't let him down."

Nick let out a deep, belly laugh as he slung his arm over her shoulders. "Your TO would expect perfection in general...and he wouldn't be disappointed." He pulled her further into him and spoke again with his voice rasping. "You are perfect." Before she could respond he pulled her to a stop and then moved to kneel in front of her.

"Nick...what are you doing?"

His eyes shone with a sincerity she had never seen before. "I know this means that we can't ride together anymore, and I'm sorry for that. But I'm not sorry I fell in love with you. You are the best thing that could have happened to me. The way that you always look for the good in people, even now that you've been on the job awhile...it amazes me. If you let me, I'll spend the rest of my life learning from you and making sure that that you're always happy."

He pulled a ring out of his pocket and held it up to her. His voice seemed to drop octave as he continued on in a deep, breathy whisper. "I've been carrying this around for two weeks." He gave a quick, obviously nervous laugh. "It's been burning a hole in my pocket. I can't carry it anymore...I have to know. Will you marry me, Veronica?"

Veronica opened her mouth to answer, but was interrupted by a barrage of gunfire.

They both flinched before they remembered where they were.

As it stopped, Veronica began to laugh, "Only you would think it's romantic to propose with the sound of gunfire in the air."

Fear and deep seeded hope filled his eyes as he spoke again with gravel in his voice. "Please, tell me that means yes."

Veronica's eyes glistened with unfallen tears as she nodded her head, her curls catching the light as they bobbed with the motion. "Yes! Of course!"

Nick expelled a breath as he slipped the ring on her finger. Standing up, he pulled her into a rib cracking hug and spun her around. "Come on. Everyone's already waiting at the bar to buy you a round. Let's tell them the good news. I think Ben might even win another bet off of this."

As Veronica started coming to the end of her happiest memories with Nick, she began to lengthen her stride and push to move faster. There was a familiar burning in her chest, telling her she should stop, but as per usual she ignored the feeling. She left the park and kept running with everything she had. Eventually she made it back to her apartment, but she did not go inside.

Instead, she loaded Ace into her car and drove to the cemetery. Once she parked, Veronica got out and ran on autopilot to Nick's grave, falling to her knees. Ace sat next to her and nuzzled her shoulder. He knew this location almost as well as she did, and he definitely knew what it meant to her.

Veronica would never doubt the intelligence of dogs. On nights like this, Ace was the only person that kept her breathing. Well...maybe not the only person.

Suddenly Veronica became aware of footsteps behind her.

"Fancy meeting you here."

She chuckled under her breath, "You need a new opening line."

"I know, but I like that one."

Veronica turned around long enough to acknowledge Ben as he came to a stop behind her.

He was having just as hard a time dealing with Nick's death as she was. They met at his grave often and spent time reminiscing and keeping Nick's memory alive.

Over the past year, he had become one of her best friends. With almost everyone else in her life, she kept a wall up around her and nobody even tried to touch her.

Ben was different. He knew when she needed someone to hold her hand or give her a hug, and he was always there for her.

He walked over to Ace and started petting him. "I decided that this time we could use some refreshments." Ben shrugged off his backpack and started rummaging through it. He pulled out a six pack of beer and set it on the ground. He opened a couple and handed one to Veronica.

"Thanks, after tonight, nothing sounds better than a couple beers." As she took a swig of her drink, Ben pulled a bone out of his bag and tossed it to Ace.

At the questioning look she gave him, he said, "What?! If we get a treat he should too!"

They started chuckling as Ace exuberantly gnawed on the bone with his hind end still in the air. He was holding it down so strongly, that his front paws were pushing the bone around in front of him, and Ace had to keep crawling after it.

Still snickering, she said, "Anything that makes him that happy is fine by me."

After a couple hours of laughing and talking to Nick's headstone, Ben became serious with no warning. He started picking at the grass at his feet and would not meet her eyes. "You know this has to stop, right? It's been a year...we have to at least try to stop coming here."

Veronica stared at the ground without reacting and finally said, "I know...I just can't yet. He was my whole life...I don't ever want to forget him."

"You don't have to. I know I never will. He was the best friend a guy could ask for, but he wasn't your whole life. There were so many of us that were there with you. Everyone at the station...we were your family. If you came back, we would all be your family again. Your medical leave of absence is almost over. Your leg is fine now. It's time to either come back or tell Blake that you're resigning."

Before she could snap back at him, Ben silenced her. For the first time since he had started the conversation, he stopped picking at the grass and looked her straight in the eye. "I know you've built a new life. I get why you don't want to come back, and I will stick to the deal we made, but I can't keep going to this cemetery and pretending he's still here. You shouldn't either."

When Veronica's unfocussed gaze remained fixed on Nick's headstone, Ben shook his head and stood up. "Call me whenever you want.

You can come over to my place whenever you need to, but don't expect to find me here again." With that, he walked away, leaving Veronica to mull over what he had said.

Noting her mood, Ace crawled over and rested his head on Veronica's knee. His comfort and warmth spread through her until it reached her heart.

"I know boy. You're as tired of these runs as I am."

She stood up and took a fortifying breath. In that moment Veronica decided to make a real effort to stop coming to the cemetery all the time. It terrified her more than she wanted to admit. She was not ready to say goodbye to Nick. She had spent every day since Nick's death avoiding this exact moment. Even when she was not healthy enough to be able to walk without a cane, she always found her way to his grave. But she knew that she needed to stop.

Her mother had been killed by a drunk driver when she was a little girl. That was one of the many reasons she had become a cop in the first place. Every drunk that she pulled over was potentially one less family destroyed. Her father never recovered, and eventually turned to the bottle to make himself numb. Veronica had been forced to raise herself, while her father drunk himself into a stupor every day. She was determined not to let that become her life. Still, Veronica had dreaded this moment for a long time.

When Veronica looked at Nick's grave, a well of sadness opened up inside of her and she did not know how to close it. She had fought for a year to keep a lid on it, but that lid had just been blown clean off.

"It's time my love. I have to leave now. I don't know when I'll be back, but I hope it will be some time... Oh God I can't breath!" Veronica fell to her knees and gasped for air.

How can I do this if I can't even bring myself to say it?

" I...love you so much. I will never...never forget you. I'm so sor-sorry. This is all my f-fault. If it hadn't been for me...you would still be here. I'm so so sorry! Please, please f-f-forgive me!" Her sobs filled the still air around her. She didn't want Ben to hear her and come back, so she covered her mouth and tried to steady her breathing.

Once she had regained control of herself, Veronica stood and picked up Ace's leash. "Good-bye my love. I will always love you." With that, Veronica started running as fast as her body could carry her, back to the parking lot. Even Ace was straining to keep up with her. She threw herself into her car and drove home. When she got inside and kicked off her running shoes, Veronica was hit by a sudden wave of fatigue so intense that she thought she would pass out right there. She managed to make it back to her room with just enough energy to climb into her bed, fully clothed, before falling into a dead sleep.

DAY 2

F ire...Sirens...Searing heat. It's like the whole world has ignited in flame and hate. The air is filled with the acrid smell of smoke and it's burning my lungs. Who is screaming? I look around to find the woman, but there is no one else here. I don't understand what's happening. I try to call for help, but I can't stop the screaming. The cry filling the night is coming from my own mouth. The sirens come closer and I can see the red and blue flashing lights. I should go get checked out and give my statement. Years of following protocol has ingrained that instinct in me, but I cannot make myself care. All of my attention is on the fire. Someone is asking me something...they're shaking my shoulders. What are they saying? I know that I should know who they are and what they are saying, but I can't think. Then suddenly I realize...

The sound of an alarm intrudes.

What?....

Veronica sits bolt upright in bed. "Just a

dream...just a dream."

She snoozes her alarm and falls back into her pillows, her exhausted body dragging her back into sleep. Before long, her alarm is going off again and she knows that she cannot ignore it this time. Gathering herself for the day to come, Veronica tries to find the motivation to leave her apartment. Rolling out of bed, she tripped over her shoes from the night before.

With that, she walked out of her room and started getting ready. She studied her collection of slacks and tops, selecting a pair of black pants and a pale-blue, button-up blouse. Once she had showered and gotten dressed, she looked in the mirror.

Veronica realized that she did not recognise the woman she saw there. She used to be a strong, confident woman with color in her cheeks, and flowing red hair that matched her fiery personality. The woman that she saw returning her stare was pale and mousy, with deep circles under her eyes that she usually covered with makeup.

Shortly after Nick's death, she had cut her mane of hair to shoulder length. She had thought to make it even shorter, but that would require styling it, which she did not want to deal with. At this length, she could throw it up into a pony-tail every day. She had also considered dyeing it, but decided that was just too much trouble. Even her eyes seemed to have less color than they used to. Nick used to say that they were the color of celery and sparkled when she smiled, but all she saw now was a dull green with no life behind it.

Looking in the mirror finally proved to her that Ben had been right. What she was doing was not healthy. She needed to start trying to move on with her life. More than that, she needed to start taking care of herself again. It was time that she started living; not surviving.

Veronica vowed to call Ben later and apologize. Her old habit of giving herself just enough time to slide into work with seconds to spare, was one of the few things from her old life that still persisted. She grabbed her car keys and ran out the door.

After Nick died, Veronica had been placed on a medical leave of absence to recover from her injuries. A year later, she was done with all of the physical therapy she had needed, and knew that she could pass the recertification. She had never done the psychological evaluation required to re-enter the force, because she could not imagine talking to a total stranger about her problems. Technically, she could come back anytime she wanted. She just needed to fill out paperwork and pass all the tests. Months ago, she decided that she was not returning to the police force. Even the idea of it used to give her panic attacks. She had not told her old boss that she was going to resign, but she was fairly certain he already knew.

She found another job to hold her over quickly. It was completely safe and a little boring, but it was what she needed. She always had a passion for art and one of her old friends worked at The Phoenix Art Museum, so she asked her if there were any openings. They had both taken a training course to become docents there after college, so Natasha had allowed her to come back to give tours. Now, it is the only thing in her life that does not feel empty. Being able to teach people about the art got her through the day. There was only one small downside; more a nuisance than anything else.

While entering the break room she literally ran into that problem; its name was James. He was the type of guy that never gave up, and he had been sniffing after her ever since she had arrived at the museum. In spite of the fact that she was clearly grieving and could barely walk at the time. He was not even deterred by the engagement ring that she still wore on her finger. Normally, she let him drop his lame pickup line then got on with her work, so as not to create drama with a fellow docent. Today however, she was simply not in the mood to deal with him. So she shoved past him before he even had a chance to open his mouth. This earned her a confused look, but she could not be bothered to apologize.

So she went to her locker and put her

things away. After making sure that it was secure and putting her lunch in the refrigerator, she went over to the bulletin board to check that day's schedule. There were no special tours expected, so it would be a normal day of guiding the few people that came in off the street. At least she would not have to deal with any high school students that were only there because they wanted to get out of class.

Veronica loved days like this, because she got to wander the museum when she was not doing tours. She got to stop by all of her favorite exhibits and study the beautiful artwork. Only when she was in this building, in the warm embrace of all of her favorite artists, did Veronica finally relax and almost enjoy her life again. She knew she had made the right decision about starting this job every time she got to eat her lunch outside on the grass.

This morning she decided to visit her favorite painting in the building. She loved all the ones by Joaquin Sorolla y Bastida, because her grandmother had given her a print of his as a child. It was like she could feel her grandmother's spirit with her when she was looking at his paintings. Today, she needed to talk to her grandma.

A shadow fell across the room, and Veronica turned to see Ben enter.

An uncertain grin spread across his face when he saw her sitting on the bench. "I knew

I would find you here...you always come here to think."

Veronica gave him a polite smile, and turned to look at the painting in front of her. "I was planning on calling you later. I should apologise."

Ben came to sit next to her, and shrugged. "Not necessary."

Without thinking about it, they leaned into each other. She pushed back against his arm, silently asking for comfort. He lifted his other hand and shifted, so that it came to rest above her knee.

They sat like that for several minutes before Ben broke the silence. "I know I shouldn't have given you an ultimatum like that, I just can't keep doing this anymore. My whole life has been at that grave site, ever since Nick died. I need you to know that even though I'm moving out of the cemetery, you will never stop being an important part of my life."

Before Veronica could stop them, tears started rolling down her cheeks. She furiously brushed them away. "Ben, you don't need to apologise. You were right. We both have to start living again...me most of all. I just didn't want to hear it last night." Veronica started shaking as Ben's arms tightened around her.

"Veronica...I know this is going to be hard for you. I want you to know that I'm here...no matter what happens."

The tone in Ben's voice made Veronica uncomfortable and she shoved out of his arms. "What the hell is that supposed to mean?"

He opened his mouth to answer, but was interrupted when Natasha entered the room.

"Veronica, you're up for the next tour. Be warned that old, handsy guy is back...Oh, sorry." Natasha stopped dead when she saw Veronica's desperate expression and Ben's apologetic look. "What have I stumbled into?"

Veronica rolled her eyes, "Nothing Tasha, Ben was checking on me...and now he's leaving."

Ben started to protest, but Veronica cut in before he could.

"Goodbye Ben. I'll talk to you later. Right now I have a job to do." She got up and left the room.

As she was leaving, Veronica heard Natasha saying, "Ben, you have a lot of explaining to do."

An hour later, Veronica had completed her tour and successfully avoided the older man with the wandering hands. Still she could not stop thinking about her conversation with Ben. She was torn from her reverie when she nearly walked into Natasha.

"Where are you today?...Or should I say, who are you with?" The suggestive quirk of an eyebrow made her innuendo perfectly clear.

"I don't know what you mean Tasha, Ben

and I were just talking."

Natasha laughed and responded, "What makes you think I meant Ben? Pretty defensive for someone who was 'just talking.'"

Veronica tried not to get angry at Natasha's assumption, but the lack of sleep and difficult night was making the fuse for her famous temper a tad shorter than usual. "Tasha, you know that it's not like that with Ben. Not only would it be so beyond weird, but Nick was the love of my life. It would feel too much like cheating on him."

Natasha backed a step away, "Calm down Ronnie, I was only joking. But you know...if you were ready to get back out there, Ben wouldn't be a terrible choice. Especially now that he's gotten over my rejecting him." Natasha grinned at her.

Upon hearing Natasha joking about the crush that Ben had once had on her, Veronica calmed down. Rather than continuing to argue, Veronica chose to just roll her eyes.

Natasha smiled and turned to walk back to her office. Before she opened the door she looked over her shoulder and said, "You know, it would probably feel a lot more natural than you think." With that she left Veronica behind and started shuffling through paperwork.

Veronica stood there in complete shock for several minutes.

I think Tasha's gone insane.

Dating somebody new seemed like sacrilege to Veronica. The idea of it, made her feel sick to her stomach. And to think that she and Ben were some kind of an item, was nuts. Ben was one of the only reasons she had made it through the last year, but there had never been anything romantic between the two of them. Veronica decided that Natasha had lost her mind, and pushed all of those thoughts away.

Crossing the parking lot after work, Veronica was lost in thought. Until she saw her car. The small, white note card stuck under her windshield wipers threatened to send her into another panic attack.

This cannot be happening again...

Logically, she knew she should call the police, but she had to be certain first. It would it be extremely embarrassing to call in all of her old colleagues for a false alarm. Her mind was screaming its denial, so she had to investigate the card. With a shaking hand, she reached to pull it off of her car. As she turned it over, she read the writing that was neatly printed on the other side.

"HELLO AGAIN."

Oh my God! No!

This is the moment I have been waiting for! She looked so at peace when she left work today. Now

all of it has been crushed again. She will never forget, and now she knows I won't either.

It would be so easy to end it all right now. One shot from a rifle and she would be down. But it'll be so much sweeter to drag it out. Every time I see her I want to make her pay...but I know the best way to make that happen is to make it last.

Oh, look! It's Natasha. She looks so concerned. Isn't that precious? She knows something is wrong. I get so much enjoyment watching the implications dawn on her. I'm sure she knows the whole story. After all...she is Veronica's best friend.

And the cell phone comes out! I bet I know who she's calling. Soon this whole area will be crawling with cops from the station. I should go.

I'll get you my pretty, and your little dog too!!

I like that...maybe I can use that in my next note.

Now my cell phone is going off. Gee, what a shock.

More sirens...more flashing lights. But Veronica did not notice. She had not moved since picking up the note. She knew she should say something...do something, but she could not. Two little words and a period were all that it took to shatter her mind into a billion tiny pieces. It was going to take a moment to make them all connect again.

After some time, she realized that she was surrounded by old friends. They all looked concerned and serious, but none of them were trying to comfort her. They knew that there was nothing to be said or done. They knew it a year ago and nothing had changed.

Finally, Veronica looked away from the note and took in her surroundings.

This isn't right.

Her two worlds had met and blended. Past and present collided in her mind making her head spin. She staggered, and everyone jumped to catch her before she hit the ground. Natasha, who had never left her side, was the first to get to her.

She helped Veronica to sit down and gently moved her hand towards a crime tech, so he could take the note.

Veronica was still comatose when Ben arrived.

Natasha knew that Veronica would not be able to say anything yet, so she got up to talk to him. "Ben, I'm worried about her. She hasn't said anything since I found her out here."

Ben stared over her shoulder to look at where Veronica still sat on the ground. He took in her appearance and noted that her skin was almost as gray as the pavement. "I should've known something like this would happen"

Natasha placed her hand on his shoulder to get his attention. "There is no way you could have known he would come after her again. We all thought that he was done with her."

Ben shrugged off her hand, unwilling to accept her comfort. "I should have known. That son of a bitch went underground right after...I should have known that when he came back he would go after her again."

Since comfort wasn't working, Natasha switched to stern. "Ben, you can't do this. She needs you not to fall apart right now. She needs you to catch him before he kills someone else. She barely survived last time. She won't make it if she loses anyone else."

Ben's frustration at the situation boiled over, but he answered in a whisper to keep their conversation as private as possible. "You think I don't know that! I know what it's been like for her. I've been there the whole time. I'm the one who's been meeting her almost every fucking night to give her someone to talk to. I know exactly what happens next if this guy hurts anyone else." With that, he walked past a stunned Natasha to go to Veronica.

"You know...if you wanted to see me again you could have just called."

A weak smile played on her lips, but it never touched her eyes. "What do I do now, Ben?"

He gave up trying to lighten her mood and sat down next to her, mirroring her posture. "You do the same thing you've been doing. You keep going...you keep living. No matter what this creep does."

Ben nudged her shoulder to catch her attention. "Remember the deal we made.You keep living and leave him to me."

Veronica sat in silence for a moment longer, then she suddenly went rigid. She had reached a conclusion. She knew what she had to do.

"No. I can't do that anymore. I tried to just keep living and look where that got me. He's back...and for some reason he is still fixated on me. I have to end this."

She stood up and walked over to a patrolman. After exchanging a few words, he led her to his car and they drove away. Leaving a baffled Ben to run the scene.

Two hours later, she was still arguing with her staff sergeant.

"Veronica, you know I want to help you, but it's been a year. I can't let you come back just like that. You would have to be cleared by a doctor and a psychologist before that can happen."

She furiously paced Staff Sergeant Howard Blake's small office. "Then set up whatever appointments you need to clear me! Either let me come back or I will do this on my own! I will not let this asshole waltz back into my life and fuck everything up again! It's been a year, and nobody is any closer to finding out who he is. I got the closest while I was on the force...I can find him now."

Blake was flooded with anger at first, but that soon melted into resignation. He knew that he could not stop her. No matter how hard he tried. She had always been headstrong. Now she was pissed.

As Veronica left Blake's office, she noticed Ben standing in the hallway. She melted against the wall, bending forward and rubbing her hands over her face. "I need to get some sleep," she groaned as she pulled her hair away from her face.

Ben walked over and leaned against the wall next to her. "You back?"

Veronica shrugged, "Not yet...not officially. Blake's gonna work on getting me cleared for duty tomorrow."

Ben nodded his head without responding. "Give me a minute and I'll give you a ride home." Before she could ask him what he was doing, Ben opened up the door and walked into the office.

Half an hour later, Ben returned. "Okay, let's head out." He walked away and Veronica stumbled to keep up with him.

"Wait! What was that all about?"

He kept walking while he pulled his car keys out of his pocket. "I was clearing something with Blake. If you are coming back, I'm going to be your partner. I know you were a patrol cop when you went on leave, but I've arranged to have you loaned to the detectives until we close this case. You can go back to the streets when this is all over."

Veronica finally caught up with Ben and blocked his path. "How on earth did you manage that?"

A slightly mischievous look entered his eyes, "I may or may not have started talking about stories from when we were at the academy together...He wasn't always the boss, and I just decided to remind him of his more...embarrassing moments."

Veronica began laughing, but sobered up quickly. Before she spoke again, she arranged her features into a stern look. "You know...normally I would be annoyed with you for doing that. But I can't imagine how uncomfortable it would be to ride with anyone else. Not to mention the fact that working with the detectives will make it easier to work this case. So...just this once...I'm gonna let you get away with that."

Ben laughed and threw his arm across Veronica's shoulders. "You don't let me do anything. Blake is making you follow my orders. He figures you're gonna be a bit rusty after a year and he doesn't want anything to go wrong. For now...I let you do things." Ben's face lit up with the most glorious smile.

Before Veronica could stop herself, she started to grin. But she quickly forced a scowl and punched him on the shoulder. "This is never gonna work. How am I ever going to take orders from you?"

Ben laughed, "Can you even fit into your uniform anymore?"

This earned him a swift punch to the ribs.

The joviality they had experienced in the hallway faded as Ben and Veronica approached his car. Veronica's car was still being torn apart by the crime tech guys and the bomb squad. As they drove towards Veronica's building, the tension level rose. They knew someone could be waiting for them.

"Are you sure you want to go back to your apartment?" Ben's concerned look only served to annoy Veronica.

"Yes, I'm sure. I decided in the parking lot that I am not going to let this guy push me around anymore. Last time, when Nick...I left my whole life behind. I got a new job and moved into a new apartment that's in my dad's name, and he still found me. This time I'm not going to be caught off guard. If he comes after me again, I'm gonna be waiting for him."

As if her statement had confirmed something for Ben, he nodded his head and continued to drive.

Ben pulled over in Veronica's parking lot. She hesitated as she opened the door. "Thanks for everything today, Ben. I know this can't be easy for you either."

He grinned and playfully punched Veronica in the arm. "Yeah, yeah...leave before you start getting all mushy on me."

Veronica resolutely pushed herself out of the car, and marched to the door.

He shook his head and pulled out his phone. After dialling a number that he knew all too well, he started speaking. "Hey man, do you mind stopping by my place and feeding Charlotte...Yeah, I know it's late... Dude, she's just a cat... just go refill her food and water. I have some surveillance to do tonight...Thanks man."

"No problem, Ben. I just left the station so I'll stop by your place on the way home. Keep her safe for us..."

That was too close. I almost laughed at his stupidity while he was still on the phone. Sometimes I wonder why I bother surveilling when I would be invited in anytime I wanted.

Asshole's too dumb to notice me sitting across the street. Only this time I'm watching a truck, rather than the window three floors up.

I should probably leave before he gets out of the car to take a look around. Gotta go feed Charlotte. He has too much affection for that damn cat.

For a full hour after Ben dropped her off, Veronica searched her apartment, looking for hints that someone had been there. There were no creepy notes, bombs, or anything at all out of place. With that knowledge held firmly in the front of her mind, she started making dinner. Tomorrow was going to be a big day for her and she needed a decent meal and a full night of sleep for once.

As she was putting food in the microwave, Veronica remembered something she had to do before tomorrow. Walking back into her living room, she picked up the phone and hit 2 on her speed-dial.

After a moment, Natasha picked up the phone with a frantic "Finally! What the Hell is going on!"

Before she could help it, Veronica laughed. "Calm down Tasha! I'm fine. I do have a favor to ask though."

Without even taking a moment to think about it, Natasha responded. "No problem. What's up?"

"It looks like I'm gonna need to take some time off at the museum. I'm gonna go solve this case."

There was a long pause on the other end of the line. "Okay...I need you to promise me that you'll be careful. I saw what this did to you last time, and I need to know that you're going to get out of this in one piece."

Veronica huffed, "Why does everyone think that I'm this pathetic headcase...Never-mind... Don't answer that. I promise I'll be fine this time."

"Okay, then take all the time you need."

After hanging up the phone, Veronica continued to pace her apartment, trying to settle her mind. This lasted so long, that even Ace abandoned her to curl up on the couch and sleep. She decided that the best way to calm down would be to follow her normal routine. Retrieving her dinner from the kitchen, she sat in front of the tv. Unable to focus, so she could not to decide what to watch. She just kept scanning through the options.

Finishing her food, she turned back to pacing her living room. Eventually, she decided to go to bed and wait for sleep to come.

For what felt like hours she counted sheep, blessings, and rotations of the ceiling fan, but her mind simply would not stop spinning. Every sound had her sitting bolt upright in bed. And every flash of light sent a rush of adrenalin through her system.

She was not making any headway. Because she had decided not to go back to the cemetery tonight, there was only one other place she could go.

Making up her mind, Veronica jumped out of bed and searched for Ace's leash. Once she found it, she tiptoed over to her couch and lifted up his head. Placing it in her lap, she started smoothing the furrowed brow that he always adopted when Veronica started messing with his sleep.

"Ace buddy, I have a little treat for you. We're gonna go visit your bestest buddy Charlotte."

With bleary eyes, Ace looked up at her. He started wagging his tail, and she knew that he was glad not to be going running again.

She attached the leash to his collar and went to grab her keys. "Damn! I still don't have my car!"

Do I find some other way...or do I stay here?

At that moment, a bird flew by her window and startled her.

Yeah, I'll walk if I have to.

She quickly exited her apartment and locked the three deadbolts that she had installed shortly after moving in. About a minute after she left her building, a truck pulled up next to her.

"Do you have a death wish, or are you an idiot?"

Before embarrassment set in, she turned it back around on him. "What the hell are you doing here!"

A sheepish look crossed his face, and she knew exactly what he had been doing. He had been sitting in his damn truck ever since he dropped her off.

"Well, unlock your doors and give me a ride then. I was headed to your place anyways."

He looked amused and said, "Oh really! What about all that 'I can do this on my own' crap?"

It was her turn to look sheepish this time. "Yeah...well...I'll be tough tomorrow. Right now I need to get some sleep. Besides, Ace's been missing Charlotte."

At that, Ben laughed and unlocked the car for her. "Ace, don't slobber all over her this time! I still have claw marks from the bath I had to give her last time."

When Ben opened his front door, Ace ran gleefully into his house and started searching for Charlotte.

Ben stood bemusedly watching, "Man, he really loves that cat."

Veronica walked in behind him. "They grew up together! It's like they're siblings."

She stumbled into his living room and crashed face first onto his couch.

"What do you think you're doing? I thought you said you needed sleep. You and I both know that you're not getting any on that couch. You're insomnia is way too bad to have easy access to a television."

She flipped over on her back and stared at him with an annoyed expression. "Well then, what would you suggest?"

He rolled his eyes and pulled her legs off the couch so that he could sit next to her. "Well...I suggest that you drag your sorry butt up those stairs and sleep in my room. I'll take the couch this time...Just know that next time you show up here in the middle of the night, you're on your own."

She giggled, but refused to move. "I'm not going to kick you out of your bed, Ben. I'll be fine here."

He took his chance and pushed her off the couch. "No you won't. Don't make me carry you up those stairs. I don't want my partner falling asleep all over the place tomorrow."

Veronica picked herself up off the floor and lunged at Ben. The next few moments were a mess of limbs and laughter as Ben and Veronica wrestled on the couch.

Without warning, the wall that Veronica had been holding up all day fell apart, and so did she. Her laughter became sobs, and her shoves became weaker and weaker. Eventually, their game deteriorated into her sitting on the couch and crying while he held her.

Ben knew that she needed his solidity and strength, so he held her without comment. As they sat on the couch, her breathing slowed and her body relaxed. Before long, both she and Ben were sound asleep and for a few hours, did not have a care in the world.

DAY 3

Fortunately for both of them, Ben still had his cell phone on him when they fell asleep. As his alarm went off, confusion caused them to cling to each other, before they realized where they were. Disentangling themselves, they tried to act as casual as possible, but eventually Veronica's calm exterior fell.

She wiped a tear from her eye. "I'm sorry, it's just that I haven't woken up next to somebody since..."

Ben tossed a pillow at her to break the tension and said, "I know, but hey...at least you slept. Now let's go get you certified to work again."

Suddenly she looked worried. "Right...that...you do know I have to talk to a psychologist, right?"

He grinned, "Yeah... they're never gonna let you carry a gun."

She tossed the pillow back at him.

"Haha...very funny. I thought partners were supposed to have each others' backs." At this, he grinned again and walked upstairs.

She was about to follow him, when she heard the shower turn on and backtracked. She started to feed Ace, saying, "So not going there."

In a few minutes, Ben sauntered back down the stairs, wearing a midnight blue shirt with the sleeves rolled up to his elbows. His short blond hair was still wet, and the five o'clock shadow he had been sporting before was now cleanly shaven.

As Veronica watched him walking towards her, she could not help but notice how his shirt clung to his muscles, and how he still glistened faintly from the water on his skin.

He noticed her appraisal, "We couldn't both go in wearing the same clothes we wore yesterday...people would talk. You know... if you wanted to change, I think I have a few things you could borrow that have been left here over the years."

Not taking the offer seriously, she laughed as she tried to come up with a retort. "Thanks, but I don't think I want to be wearing anything that one of your...umm...dates left here."

He let out a sarcastic snort and tossed something satiny and purple at her. "At least change your shirt. Ace drooled all over yours last night."

Veronica looked down at her own pale

blue shirt and noticed the spots on it that Ace had left behind. "Give me a sec." Then she turned and walked into the bathroom.

After putting on the button-down blouse Ben had given her, she turned and looked at the mirror. Immediately, she was struck by how different she looked in a day. The deep purple of the blouse set off the red of her hair and brought out the color in her cheeks. It clung to her curves enough to enhance them without looking slutty, and showed off a hint of cleavage.

I haven't let myself look this good in a long time.

She looked at her own shirt sitting on the counter. She knew that a simple washing would set it right, yet she hesitated. After only a moment of indecision, she picked up the shirt and tossed it in the trash bin.

Grabbing her purse, she walked back out into the hallway. As she turned the corner, she caught Ben staring at her with an awed look, before he was able to school his expression. She racked her brain for a way to ease the tension in the room.

"How is it that one of your dates left your house without her shirt?"

A mischievous grin lit up his face again, "Maybe one day you'll find out how distracting my presence can be."

She looked scandalized as she picked his keys up off of the table and tossed them at him.

In what felt like no time at all, Veronica and Ben were standing side by side at the entrance to the station. Mustering her courage, she pushed through the door.

"Well, it's now or never."

As she entered the room, she was inundated with a rush of old friends and colleagues wishing her luck and congratulating her on returning. Cheyenne and Tyler were the first to hug her. Andrew and Jennifer had both transferred to other precincts, or they too would have pulled her in for a hug. She glanced across the room and caught Erica's eye, who gave her a curt nod. Coming from her, that was the equivalent of blowing a kiss across the room, so it kind of blew her away. In public, Erica had always played the role of the division's "Ice Queen," so Veronica had expected to be ignored until later. After that, she was assaulted by many of her old superiors as they came forward to welcome her back. Jack had always treated her like a daughter when she was there. The tears forming in his eyes were enough to have her doubting whether or not she could get through this while keeping her own eyes dry.

She was so busy trying to thank all of them and politely get them to leave her alone, that she did not notice when someone crossed behind her. After accidentally backing into them, she turned to apologize. Recognizing her old friend, she went in for a hug instead.

Mark kept a stern expression on his face. "Only you would think it is okay to walk into someone and not apologize."

She stared at him, flabbergasted until she noticed the corners of his mouth ticking up as he fought to hide a grin. Eventually, he gave up and cracked a smile that lit his eyes. "It's nice to see you back here again, Veronica. The place wasn't the same without you."

She gave him a quick hug in thanks, then headed over to Blake's office.

It took almost all day for the psychologist to be satisfied that Veronica would not fall apart working again. Then another two hours before she could prove that she was still physically up to doing the job. After that, all that was left for her to do was a mountain of paperwork.

When she finally left Blake's office, she found Ben leaning against a desk, clearly bored out of his mind. She laughed aloud at the stir-crazy look in his eyes. His hair was sticking up in odd places, like he had been running his hands through it all day.

"Do you know how long it's been since I've spent this much of my day sitting in this building?"

She knew he was joking. Since he had become a detective, she knew he had been spending more time at his desk then he would have liked. Not enough to make the job boring, just enough for his mother to stop being terrified every time her phone rang. His mother was a high school math teacher, and had never understood why her son had chosen such a dangerous profession. Ben had enjoyed his time as a patrol cop, but when a position had opened up as a detective, he could not let the opportunity pass.

Veronica had met him at the same time she had met Nick. In fact, he had witnessed the radio incident, and still brought it up every once in awhile when he felt the need to embarrass her. Ben had always been intelligent and observant. That, and his natural ability to lead and put people at ease, made everyone sure that he would rise in the ranks quickly.

After achieving his promotion, he had often requested that Nick and Veronica work with him. He knew they were good investigators, and he missed the camaraderie he had with the uniformed officers.

They had all been working together, when Veronica made a discovery that had given them a huge lead in a case where everyone was coming up empty. It had also gained her the attention of the higher-ups, putting her on the fast track for becoming a detective as well. Unfortunately, that same discovery had led to Nick's death, and all of the other repercussions that followed.

Now that she was working with him again, she was worried that she would not be able to shake the memory of Nick. However, she was more worried that if she did not work with him, she would be stuck in a squad car not working the case at all.

Taking a steadying breath, "Well, it turns out I'm not crazy. You still willing to be my partner?"

Staring at the badge and gun that were now attached to her belt, Ben also took a deep breath before answering with, "Wouldn't have it any other way."

Confusion dominated Veronica's thoughts as Ben led her back out into the parking lot, rather than to the detective's office. She did not understand what they were doing.

"Shouldn't we be getting started? The sooner we figure this out, the sooner it'll all be over."

Ben tossed a slightly irritated look over his shoulder. "Do you have any idea how long that took? The day is over. We can start our investigation, but if you stay here all night on your first day back, they will yank that badge away faster than you can blink. If anyone even starts to think that you're unhealthily focused on this, you'll be done. I kind of set up a makeshift office awhile back that we can use for now. But I'm telling you that tonight is all about getting reacquainted with the evidence. We are not staying up all night so that on your first official day back, you fall asleep in front of the boss. You're going to be under a magnifying glass for the foreseeable future, so we have to play it safe." With those words he turned around once more and escorted her to the truck.

As they drove to the office that Ben had mentioned, Veronica started to recognise the route they were taking and dread filled her body. She suddenly knew exactly where they were going, and she knew that no amount of preparing could make her ready for what she was about to face.

She was going home; her old home at least. As they turned the corner onto her old street, Veronica saw the burned-out husk that used to be the home she shared with Nick. With all of the bad juju floating around this property, it had never been bought. So now, it stood as a sort of memorial to the officer that had lost his life there.

"Why did you take me here?", was all she managed to croak out as her throat had gone suddenly dry. She could not understand why someone who claimed to care about her would be taking her back to this place.

Ben glanced over to her, an apology written all over his face. "Long story short; I've been continuing the investigation into Nick's killer on my own, ever since it went inactive. This seemed like a fitting place to work from."

With that, he pulled into her old driveway, exactly where she had parked that night, and got out of the car. "After you left, no one ever came here, not even the homeless people. I don't think it's safe to be in there for too long, so I've set up in the backyard."

Veronica could feel her breath coming faster as she stared at the charred remains of her home. With her vision narrowing and throat tightening, she thought she was going to pass out.

When Ben's door slammed shut, she jumped in surprise and instinctively reached for her gun. Before she could draw it, she shook free of the panic and started counting her breaths to give herself something to focus on.

Once she felt she had gotten herself back under control, she forced open her own door. With a shaking hand, she unbuckled her seatbelt and jumped out of the cab in an awkward tumble.

As Veronica entered her backyard, she tried desperately to quell the memories that were still bubbling to the surface of her mind. That became easier to do when she saw the shed in the corner of the yard.

We didn't have a shed.

Ben walked straight to it and opened the door. "After you."

She walked past him and into the shed. As Ben turned on a few lamps, she felt as if she had entered one of her nightmares.

One wall was covered with pictures and documents, all having to do with the man that had killed Nick and so many others, but none of them held any answers. It took all of her self control and the knowledge that there was someone standing right next to her, to stop herself from curling into a tight ball on the ground.

"Without anyone out there gathering new evidence, there hasn't been anything new lately. Basically, the only thing you haven't already seen is the analysis of the bomb, and the card that was on your windshield."

The apologetic look intensified. He was starting to wonder if it had been a mistake to do this. She was clearly struggling to hold herself together.

Veronica closed her eyes and focused on her breathing again. She stopped listening to Ben talking, because she already knew everything he was saying, and fought to control herself.

She slipped the ring she had been wearing on her thumb off and flipped it between her fingers until she could think straight. Regaining composure, she started to take a more calculated look around the room.

Interrupting Ben, she went to the professional side of her mind, treating this like one of the cases that she had worked with him in the past.

"Why don't we start from the beginning.

It's been a year since I've looked at any of this stuff, so I'm bound to be a bit rusty on some of the details."

Remembering where she was, her professional demeanor cracked and her eyes began to glisten. She turned to Ben, "Do you have copies of this stuff?"

He turned and pulled a thick file out of a cabinet and held it out to her.

After snatching it from him, she left and returned to his truck. She fixed him with a stare when he climbed into the driver's seat. "I won't work here. This was my home. If you ever bring me back, I will tell Blake that I don't want to work with the detectives, and I will go back to the streets. I will work this on my own. Understood?"

With anyone else, Ben would have rankled at the command in her voice, but looking at her, he saw the same authoritative, pain-in-the-ass that she used to be, and he was glad for it. He started the engine and asked her where she wanted to go.

In the end, she decided to go back to Ben's house. It was the only place she could think of where they could work in private, plus it had the added benefit of being near Ben's kitchen. He had fantastic taste in food. Ace was also still there, so she would have to go back to collect him before she went home again anyway. This time, she was determined to stay the whole night in her own apartment. But before she could do that, she needed to clear up one thing.

"Did I pass your fucking test?"

If possible, Ben's expression seemed to be getting guiltier by the second. It had been a while since he had looked her in the eye.

"If you could get through that and not have a panic attack, I don't need to worry about you while we're out there."

She nodded and the rest of the trip was made in silence.

When they got back to Ben's place, they were greeted by an overly-exuberant Ace jumping all over them. Veronica was grateful that she had clipped Ace's claws as she felt them raking down her legs. After getting him to calm down and giving him some food, Veronica went to the coffee table in the living room and started to clear it off.

Once she was finished, she began pulling pictures and documents out of the folder and started to organize them. As she was looking through the evidence, both new and old, she began to fall back into the familiar pace of working a case. She let this feeling take over, so that she could hold up the pretence of objectivity. As she sorted through the evidence, she flashed back to what sometimes felt like another lifetime; when she was first introduced to this monster.

Ben Becker rushed into the briefing room and pinned a new picture up onto the cork board. "Ladies and gentlemen, we have another. We just received the email. Our lab techs are checking out the video as we speak."

A new urgency filled the room as people began to prepare themselves for what would come next. Veronica had recently taken time off to visit her father in New York to tell him about her engagement, so she had yet to be involved in this case. Of course...she had heard all about it.

For the past week, the Phoenix Police Department had been receiving anonymous emails. The first had contained a picture and a web address. All of the subsequent ones had been anonymous jeers and taunts. After checking the web address, detectives had found a live video of a woman that appeared to be buried alive. They had already been forced to watch her suffocate as they futilely searched. Now it appeared that they had another.

As of yet, they didn't have anything to go on. There was nothing to identify the woman or her location in the video. It was only after she expired that a name had been anonymously sent to them so that they could inform her family. They still had not found her body. Every cop on the force was itching to get their hands on whoever was doing this.

With the new video up, they were all partially terrified that they would not be able to find her, and partially excited with the possibility of new evidence. As everyone flurried about the room getting ready for Ben's briefing, Veronica retrieved the file that she had received earlier that day, and went about familiarizing herself with the case. The sinking feeling in her stomach got worse and worse as she dug deeper into the provided information. As her pessimistic side took over, she pulled her necklace out of her uniform and began spinning her engagement ring around. Trying to force some happier thoughts into her mind.

As Ben pulled the video up on a computer in the front of the room, he began to speak. "So far, all we know is that someone, a man judging by the profile, has now abducted two women and buried them alive in an undisclosed location. This guy wants attention. He's calling us out and asking us to try to catch him. He thinks that he's smarter than us. Let's prove him wrong this time."

When the video finally came up, everyone in the room sucked in a breath. They were shown a video of a woman, clearly terrified, in a small box that had dirt filtering in from cracks in the corners. Everyone went pale as they realized that this video was the same as the first. There was little chance that they would be getting any new information from it.

As Ben was moving the mouse to the side of the screen, Veronica noticed something. She could have imagined it, but she had to be sure. She quickly got up and walked over to Ben. "Move over for a sec?"

He gave her a quizzical look, but said nothing as he slid away from the keyboard, allowing her access to the computer. She took hold of the mouse and slowly scrolled across the screen again. When nothing happened, she took a deep breath and tried one more time, focusing on a different area. Sure enough, for a brief moment, the cursor morphed into a hand. She held her breath and went back to that spot.

Ben gasped and eagerly moved back in to take control of the computer. "Look alive people! We've got something new!" Taking a moment to make sure he had everyone's attention, he clicked on the hidden hyperlink.

They were greeted by several images that were obviously meant to infuriate them. The first few were jpegs of recent news articles. All which had headlines like "Clueless Cops Still Stumped." There had been several articles lately that talked about this case, and how the cops were no closer to solving it than they were when they got the first email. Looking around the room revealed a large amount of faces changing color as their anger grew to a new level.

This guy was cocky.

As the next message scrolled across the screen, several of them jumped up in rage, wishing they had someone to pummel.

"THOUGHT YOU COULD USE SOME AS-SISTANCE."

Veronica's mind clouded over with fury as she watched all of this. In a moment, all of that was forgotten as her mind went blank in shock. A new video popped on the screen, but this one wasn't live. In fact, no one knew what to think of the video at all.

The video showed a woman walking down the street at night. The person filming was clearly sneaking up behind her and getting closer. In almost no time at all, a hand reached out from behind the shot and wrapped around the woman's face.

This is when they all noticed the white piece of cloth in the mystery hand.

The woman struggled for a moment and then went limp. As the man lowered her to the ground, they finally got a clear shot of the woman's face.

Everyone leaned away from the screen as they realized this face did not belong to the most recent victim. Nor did it belong to the original victim, Sylvia Clark.

"MORE TO COME."

The screen went black as the implications dawned on all of the cops in the room. The killer had not one, but two women...and this time he was going to walk them through the whole thing.

Exactly twelve hours later, they received another email.

The subject line on this one had read, "NEED MORE?"

With their hearts in their throats they watched another video. This time they saw a man digging in the middle of the desert, depositing a coffin sized box into a large hole, and then covering it back up again.

As Veronica watched, a memory stirred, but she was unable to fully pull it to the front of her mind. Disturbed that such a horrifying moment could remind her of something from her own life, she decided to ignore the feeling and continue working the case.

When her shift was officially over she went back to Nick's house and continued to pour over the videos. She knew she would never sleep anyway. This case was keeping everyone up at night. Even Blake, who was about to be promoted to Staff Sergeant, was looking a little worse for wear.

Having already watched the earlier videos many times, she focused on the most recent two that had come in. She was sure if she concentrated enough she would be able to find something useful in one of them. But all she managed to achieve was falling asleep at the dining room table, with her laptop still open and playing the videos in front of her.

When Nick staggered exhausted through the front door later on, he found her still asleep. He was far too tired to pick her up and he did not have the heart to wake her, so he grabbed a large blanket and pulled a chair up next to her. After placing the blanket over both of their shoulders, he fell asleep hugging her in a grip that would not let up.

Just before he lost consciousness, he heard Veronica talking in her sleep.

"Bad baby pie, please."

He let out a silent chuckle and then his world went black.

I'm sitting in that diner from that movie The Waitress. What am I doing here? Whatever, I've had weirder dreams before...at least the diner isn't on fire.

As Keri Russell, wearing her costume from the movie, arrives at my table I give my order and she walks away again. I start to relax, because I haven't in so long. I know there is something else that I am supposed to be doing, but I can't be bothered right now.

Keri Russell comes back to my table and sets my pie down. "Why won't you see me?" Her voice is begging me to understand her.

I stare at her, confused because I can't imagine what she could be talking about.

The next thing I know we're walking down a dark street. I recognize this scene, but I can't figure out why. I'm about to ask her what is happening, when a man comes up behind her and holds a cloth to her mouth. Keri struggles at first, but in moments she is lying limp on the ground.

As I look at her face, it suddenly morphs and I understand.

"Can you see me now?"

Veronica sat bolt upright, so fast she knocked Nick off of his chair.

"What the Hell!" he yelled in surprise, scrambling to get back up.

Quickly, she grabbed him and said, "I figured it out!" She woke up her laptop and queued one of the videos to start. She stopped on the image of the woman lying on the ground.

"Look at her clothes...she's wearing a uniform!"

That was all it took. Nick had taken his phone out and within a few hours they knew where she worked, and it did not take long after that to figure out who she was.

Her name was Jennifer McCordell. Finally they had a clue.

While the detectives were following up on the lead she had provided, Veronica and Nick had been forced to go back to their job as patrol cops.

All day in the car, they went through the case over and over again, looking for something they had missed. They only had a few hours left to find the latest victim or they would be too late. Every cop in the city wanted to solve this case.

Veronica had given them something to work with, but she still felt like she should be doing more. She was missing something important and she knew it.

   They had not been able to save Jennifer McCordell.

Nor did they save the many women that came after her. It took almost seven weeks for Veronica to finally figure out what she was missing.

She was watching all of the videos again, as she did most nights, and it finally dawned on her. The video of Jennifer being buried got her there. She understood.

She had been there before, or at least somewhere near there.

When she was a teen, she had gone hiking with her grandfather most weekends. They had climbed the mountains in the background of that shot at least a hundred times.

It took some time, searching through pictures, but finally she found one with the same mountains silhouetted in the background. Luckily, her grandfather had been anal and labeled the back of all of his photos.

Two days later, the PPD was digging up women's graves in the middle of the desert, and it was all because her grandfather believed that she was not spending enough time outdoors as a kid.

She felt proud that she had provided vital information, and that they were now that much closer to catching the man, but she also felt sick. Of course, that could have been the pregnancy talking. She had found out only the day before that she was going to have a baby with Nick.

Later that day, the precinct received one last email from their mysterious killer. This one did not have a video attached; there was only a message.

"YOU MAY HAVE FOUND THEM BUT YOU WILL NEVER GET ME. I WILL BE GOING ON A SHORT HIATUS TO ENSURE THAT FACT. BE WARNED THAT YOU WILL SUFFER FOR STOPPING ME AND TAKING MY SANCTUARY AWAY."

He had been true to his word. They never did find him. Not long after that, she found a note that was meant for her. Then her whole world had changed.

Veronica was driving home from work

after an amazing day.

Sergeant Blake had told her that she was being considered for an open position as a detective in training. Most people had to wait years to gain admittance into that group, but she had shown a real knack for it.

Veronica knew that she owed Ben big time. She was going to have to set him up with Tasha for this one. He had been begging her for years, and now she had no choice but to do it. She had not wanted Natasha to start dating a cop, because she did not want that life for her. But who knows, maybe if she and Ben hit it off, they could all grow old together. Now she was really getting ahead of herself. She had not even talked to Tasha about going on a date with Ben yet.

While she was driving, "Footloose" came on the radio, and she could not help but blast the music and sing with all she had. She loved singing in the car, because she could do it as loud as she wanted and no one would hear her.

It had been a beautiful day and now she was driving home to be with her wonderful fiance. Life couldn't get much better than that.

When the song ended, she turned the radio down again and focused on where she was going. For a cop, she had always had a terrible sense of direction, so she had to concentrate on what she was doing.

After about ten minutes, she found her street and turned down it. When she pulled into her driveway, she saw that the lights were on in her living room and her heart leapt. In only a few moments, she would be able to share her fantastic news with Nick.

While she was walking towards her door, she noticed a card on the windshield of Nick's car.

Rolling her eyes, she snatched it up. "I swear, one day he's going to get into and accident, because he's distracted by another flyer that he left on his car."

She flipped it over and saw only one line of hand-written text. Thinking this odd, she paused for a moment to read it before she tossed it into the recycling bin.

"VENGEANCE IS BEST SERVED COLD...I THINK NOT."

She had no clue what that meant, but it set off warning bells in her mind. She turned to walk into the house so she could tell Nick about it and ask his advice.

Before she could take one step, she was thrown backwards by a wave of heat and glass. She felt some of the larger pieces ripping through her clothes and slicing her skin. As she landed on the ground about five feet away, she looked up to see fire blazing inside of her house.

All of the windows had been blasted out, and the walls looked as if the were about to fall in on themselves. She picked herself up, but she had a hard time standing. She looked down to see blood oozing from a particularly deep gash on her leg.

She knew that she should feel more pain than this, but it was as if her whole body had gone numb. Nick was still in the house.

Nick IS STILL IN THE HOUSE!

All at once, it was as if she was flying towards the front door.

She had to get to him!

Her left leg did not want to support her weight, but she pushed forward anyway. Before she could get to the door, she felt another wave of heat roll over her as the walls started to collapse in on themselves.

At that moment, it was as if all of the fight left her body. She knew she was too late. She stood there, unable to move, or think, or even breath.

She heard sirens approaching as the fire truck arrived. She knew that it would only be a matter of time before her entire precinct showed up, too. The moment that they heard her address over the radio, they would be jumping into their cars, calling the detectives and everyone that was off duty.

A fireman ran up to her and Veronica knew that she should at least try to understand what he was saying, but she could not focus.

She knew this fireman. They had run into each other before. She glanced at his face and tried to remember what his name was, but it was like her mind had gone numb along with her body.

She could tell that he was trying to ask her something, but nothing was working anymore. She was trying to think of where Nick would have been in the house.

Was there any chance?

When he saw her headlights, he usually went to the kitchen to get her a beer. Maybe if he was in the kitchen when it went off, he could still be alive.

This thought...this hope, gave her fire.

She sprang into action like a cat. One second she was standing next to the fireman, and the next she was trying to sprint for the structure that used to be her home.

Just before she reached it, she felt someone drag her back.

"Let me go!" Her scream filled the night.

Ben's strong arms coiled around her and Mark joined in as she fought him. "I can't let you go in there Veronica. Nick would never forgive me if I let you die by running into that house."

Veronica continued to struggle against Ben and Mark, "I will NEVER forgive you if you don't let me save him!"

Ben spun her around and held her by the shoulders, with tears in his eyes he made one final plea. "Ronnie...he's already gone. I know why you want to go in there. I want to go in too. But there's nothing that anyone can do for him now."

She struggled for a moment longer and then slumped against him and started sobbing. "I have to save him. It's all my fault."

Before he could answer her, she shoved away from him and hobbled over to Nick's car.

Ben tried to help her, but she pushed him off.

She picked up the note and handed it to him. "I found this right before it went off. I think he wanted me to see."

Ben stared at the note for a moment and then took it from her. "I'll be back in a moment." Then he turned and went over to where Blake was standing, talking to the fireman in charge.

Veronica watched them talking for a time, but then her vision started to darken and a tingle started to spread from her fingertips. She looked down to see that her entire pant leg was soaked in her own blood. She tried to call out to the paramedics, but before she could, her vision went completely black and she felt herself falling.

Veronica woke to the sound of beeping. She recognized the sound, but could not place it in her memory. She struggled to remember the sound, and then in a flash she understood. It was the medical equipment they had her attached to.

Opening her eyes, she found herself in a bland room on an uncomfortable bed, hooked up to a bunch of machines. She looked around to find half of her precinct watching her and the other half pressing their noses up to the window in her door. Normally she would have been embarrassed, but she could not manage to summon any emotion.

She tried to sit up, but she found that she did not have the strength to.

Blake finally spoke up. "Be careful, you came close to losing your leg. For once, do what you're told and take it easy."

Groggily, she tried to remember being brought to the hospital or anything after that, but there was nothing.

"How long have I been out?"

Everyone looked uncomfortable.

"You've been unconscious for about two days."

A doctor walked into the room, so everyone got up to leave.

For an hour, Veronica laid there as the doctor described everything that was wrong with her leg, and how much rehab she would have to do before she could walk properly again. It turned out that the glass had cut deeper than she had originally thought.

Veronica wasn't listening, because she didn't care. She knew that she would do the rehab, but she didn't care if her leg ever went back to normal. Her life would never be normal again, so why did it matter if her leg worked?

The doctor knew that she was not absorbing anything he said, but he had one more thing to tell her that she could not ignore. He clicked is pen to make sure she was paying attention before he went on.

"There is one more thing that I have to tell you. It will not be easy to hear, and I am sorry to be the one to have to tell you. It seems that... with all of the emotional trauma...and the blood loss...I'm sorry. Everything that you suffered that night. I'm afraid you lost your baby." He mistook her stunned silence for understanding, apologized once more, and left the room.

Veronica stared down at her stomach and began sobbing once more.

She had only known that she was pregnant for a short time. She and Nick had only recently decided to postpone the wedding so their child could be there. She had been planning on calling her father in a week or two, to tell him that he was going to be a grandfather.

It could not be possible that she lost the love of her life and her child all in one horrible night. It could not be possible that someone could be so evil as to do this to her on purpose.

There was only one person on the face of this Earth that could hate her enough to do this. At least she could tell Blake exactly that, so that he would not waste his time hunting down someone else.

Her only comfort was knowing that one day, they would find him and he would be brought to justice. Until then, she would wait.

"Veronica...Veronica! Earth to Veronica Taylor!"

Slowly she came back to the present, and was staring at Ben in the middle of his living room floor. She was surrounded by papers and pictures.

"Where did you go?"

Shifting into a more comfortable position, she hugged Ace. "I was running through it all in my head again."

Ben looked like he wanted to ask her more, but he held his tongue. He knew exactly what she had been doing, and could not bring himself to ask her any questions about what she had remembered. It was bad enough that she had to think about it at all.

They spent the next few hours going over everything that they knew about the case, and all of the things that Ben had found. Unfortunately, there was not much.

When Veronica pushed up off of the floor

suddenly, she startled Ben.

"Where are you going?", he half asked and half yelled.

Before he had a chance to stop her, she grabbed Ace's leash and attached it to his collar. "We've gone through everything we have and I'm tired. I promised myself that I would sleep in my own apartment tonight, so I'm going home."

Ben bounced up off the floor and grabbed his car keys. For a moment they stared into each other's eyes. He knew that he could not talk her out of going home, and she knew that she could not talk him into letting her go home alone.

When their gazes held for a fraction of a second too long, Ben shifted awkwardly and said, "Let me add more food to Charlotte's dish."

As a response, Veronica scooped the cat up into her arms and walked out the front door with Ace in tow.

Ben gently shook his head and followed behind the odd parade.

They drove to her apartment in complete silence. Neither of them was willing to admit how scared they were.

When they reached her apartment building, they sat in her parking lot for a full ten minutes before Ace started whining, and they got out of the car.

They approached her front door hesitantly, and were relieved not to see anymore notes. When Veronica unlocked her door, they both drew their guns before entering.

Opening the door, they were both ready to take out anyone that was in the room...but no one was there.

Working as a team, they cleared every corner of her apartment before they sheepishly holstered their guns.

Ben flopped down on her couch and flipped her television on. As Charlotte curled up on his chest, Veronica noticed how comfortable they both were.

Shaking her head, she walked over to the linen closet and pulled out an extra blanket. She threw it at him, careful to get only his face and not his cat.

He tossed an annoyed look in her direction and opened his mouth.

"See you in the morning," she interjected before he could speak. With that, she turned and practically ran into her room.

How long has it been since I showered?

She honestly could not remember.

Upon walking into her bathroom, she looked in the mirror and groaned. She had terrible dark circles under her eyes and her hair was a greasy mess. Without any more thought she stripped off her clothes and jumped into the shower.

Never had it felt so good to stand under the blast of hot water. As she felt the it wash over her, it seemed like all the tension fell off of her body and ran down the drain. She must have stayed in there longer than she thought, because there came a hesitant knocking at the bathroom door.

"Everything cool in there?"

She rolled her eyes and felt the sudden urge to open the doors and splash water at him. Before she could act on that impulse, she remembered that she was completely naked so that would have been a horrible idea. "I'm fine Ben. Enjoying the warm water."

As if on cue, the warmth ran out and she was suddenly blasted with a shot of ice cold water. She squealed and desperately tried to dance out of the stream.

Ben must have heard her, because suddenly the door burst open and he came running in, looking for something wrong.

For a moment, he stood transfixed in the middle of the room. Then he burst out laughing at the sight of her cowering in the corner of her shower, trying to avoid getting hit.

In an outrage, she slid open the glass door. She simultaneously grabbed a towel and stepped towards Ben.

He was so distracted by her attempts to cover herself, that he was taken by surprise when she gripped him by the front of his shirt and dragged him bodily into the shower with her.

"How do you like it?", she asked as he tried

to squirm out of her grasp.

She turned the spray of water off and tried to vacate the shower. Unfortunately, Ben was trying to do the same thing. They crashed into each other and tumbled out of the shower stall together.

They landed in a pile of limbs and wet fabric. For a few moments they laid there laughing on her bathroom floor. Then it became painfully obvious how naked she was, and how soaked his clothes were. Desperately trying not to be caught looking at each other, they disentangled themselves and Ben fled the bathroom.

Once she was safely in her pajamas, Veronica went back into her room and tried to find some clothes Ben could wear while she dried his. She landed on an old t-shirt of Nick's that she often wore as a pajama top, and a pair of baggy sweat pants with an elastic waistband.

When she walked into her living room to give them to him, she was stunned to a halt by the sight of a nearly naked Ben. He was in only his boxers, with a pile of dripping wet clothes at his feet. There was also a towel lying on the couch that was clearly meant to cover him while he waited for clothes.

As she watched his thumbs hook the top of his boxers, she was startled into speaking. "Not another inch."

He froze.

"We have to stop meeting like this."

He turned with a mischievous glint in his eyes. "Well, if you hadn't been so intent on getting me wet..."

She tossed the clothes at him before he could continue, and tried to go back into her room.

She lost her balance as she turned too quickly and fell into her door frame.

"Ow...that was embarrassing."

Strong arms closed around her, "Nothing to be embarrassed about."

She leaned into his grip for a moment before speaking. "You had better have at least gotten those sweatpants on."

He laughed and she noticed how much she enjoyed the rumbling feeling that it created on her back.

"I should get some sleep...you should too for that matter."

He straightened and backed away from her with a slightly bewildered look on his face. "Right...sleep...see you tomorrow." Then he turned and flopped back down on her couch.

She walked into her room and quietly closed the door.

DAY 4

O nce again, Veronica awoke to an alarm that she desperately wanted to snooze.

The only reason that she left the bed was the scent of bacon wafting into her bedroom. For a moment this confused her, but then she remembered her roommate for the night.

Grinning, she rolled out of bed and stumbled into her living room. She tried to make her way over to the kitchen without embarrassing herself again, but she kept tripping over Ace and Charlotte.

"Is this some sort of conspiracy? Do you not want me to get breakfast?"

She finally made it to her kitchen to find Ben with a pile of waffles, bacon, and orange slices. "Why is it that when we stay at your place with all the good food, I get nothing. But when we stay here, you raid my pantry and probably use all of the edible things left in it?"

He chuckled softly before turning around. "It's true. You do need to go grocery shopping. And besides, yesterday we barely woke up in time to get to the station. Shouldn't you be used to that? You were the one who only barely managed to make it to work on time, right?"

She smiled evilly at him, "The only reason you are getting away with that one is, because I'm hungry and you made the food." She filled a plate and went back to the living room.

Shoving the pillow and extra blanket out of the way, she tucked into her food. She was too preoccupied with eating to notice when Ben re-entered the room.

"How does a person eat like you do and still have that body?"

Having heard this questions many times in the past she had long since perfected her answer. Without looking up from her plate, "I have excellent genes."

He snorted, "Whatever...you should be studied. Eat fast. We need to stop by my place so I can get some more clothes. We should take Ace with us. I have a yard and Charlotte misses him. I've never seen a tabby-cat and a German shepard get so attached to each other."

An hour later they were both fed, dressed, and on their way back to the station for Veronica's first full day of work. With Ace and Charlotte happily lounging on Ben's couch, everyone was having a fantastic morning.

Once again, the ride to the station was made in silence as they both contemplated what the day was going to bring. Upon reaching the station, they parted ways to go to their separate locker rooms.

Ben mostly went to the men's locker room to socialize with his friends that were still on patrol, but Veronica had to change into her uniform for the first time in a year. She had never been a particularly sentimental person, but this was a big moment for her. In spite of the uncomfortable fabric and the unflattering fit, it felt surprisingly amazing to be back in uniform. She expected to feel apprehensive or sad, but instead she only felt excited. The adrenaline flowing through her veins made her feel strong again, for the first time since she saw her home blown up in front of her.

When she left the locker room, she found Ben leaning back on the wall opposite the door.

"Time to get to work?"

She smiled and nodded as she walked by him.

He moved to follow her. "Like I told you before, I arranged for you to partner with me while we work this case. I've been partnered with Mark for about nine months, so he will be working with us too. This arrangement will only last, as long as the top brass believe that you are mentally and emotionally fit enough to work the case. For the time being, you will follow every order given to you. Understood?"

Veronica spun on a heel and saluted him, "Sir, yes sir." She laughed, spun again, and walked calmly towards the detective's office.

Ben watched her for a moment, aware that everyone else in the building was watching her too. He hoped he was the only one who noticed the telltale stiffness in her back that indicated just how uncomfortable she was with everyone tracking her every move.

When they reached the semi-privacy of the detectives office and closed the door, Veronica's shoulders sagged.

"For the first time in my life, I understand what people are saying when they talk about living in a fish tank."

A tall beanpole of a man with shaggy black hair stood up from his desk. "This is what happens when you disappear for a year and then show up again out of the blue."

Veronica straightened up again and walked over to the man. "Mark, we didn't get to catch up yesterday. It's so great to see you again!"

They hugged for a moment before pulling apart.

"Yeah, yesterday you were too busy paying attention to everyone else in the room to talk to me. That's okay...I forgive you. But now you owe me at least a makeup lunch. Free food fixes all problems between coworkers. Speaking of which, I hear I'm going to be forced to work with you again."

This time Ben joined in on the conversation. "Oh, come on! You know you were excited when I told you about it. Everyone loves working with Ronnie."

Everyone in the room began to laugh as they remembered similar conversations in the past. The men of the division had always enjoyed making Veronica feel uncomfortable by complimenting her. It was like a competition to see who could make her blush first.

"Okay, I want you both to shut up before all of this starts again."

The first half of their day was devoted to going over what they knew and organizing their information. This was mostly for Mark's benefit, because Veronica and Ben had done the same thing the night before. It was good to have someone looking at the information with fresh eyes.

They spent their entire lunch break discussing different ways to come up with new information on the killer. The first thing that was agreed upon, was that Veronica would have absolutely nothing to do with the investigation into the bombing that killed Nick.

It was also decided that Veronica and Ben would be focussing on studying the lives of the women that the killer chose. After the killer had stopped providing them with the names of his victims, they had struggled to identify them. This became easier when they had found the bodies, but it still took a long time. Some had only been identified recently. They hoped that by studying their lives, they would be able to see what it was about them that drew the killer's attention.

After lunch, Mark disappeared so that he could work on the bombing without tempting Veronica to involve herself.

Ben and Veronica proceeded to cover their bulletin board with every detail they could come up with about Jennifer McCordell and the other 18 women that they had found buried in the desert. By the end of the day, their board was filled with the life stories and photos of all of the victims. Beyond sharing similar height and hair color, they did not find much to connect them. The closest thing that they could find other than their basic physical appearance, was the fact that they all had jobs that kept them on their feet or had them working with their hands. None of them had a typical 9 to 5 office job.

Throughout the day, they would occasionally see Mark as he would come in to grab something from his desk or look up some information in one of his files. Every time he entered the office, he would nod a greeting at Veronica and Ben then quickly drop his eyes.

Veronica understood why he was having a

hard time meeting her stare, but she wished that she could get Mark to look at her. She had a feeling that she would be able to tell how his investigation was going if she could get a look at his expression.

Other than Mark, nobody entered the office to disturb them all day. Veronica had the feeling that the other detectives who worked here had been told to give them a wide berth, and was not sure how she felt about that.

Every once and awhile, they would look out of their glass walls to see someone watching them. It seemed the novelty of having Veronica back in the station had not worn off. Her fellow patrol officers would stop and watch every time they came back in to fill out paperwork or drop off a suspect.

After double checking they had all the information they could on the women, they found themselves back in Ben's truck on the way to his house.

"I expect real food this time. None of this 'we only eat well when we're eating your food' crap."

The laughter that had subsided while they were focusing on work, reemerged with that statement. Like flipping a switch, they went from being total professionals to two people who could not keep a straight face if they tried. It was like they had stored up all of their laughter and humor for the day, and were letting it out in that truck.

When Veronica could finally speak, she said, "It feels so good to be smiling again. I felt like I had to be completely stoic while I was there or people would think I was going to crack. I hate that they watch me all the time."

Ben pulled the car into his driveway and shut it off. "They'll get over it eventually. Someone will screw up. Maybe one of the rookies will accidentally shoot a chair or something. That will take attention off you, and then one day they will all forget that you ever left."

They both climbed out and entered the house.

Making their way to the kitchen, he started pulling ingredients from the cabinets and refrigerator.

Once they were all assembled on the counter, Veronica was finally able to figure out what Ben's plan was. "Seriously! I say I want real food and you are going to make a pizza!"

Ben grinned while he began measuring out ingredients to make the crust. "No, I'm going to make two pizzas. You forget that I know how much you can eat during one meal. Remember your plate this morning? Besides, I worked at a pizza joint in high school. I make a damn good pizza. I can even do the dough toss."

Veronica was certain he was bragging, so she tried to call his bluff. "Prove it."

The cocky smirk that his 'dates' love so much, emerged as he kneaded the dough. The next few minutes passed in silence as it was worked to a perfect consistency and malleability. Then he pushed it out into a circle and rested it on his upturned fists. He bounced it there a few times to make sure it would not stick before tossing it up.

Veronica watched as it rotated in the air, then landed once again on his fists.

Once it had landed and settled, he turned and stared at her with triumph written across his face.

Veronica paused for a moment. She was clearly trying to think of a comeback to his silent gloating, but could not come up with anything. "Fine...I will admit that was cool. Can you teach me?"

They spent the next hour tossing dough around and usually hitting each other with it. Once again the uncontrollable laughter emerged, and they were able to forget about the day they had spent searching for a deranged killer by digging through the lives of dead women. Eventually, they wound up with two fairly decent pizzas.

"I guess I should be heading back to my place. Can I get a ride from you? Or do you want to follow me the whole way there?"

Ben stood up and walked over to the table to retrieve his keys. "Normally, I would argue with you, but I'm fairly certain you're stubborn and stupid enough to sneak out of here in the middle of the night to walk home with Ace as your only protection. I'll give you a ride back to your place and I'll come get you in the morning."

Veronica retrieved Ace's leash and put it on him. He clearly wanted to stay with Charlotte, but she was determined to go home and spend a night without a bodyguard. "Don't even think about pulling sentry duty in my parking lot tonight. I want you to come straight back here after you drop me off. We both need to get some sleep tonight, and neither your truck nor my couch are comfortable enough for that."

Ben opened his front door and pushed her out of it. "Yeah yeah, get in the truck smart-ass."

When they reached her parking lot, Veronica turned to Ben, "I'm calling your house in fifteen minutes. If you don't answer, I will assume that you are still here and I will be severely pissed off." With that, she popped the door open and climbed out.

Once Ace had joined her, she closed the door and walked back to her apartment building without looking back.

Ben watched her walking, "I get it. You're brave. You can take care of yourself. I hope this stubbornness doesn't get you killed." He put the truck in gear and left the lot.

Meanwhile, Veronica was walking up the staircase to her floor, desperately trying to curtail the panic attack that had been building ever since she left Ben's truck. She could feel her breaths becoming more shallow, and her vision was darkening, but she refused to stop. That silver beast of a truck felt safe to her, but the second she left it, all of her anxieties crashed down.

At first, she assumed that it was all of her old anxieties being magnified because of recent events. But the closer she got to her apartment the more she felt like something was wrong. She knew she was going to find something in her apartment, she just did not know what. As she approached her front door, she pulled the gun out of the holster on her hip and readied herself for what might be waiting for her. As quietly as she could manage, she inserted her key into the lock and turned it. She waited a beat before she pushed it open, while remaining covered by the wall and door jam. She raised her weapon and swung through the open doorway. Her heart stopped in the same instant as her body did. Once she was able to restart her brain, she reached into her back pocket and pulled out her cell phone.

Ben's phone went off, and he knew there was only one person that it could be. So he pulled his truck over and started digging around in his pockets. When he saw his caller id, he let out a quick laugh and slid his thumb across the screen to answer it. "It hasn't even been five minutes. You can't expect me to be home yet."

He started to get concerned when he only heard silence on the other end of the line. "Ronnie, what's going on? What happened?" When she finally spoke, he breathed a sigh of relief, but it was short lived.

"Come back. This message is for you too."

She hung up before he was able to question her on what she meant. Without hesitation, he pulled back onto the road and made a dangerous u-turn. When he entered her parking lot he pulled out his gun and cocked it before he left the vehicle.

Making his way to the building, he had his gun raised and cleared the lot like he was trained in the academy. He repeated this as he climbed the stairs up to the third floor. Becoming more and more cautious with every step that took him closer, he also moved faster and faster because he knew that she was alone and needed him.

When he entered the third floor hallway and saw her standing there waiting for him, he rushed forward.

She had put her gun away after clearing her apartment, so he put his back in its holster as well. She ran to him and collapsed into his arms.

"He was in my apartment."

Ben held her to him so that he could prove to himself that she was there and okay. "I know. Let's go check it out."

When Ben pushed her door open, his breath left him. He entered her living room to find the walls plastered with papers. Upon closer inspection, he found that it was all of the evidence that he had collected and obsessed over throughout the year.

"It all came from your shed."

Looking across the wall, he noticed that it was all laid out in the same order it had been in the shed. There were even lines of string connecting documents, the same way that he had connected them when he was setting up the test for Veronica.

"We have to call this in. They're gonna want to go through this apartment with a fine-toothed-"

Veronica cut him off before he could get the words out. "If Blake sees or hears about this, he's going to take you off the case. And if you get kicked off, I get kicked off. We can't call this in."

Going into his by-the-book, command mode, Ben pulled out his cell phone and began dialing. "Veronica, everything in this apartment is evidence now. If we don't call this in and someone finds out, we will both be without a job. You may have another career to fall back on, but I don't. I might be able to talk Blake into letting me stay on the case, but if I hide this, I have no chance when he finds out."

By the time that he finished this speech, Veronica had been silenced and the desk sergeant had picked up the call. "Stanton, I need a unit and techs at Veronica's apartment ASAP. There's been a breach. Blake is gonna want to be here too. The apartment has been cleared, so for the moment there is no danger. All the same, tell the guys to keep their eyes open on approach. I get the feeling that this unsub likes to watch."

It's like they are puppets and I am pulling the strings. They do everything I want them to, exactly when I want them to do it. They think they are so clever with all of their evidence gathering and investigating. They think they will catch me...what morons.

I eagerly await the day when Veronica and Ben understand what their fatal mistake has been for all this time. Sometimes it amazes me that they cannot see it.

They could not catch me then, they will not catch me now. They all assume that I could not possibly be one of their own...part of their precious brotherhood.

"We protect our own." What utter bullshit. One day they'll understand. One day they will see me for the genius I am. I will get the credit that I deserve.

Then I will kill them and be free.

Until then, I will revel in the knowledge that they think they can trust me.

In fact, I should be getting a call any moment now.

"Why are you calling me this late? Has Ronnie gotten tired of you already?"

Ben wanted to smile when he heard this, but the situation was too serious. Everyone else that he called, had already come up with similar greeting when they saw his name on the caller ID. He had set them straight, and they said they would come without asking too many questions, but he knew this was going to be the most difficult call.

"No sir, Ronnie and I are doing okay. There's something you need to see. The unsub broke into her apartment...he left a message. I wanted you to see it for yourself and I wanted to be the one to tell you. I wanted there to be no question of whether or not I...we tried to hide this from you."

Veronica was listening in on the phone call and heard Blake's tiny voice respond, "What happened Ben? Why would someone think you were trying to hide it from me?"

Ben was cringing away from the phone because he did not want to have this conversation, but knew that it was inevitable. He settled for delaying it, "Come to her apartment, sir. I'll explain everything then. It's better if you see it anyways."

There was a pause while Blake considered his options. "Okay, I'm on my way now. I want a full explanation when I arrive. Is that understood?"

Ben looked around the room and knew that this was going to be a long and difficult conversation. "Yes, sir."

They only had a few moments of silence before they heard a siren and saw red and blue lights bounce around the room. Shortly after the lights and siren cut out, Officers Cheyenne Bellows and Ryan Foster entered the apartment. Both of them stopped short, and drew a quick breath when they looked around the room.

Ace, feeling the tension in the room, stood at Veronica's side. Normally, he would have gone in for a sniff of the newcomers, but he felt that his person needed protecting.

Cheyenne went over to comfort him, while speaking to Ben and Veronica. "The techs are coming in to photograph the scene and dust for prints." They arrived before she or Ryan could ask any questions.

More people entering the room made Ace uncomfortable, so he crouched in front of them and growled. His hackles were raised until Veronica stepped forward and calmed him down.

They nodded at Veronica and started going about their business. In spite of working together before, Veronica had never gotten to know many of the techs that came to their crime scenes. She was friends with a couple, but unfortunately neither of these two were among them.

Ryan set about putting up crime scene tape across her front door, while everyone else stood and watched the techs take pictures of everything.

They were not able to stand idle for long.

Blake and Mark entered the room together and took a look around. Mark looked shocked, but Blake looked more angry than anything else. Clearly he had come to some conclusions about what he was looking at.

He spun to Cheyenne and Ryan, who had finished with the tape, "What are you doing standing there? Go wake the building manager and see if there are any security cameras on this property. Once you're done with that, go to the neighboring buildings and see if any of them have cameras that point to any of the doors into this building. When you are done with that, start canvassing the neighborhood and see if anybody has seen anyone suspicious lately. This is rookie stuff guys. I know that this one hits close to home, but Ryan, you've been doing this for seven years now. This should be habit for you. And Cheyenne, I get that Veronica is your friend. Do not give me a reason to take you off this call and send you home."

Sufficiently shamed, Cheyenne and Ryan nodded and spun on a heel to duck under the tape.

After that, Blake spun to Ben and Veronica. "Explain."

While Blake had been chastising Cheyenne and Ryan, several other officers had heard Veronica's address over the radio, and arrived to make sure everything was okay. When they heard the anger evident in Blake's commanding voice, and saw the way his bulky form was tightened like a spring ready to explode, they knew this was something they would not want to witness. Five senior officers and one scared rookie made their way to the door, in a race to see who could make it under the tape and out of the room first. The rookie won.

The only person who stayed to hear Ben and Veronica's explanation besides Blake, was Mark who loyally decided to stay.

Ben and Veronica instinctively moved closer together so that they could gather strength from each other, while Mark earnestly paced around the room, occasionally stopping to read a document or study a photograph.

Howard Blake stood firm and tall in the center of the room waiting for the promised explanation.

Ben started to speak before Blake lost his patience. "After the case went inactive, I sort of kept it running. I, uh...I set up an office for myself in Nick and Veronica's old backyard and kept all the stuff there. I didn't get very far. Nobody was collecting new evidence, so mostly it was me going to the shed and looking over what we already knew, to see if anything popped out at me. If anything had, I would have brought it to you. I never intended for this to turn into an independent investigation. It appears that the unsub was aware of this and stole everything out of the shed. He broke into Veronica's apartment sometime today and did this. She found it when I dropped her off about twenty minutes ago. I realize that you told me not to get too involved with this investigation while it was inactive, and if you feel I should be removed from the case I will not argue. I only ask that you let Veronica stay on it. She was entirely unaware of my outside investigation until yesterday, when I took her to the shed as a test. She hasn't lost any of her old skill. She was only in the shed for a moment, and was the first to recognise that the layout of these documents is the same as it was there." Having finished his speech, Ben fell silent to await Blake's response.

The first words spoken after his nervous ramble, came from an unexpected source.

Mark stepped forward to defend his friend. "Sir, if you see fit to allow Ben to remain on this case, I would be willing to supervise and make sure neither he nor Veronica cross any lines. They're both good investigators with a history of finding things that others don't see, especially when they're working together. I think this investigation would suffer if either of them were removed from it. Truthfully, I'm gonna need all the help I can get with this one. There's too much to look into for me to do it alone." With his two cents added Mark returned to studying the room.

Seconds that felt like hours ticked by before Blake finally came to a decision. "You may both stay on the case...for now. But I want a clean investigation. If I hear from anyone that either of you is taking things too far, you will both be removed. And Ben, anymore things like this happen and I will bust your ass back down to the street so fast you won't know what happened. Now, I want you to take a couple uniforms and techs to the shed you were telling me about, and run that scene. Mark and I have got this one."

Ben and Veronica looked at each other and grinned. They then turned to Blake and thanked him profusely.

Before they left the room, Veronica spun and addressed Blake. "Do you mind if we take Ace to Ben's house before we go to the other scene? He'll only be in your way here and he's spent a lot of time at Ben's lately."

Blake thought for a moment. "Go ahead. Drop him off, then go straight to the house. I want this shed checked out... and be careful. I know nobody wants to think about it, but it wouldn't be the first time the unsub set a trap."

Ben and Veronica nodded, grabbed Ace and left the room.

Once they left, Blake turned to Mark, who had stayed silent after speaking up for his friends. "Do you really think it's smart to keep them on this case? Aren't they are too close to this?"

Mark crossed the room to stand in front of him. "Answer me this...who at the station isn't too close to this case? Everyone loved Nick. Obviously they're gonna be closer than anybody else, but I can keep an eye on them. I'll make sure they don't let things get to an unhealthy level. Besides, do you think either one of them would drop this case if you told them to? If they're part of the official investigation it'll be easier to keep them safe."

Blake nodded and went back to supervising the crime scene.

For what felt like the thousandth time in the past few days, Ben and Veronica rode in total silence. Neither of them knew the words to describe what they were feeling.

When they reached Ben's house, they both climbed out of the truck to let Ace in.

"You can stay here for as long as you need.

After they get done with your apartment, we can go back and pack up a few things for you."

Veronica slouched against the wall for a moment, before pushing off of it and heading back towards the truck. "I was ready to fight you on that, but I don't want to stay in a hotel. And I don't think I can be in that apartment right now."

Ben pushed forward and opened the passenger door for her. "I get it. You've got a home here for as long as you want."

When they arrived at Nick and Veronica's property, they found a familiar scene. It made Ben stop the car at least a hundred meters from the house, and turn in his seat to make sure that Veronica was okay.

It was clear that she was finding it difficult to hold it together, but the more time they spent there, the stronger she appeared. He noticed her fiddling with the ring she normally wore on her thumb.

After about two minutes, Veronica turned to Ben with a determined glint in her eyes. She looked like she always did when a case was pissing her off.

He put the truck back in gear and approached the house. He parked as close as he could, then got out and approached the fire captain, who was talking to Tyler McFarland. Tyler had been the first on the scene.

When Ben and Veronica reached the pair,

he took over as the most superior officer on the scene. "What happened here?"

Tyler faced Ben and began his report. "When we got here, the shed was on fire. Judging by how far gone it was, I'd guess it went up sometime in the last hour. I talked to Captain Hastings here and he agrees with my assessment. If I were a betting man, I'd say that the unsub torched this place around the same time that you found the stuff in Ronnie's apartment."

Ben was nodding through the entire explanation, "I think you are right. In fact, I'll do you one better and say that he watched us find the stuff in Ronnie's apartment, and then came here because he knew that it was our next stop. I'm not sure how he is getting his information yet, but this guys knows more about all of us than we would like to think."

After getting confirmation from the fire captain that it was safe to enter the yard and shed, Veronica slipped on a pair of gloves and made her way through the sea of people that included firemen, cops, and crime techs to the shed.

After a careful inspection they found a few finger smudges, but none that contained clear prints. This led all of them to believe that the unsub had worn gloves while he ransacked and set fire to the shed. He came prepared. This only confirmed that all of this had been a plan from the start.

The only concrete piece of evidence that they were able to find was one muddy shoe print heading back towards the street. It was not much, but it was the first real mistake the killer had made. That one shoe print was the first piece of evidence they had been able to find that was actually something the unsub had left behind.

It may have only been a shoe print, but to Ben and Veronica it was the Holy Grail.

This was their sign that the man they were hunting was starting to get sloppy. He thought he could not be caught so he was becoming less cautious. Whoever he was, he still knew far too much about them and held too many cards. But for the first time in a long time, they had real hope that they were going to find him.

Shortly after they finished combing through the scene they received a call from Blake saying that he and Mark had finished up at Veronica's apartment for the night. They were cleared to return so they could pack a bag for her and then they were to turn in for the night. Blake wanted them back at the station bright and early in the morning for a meeting.

When they arrived at Veronica's apartment they were ushered inside by Cheyenne and Ryan.

"Blake told us wait for you two here and then escort you back to Ben's place. When we get there, we are going to be relieved by two officers that have just gotten on shift. They're gonna be in an unmarked car. They are gonna be watching you guys all night...It looks like this protective detail is gonna last a while." Ryan looked incredibly uncomfortable while he told them about Blake's orders, but he also made it clear that there would be no point in arguing.

Cheyenne piped in. As she spoke, the petite woman began to turn pink, then red as she blushed. "It seems Blake doesn't think you guys are safe on your own anymore...He also assumed that you would both be staying at the same place...Should we tell him otherwise?"

Once again both Cheyenne and Ryan looked uncomfortable and would not meet their eyes. Everyone in the room knew what was being insinuated and none of them wanted to be having that conversation.

It seemed that Blake was getting his revenge for Ben continuing his investigation and Veronica not telling him when she found out. He was not going to take them off the case yet, but he was going to have his fun with them.

Veronica took over the conversation, "Ben offered me his couch for now, so I'll be staying there. It's cheaper than getting a hotel and Ben likes my dog."

Cheyenne and Ryan were happy to leave it at that and as far as Ben and Veronica were concerned that is all there was to it.

Ben wanted to argue against being

watched around the clock, but he knew that was something that should wait until the meeting in the morning, when Blake had time to sleep and calm down a bit.

After Veronica had collected her things, piled into their cars to drove over to Ben's home. When they arrived there, Veronica noticed a car parked on the corner populated with familiar faces. Exiting the vehicle, she and Ben nodded to the officers that would have their backs for the night and then waved goodbye to Cheyenne and Ryan.

Once they were settled in the house the inevitable subject of sleeping arrangements came up.

Ben went to the hall closet and started pulling out sheets, blankets, and a pillow. "I know you told the guys that you'd be sleeping on the couch, but you're welcome to my room for the night. Last time you stayed here I told you that you could have the bed for one night and that offer still stands. I'll give you the bed for one night of decent sleep and then its couch city for you."

Veronica started laughing, "How gentlemanly of you. I have a counteroffer. We're both adults and you have a large bed. If we both stick to our sides then there is no reason why we can't both have a decent night of sleep."

This time it was Ben's turn to laugh. "Okay, but remember this; Nick was my best friend and men talk as much as women do. We don't like to admit it, but it's true. If you kick or punch me in your sleep I will push you off the bed."

Veronica let faux-shock fill her face, "I can't believe he told you about that! He told me that everyone bought the story about the black eye...and I only hit him once."

He looked at her skeptically. "Yeah, you had a bad dream and punched him in the face while you were sleeping. Something gives me a feeling those dreams come a little more frequently now. If I show up at work with a black eye tomorrow A) no one will believe you slept on the couch and B) everyone in the station will be wondering why two men who slept in the same bed as you came into work the next morning with a black eye. Now...I would find that whole scenario pretty funny, but I think you'd rather avoid it."

Veronica stuck her tongue out at him and listened to him laughing as she marched up the stairs. She threw a comment over her shoulder, "Keep laughing at me and I will lock you out of you room and take all of your precious bed."

The laughter quickly ended and she could hear Ben racing up the stairs behind her. She smirked and started running too.

Twenty minutes and some roughhousing later they were both in pajamas and ready for bed. For a moment they stood staring at it.

Ben was the first to speak, "Right or left side?"

Veronica looked around the room for a moment, "I'll take the right."

Ben nodded as he made his way around the bed, "The side closest to the door. I should have known."

With that, all conversation ended. They settled on their respective sides of the bed and turned so their backs were to each other.

Veronica spent the next half hour trying to quiet her mind. After a few minutes Ben fell asleep leaving Veronica to listen to his breathing, envying his ability to pass out whenever he wanted to. Eventually she was able to drift out of consciousness as she counted the breaths that he took.

DAY 5

Fire...Sirens...Searing heat. It's like the whole world has ignited in flame and hate. The air is filled with the acrid smell of smoke and it's burning my lungs. Who is screaming? I look around to find the woman, but there is no one else here. I don't understand what's happening. I try to call for help, but I can't stop the screaming. The cry filling the night is coming from my own mouth. The sirens come closer and I can see the red and blue flashing lights. I should go get checked out and give my statement. Years of following protocol has ingrained that instinct in me, but I cannot make myself care. All of my attention is on the fire. Someone is asking me something...they're shaking my shoulders. What are they saying? I know that I should know who they are and what they are saying, but I can't think. Then suddenly...

The world shook and there was yelling.

Veronica woke suddenly as Ben grabbed her by the shoulders and shook.

"Veronica, you have to wake up!"

Before she was fully able to pull herself out of the nightmare, Veronica thrashed and screamed.

Ben tried to hold her down to keep her from hurting him or herself, but she was strong and entirely unaware of what she was doing.

Once she woke up she laid there, drenched in sweat, trying to catch her breath.

Ben was still leaning over her holding her down by her shoulders.

"What happened?"

Now that she was coherent enough to be aware of the world beyond her dreams Ben let go of her and flopped down next to her. "Amidst the screaming...you said a few things in your sleep... mostly Nick's name. How often do you get that dream? Is that why you always went to the cemetery?"

Veronica stared at the ceiling for a moment and then turned over to face Ben. "It's always the same dream. It never changes, even a little bit. I've had it on and off ever since Nick died...I usually don't have it this often."

This time it was Ben's turn to flip over to face her. "I wish you would have told me. I could have at least tried to help."

Veronica sighed, "What would you have done? It's a dream Ben. I'm sure that with enough time it will fade away. Until then...I wake up abruptly sometimes."

Ben inched closer and placed his hand on her arm. "Veronica, you were screaming. Maybe you should see someone...talk to someone about this. It might help."

Veronica looked him right in the eye, "I do talk to someone. The dreams mostly faded out when we started meeting up at the cemetery. They've picked up again recently."

Ben's sighed. "Because I stopped meeting with you. I knew I shouldn't have..."

Veronica placed a hand on his cheek so she could stop him from talking. "No, not everything is your fault. The dreams started again a few days ago because I went to bed thinking about what happened to Nick. It came again tonight because of everything that's been happening lately. I'm surprised I'm not having the dream more often. I think it's better with you."

They stopped talking and comforted each other for a time. Falling asleep wrapped in each other's arms, they both slept soundly. When they woke up again they were still tightly wound around each other. Having woken up like that recently, they were far less uncomfortable with it. This time there was no awkwardness or tears. They were just two people, currently living together, that slept in the same bed.

Getting ready for work that morning, they formed a rhythm. While Veronica showered, Ben made eggs. While Ben was in the shower, Veronica cut up a couple apples. Once they were both in the kitchen, Ben brewed coffee and Veronica made them some toast. Then they both sat down to eat the feast that they had created.

Most of this occurred without words except for a few comments about the quality and quantity of the food. Neither of them were morning people and they both knew each other well enough not to try to hold a conversation until the caffeine had a chance to enter their system. They had both had a big night and not enough sleep to recover from it fully.

The rhythm continued as they got ready for work. Veronica had always been the type to barely make it to work on time so she was unused to waking up with the ability to make a real meal for breakfast and take her time getting ready. All the same, it was like they got ready together every day. Ben pulled their guns out of his lockbox while Veronica got her uniform together. Veronica fed the pets while Ben loaded up the truck. Then they took their usual seats with Ben driving and Veronica on the passenger side and went to work.

Look at them. Their cozy lives. Their easy routine...Maybe it's time to shake things up a bit. I only have to find the perfect way.

When they got to work everything was the same. The room was busy with the same level of activity, all the faces were the same. Still, everything felt different. Yes, they were in trouble. Yes, there was still a psycho after one of them. Yes, they were still far away from catching him. In spite of that, they felt a new energy coming from everyone in the building. As terrible as it was that the killer was active again, no one else had died yet. They had new evidence, while it was not much, it was there. Most importantly, for the first time since Nick died, they felt like the team was back together again. It could never be full again, with Nick gone. But with Veronica back, they all felt like they had a better chance at finding the man responsible for so much pain. That's the energy that Ben and Veronica walked into and it was infectious. In spite of the fact that they were about to walk into a meeting where they were most likely going to be reamed out by their boss again, Ben and Veronica could not help but feel optimistic . Even though she had only been back for a short time, Veronica already felt home again at the station. She had tuned back into the life there, and it felt good.

She was practically glowing when she and Ben walked into Blake's office.

The happiness on her face and in her body language made Blake pause for a moment. He enjoyed getting to see her like that.

She was always so happy and vibrant

while she was with Nick and ever since she lost him he had been missing that look.

He, Nick, and Ben had all gone through the academy together. Although he had risen in the ranks faster than either of the other two, they had all remained close. They had all trusted each other with their lives at times, and when Veronica started dating Nick she had been become the fourth musketeer.

It seemed now she was finally coming back to herself and into the fold.

However, he was still the boss and he had to act like it.

Once the door was closed and Ben and Veronica had taken seats opposite to Blake he began speaking. He let command deepen and strengthen his voice, "I want to make it clear that I do not condone your outside investigation. If that's what you call it, Ben. And Veronica, you should have told me when you found out about it. You've disobeyed my direct orders and for that I would be well within my rights to take you off this case. Ben, if I wanted to I could take you upstairs and have you suspended...if you were anyone else I probably would. Out of respect for our friendship and our mutual...connection to this case, I'm letting you stay on and I'm not going to turn you into the higher-ups. Both myself and Mark will be keeping a close eye on you now. If one of us gets a whiff of impropriety from either of you I'm taking you off the case. I care too much about both of you to let this kill you or your careers. You will come in every day and work. You will tell me what you are doing every time you leave this building. You will brief me at the end of every day on what you have done and what theories you are working. Most importantly...when you go home at the end of the day, you are going to leave this case here. No paperwork, nothing is leaving this building with you. When you leave this place, I want you to at least try to live as normal a life as you can. By now you know I've ordered that you two be watched while you are not here for your own protection. Ben, don't bother trying to talk me out of it. It's for your own good, and it means that you can rest easy when you leave here at night. If you want to stay on the case, those are the rules. Break any one of them, and you're done." Blake looked them both in the eye as they considered what he had said.

Once a chorus of "Yes sir," had come from them he went to dismiss them. "Good, now go get to work. The sooner this ends the better off we'll all be."

Upon leaving Blake's office Ben and Veronica turned to one another.

"Well, that was inspiring. I knew I was going to be watched when I came back but...we have to check in every time we leave the building...Mark has to babysit us. It's almost not worth it."

Ben shoved her playfully into the wall, "Of course it's worth it. The moment we catch that crazy bastard everyone will stop questioning if you are fit for duty. Think about it...if you and I come up with enough evidence to put this guy away...this'll all be over. We can both start to move on."

Veronica was nodding throughout this speech, "Then I guess we better get back to work." She shoved him back for good measure, walked past him, and entered the detective's office.

Once again, Ben stared after her as she crossed the room. He shook himself out of his reverie and followed after her.

Behind him, Blake could be seen watching him through the glass walls of his office and nodding.

Nobody else seemed to notice.

When Ben and Veronica made it into the detective's office, they were met by Mark.

"I know you guys probably aren't that keen on having me watching you during this investigation, but it's probably the only reason why Blake let you stay on the case. I swear I'm going to stay out of your way. I know you guys are good cops, I'm not all that worried. I'm here to make sure that when we go to prosecute this guy, nobody can file harassment charges and you two won't be ripped apart on the stand.

Plus...I'm a pretty good cop myself. I can help if you ever need someone to bounce ideas off of."

He poured this speech out in such a rush that neither Ben nor Veronica had a chance to silence him.

Ben was certain he did not take a breath the entire time.

When he was finally done, and a little red in the face from lack of oxygen, Veronica stepped forward. "We get why you volunteered to watch us for Blake. In fact, we kind of owe you one. If you hadn't been there last night I don't think Blake would have ever stopped screaming at us. Thanks to you, all we got was some minor yelling and teasing. As much as it sucks that we have to be watched this closely, I'd rather you do it than anyone else. I trust you, and Blake will listen to you when you tell him that everything is going fine. This is way better than having some IA jackass following us around 24/7."

Once Veronica was finished reassuring Mark that they were not mad, Ben chimed in with his own two cents. "As much as I'm loving this heart to heart, I think we all better get back to work. The sooner we can catch this guy the sooner Mark can stop feeling like a narc for having to report our actions to Blake. Veronica's right, I'd rather it be you than anyone else. However, all of these offices have glass walls. People are literally watching our every move right now. That means that Blake can see everything we are doing and he will know if Ronnie and I are trying to influence you, so the best thing we can do right now is just do our jobs."

With that, Mark and Ben went back to their desks while Veronica worked to move an extra chair over to Ben's.

They spent the next few minutes updating their board with the information collected last night. They had a timeline containing the dates that the police had received emails with stills of the victim's face from the video and the autopsy reports underneath. Plus, a description of their lives up until they were buried in the desert.

By compiling all of these descriptions, they had come up with a general profile of the victims he chose. The killer liked tall women with wavy, brown hair. He prefered that the woman's hair be long and he liked it when it was their natural color. None of the women were wearing much makeup when they were abducted, suggesting that he prefered women to look more natural. He also liked to take women that worked with their hands or had jobs that kept them on their feet.

The medical examiner had confirmed this for them during the previous investigation. It appeared that he liked to speed up his timetable for taking women. In the beginning, the police would only be getting emails from him once a week, by the time that they found his burial site, they were receiving emails every other day.

There was only one anomaly; when he had two women buried at one time. They had yet to explain that one. All in all, they had found 18 victims at the burial ground, which exactly corresponded to the amount of emails they had been sent with new victims on them. They knew that he liked burying the women in the same place every time. He had stopped taking new victims right after they found his site; suggesting that particular place had a special meaning for him.

The most striking thing about him was the way that he taunted the police.

This killer clearly had problems with authority figures and considered himself to be smarter than everyone else. He was incredibly cautious while he was doing his "work." Until last night, nobody had ever been able to find any physical evidence that he even existed.

Given the grainy image that they had of him from the videos and the shoeprint that they were able to find at the shed last night, they knew that the killer was at least 6 feet tall, but he was stooping in the video so he could be taller. They knew that he wore a size 13 shoe. It was difficult to determine his build because of the baggy clothes that he wore. He always wore a hood with long sleeves, pants, and gloves so they were unable to determine his ethnicity, hair color, and they had no sketch of his face yet.

They knew that he was meticulous. He recreated Ben's shed down to a "t" in Veronica's living room and he did so without leaving any trace of himself.

They also knew his main focus: Veronica. Ever since she went to her superiors and helped them find the killer's victims, he had come after her.

First he had blown up her house with Nick in it. He waited until she got home, which suggested that he was watching her while he did this. A year later, he had left a note on Veronica's car. For some reason, she was still his obsession, and judging by last night he was still watching her.

While Ben and Veronica rankled at the idea of being guarded when they left the station, they knew that this was a strong argument not to fight against it. If they managed to catch the killer because he was watching Veronica, it would make all of their lives that much easier. As agreed upon the day before, Ben and Veronica refrained from investigating the explosion at Veronica's old house and allowed Mark to run that end of the case without them.

As they stood looking at their board, full of all the things they knew, Ben and Veronica felt the hope from last night flare brighter. They still did not have much, but they were slowly building a net around their suspect and they were sure that someday soon they would catch him. Any more slip ups like last night would only serve to speed things along.

In their minds, the results of this investigation were a forgone conclusion. Once this case was over, Nick's killer would be rotting behind bars for the rest of his existence. All they had to do was find enough evidence to put him away. For an investigation that had been re-opened less than a week ago, they were already doing well.

Veronica was the first to make a suggestion, "I think we should talk to the victim's families and friends. Maybe they've remembered something over the last year that can help us. This is the best we've got right now, so let's run with it."

Ben nodded and pushed up out of his chair. "I agree that's our best option right now. Let's go talk to Blake and clear it with him." Before he left the room he turned to Mark and explained what they were going to do.

Mark only smiled and went back to his work.

When Ben and Veronica left the office they had to cross a more open area where all of the patrol cops worked when they had paperwork to fill out or research to do. As they were walking they could feel all eyes upon them.

More specifically, everyone was looking at the hand that Ben had placed on the small of Veronica's back to guide her across the room. This was not an uncommon gesture. They had all seen it before. This was Ben telling Veronica that he had her back without having to speak. Yet for some reason, this gesture seemed far more intimate with these two.

They all noticed how comfortable the two were with the contact and could not force themselves to stop looking.

When Ben noticed what had caught all of their attention he became self-conscious and let his hand drop. He did not realize that as it swung by his side after that, he was continuously clenching and unclenching his fist.

A few people shook their heads, others exchanged knowing glances, some were smiling. Even the new rookies who did not know them reacted as if they did.

Across the room, Erica could be scene grinning in a very un-Ice Queen-like manner.

Ben and Veronica entered Blake's office to get permission to leave the building so that they could conduct their interviews. They were sure that it would not be a problem, but according Blake's rules they had no choice.

Because Ben was by far the superior officer, he took the lead with Blake. "You told us that we need to talk to you if we're planning to leave the building. We decided to go talk to the families of our victims. I know that we talked to them the first time around, but they might have new information.."

Blake was sitting at his desk, filling out papers. Without even looking up he responded, "That's fine, but be gentle with them. They've already been through alot, and they are under no obligation to answer your questions. Start with the most important stuff and go from there because they can end the interview anytime they want."

Veronica took this speech without comment because she knew why he was saying it; she had been gone for a long time.

Ben was another story. He was offended that Blake felt the need to talk down to him. "Sir, I get what you're trying to do here, but it's unnecessary. With all due respect, I know how to do my job. I've been a detective for a while now and I know how to conduct an interview. I'm not trying to be insubordinate here. I need you to know, in spite of recent events, you don't need to worry about me."

For a moment, it looked like Blake was going to push back but he decided to let it slide.

When they left the building Veronica turned to Ben. "Dude, you need to chill. I know that this is a sucky situation and I get that you and Blake are old friends, but you can't snap at him like that. No matter what your history is with him, he is still the boss. He wears the white shirt, so he can say whatever he wants. If we are going to stay on this case, we have to stay on his good side."

Ben continued to stomp to his truck as he ripped the keys out of this pocket. "I get that, but I know how to do my job. I won't walk around this building having people doubting every move that I make. I didn't walk out on my job for a year. They have no justification to doubt me."

The moment that those words left his mouth, Ben regretted them. He stopped in his tracks and turned to apologise to her.

The hurt and furious expression on her face scared him because he had never seen it before. As per usual, this did not last long because she covered it up with the calculatedly bland mask she always wore with suspects and people she did not trust.

Having known her for so many years, Ben could still see the fury boiling below the surface. Most especially in the angry tears that were building in her eyes.

"Ronnie...I didn't mean that....You know I never held that against you...And you know I think you're a good cop...No matter how much time you spent away..."

His stuttered apology did little to appease her.

"Save it Ben. Like you said...we have a job to do. Wouldn't want people doubting me even more...you know since I lost it and left before. Heaven forbid a person take time off to do physical therapy."

Veronica shoved past him as she grabbed the keys out of his hand and marched to the car. Once she pulled herself into the driver's seat she rolled the window down. "If you don't get in I'm going to leave without you."

Ben was still frozen in place. Before he turned around to follow her to the truck, he bowed his head to stare at the ground then slapped his palm to his forehead. As he was walking he could be heard muttering, "Stupid, stupid, stupid."

This time the cab of the truck was not filled with a comfortable silence. This ride was full of a tense, angry silence that made Ben fear for his well-being when Veronica finally got around to lashing out.

She had a reputation for a long fuse and low blows. Ben once saw her kick a guy right in the nuts because he had punched her in the breast, accidentally, three months before.

And that was all in jest.

There was no telling what she was going to do to him, or when she was going to do it.

From across the cab of the truck Veronica heard him mumble, "I guess it's couch city for me..."

For a moment he thought that Veronica had not heard him, then she leaned over and whispered in his ear. "I think that's probably safest."

If this had been happening to anyone else he might have found it funny, but in that moment he was justifiably terrified.

It appeared that fiery, redhead temper that he had always loved about her was finally back and it had found its first target.

"This is going to be unpleasant for me."

Veronica's cold smile brought him no comfort, "You have no idea."

Me and my big mouth...

Having already mapped out where all of the people they wanted to talk to lived, there was no discussion of where to go first. The giant circle they had plotted starting at the home of Jennifer McCordell's father.

When they arrived, Veronica paused for a moment. "The second we leave this truck we have to start acting like partners again. I need to know you aren't going to be questioning me in there. I need to know that we have each others backs at least while we're in the field."

She still was not looking at him, so he knew he was still in trouble. He also knew that she was right. Personally they might be having problems right now, but she needed to find a way to trust him professionally. Otherwise, she might as well get in a patrol car now because it would only be a matter of time before Blake separated them.

"I've always got your back Ronnie. You

know that."

Still not looking in his direction, Veronica nodded and climbed out of the car. Without waiting for him to follow she walked up to the front door and rang the bell.

Ben caught up to her and gave her a mildly annoyed look before an older man opened the door.

Sam McCordell was frail with graying hair and pasty, white skin. His wife had died of cancer about ten years ago and now he had lost his only daughter as well.

Veronica softened upon seeing him. To her, it felt like looking into a mirror. She too had lost everything and she had deteriorated since then as well.

She had never been involved with the interviews during the initial investigation, but Mr.McCordell recognised Ben.

"Unless you're here to tell me that you finally caught that murderous bastard, you are not welcome in my home."

Ben flinched at the accusing tone to his voice but recovered quickly.

"Sir, the investigation into your daughter's murder had been reopened recently. We were wondering if we could maybe ask you some questions about what happened."

Both Ben and Veronica held their breath as they waited for his reply.

Anger darkened his face once more. "So

you haven't caught him. I answered all your questions last time and it didn't do a damn bit of good! If there was anyone following her, she never said anything about it. You know everything there is to know about her life. She was a good girl who never did anything wrong. She worked hard and she never complained. All she wanted to do with her life was help people!"

Throughout his speech, Mr McCordell's voice had grown louder and louder until it ended with him yelling. Once he had said everything he wanted to say, he slammed the door in their faces.

After turning to walk back down the driveway Veronica spoke. "That went well."

Although they did not always receive the same violent reception, Ben and Veronica did receive the same information.

Every woman that their killer chose was a good person, but the only specific commonality was their appearance.

When they returned to the station to check in with Blake at the end of the day, they had no new theories to give him. Neither one of them could look him in the eye for fear of reading the disappointment there.

Worst of all, they feared finding out that Blake knew they were not going to get anywhere with this line of questioning and they had just proved it to him. All they could hope was that Mark had more success today than they had.

When Blake released them, they returned to the detective's office to see if Mark would share any information with them.

"I know what they used to make the bomb. I've talked to everyone in the area to see if they can remember anything. I'm also having the lab run more tests on the notecard that was on your car. Hopefully, I'll come up with something soon."

They realized that after a whole day of work nobody was any closer to coming up with new information. Glumly. they trudged over to their respective locker rooms to cool down a bit before leaving for the night.

Although much of the anger that Veronica had been feeling before had faded away, a deeper depression had settled into her heart.

After starting the day in such a wonderful mood it was twice as horrible to feel like this now. As she crossed the building to get back to the parking lot, everyone who saw her noticed the change. She had been bouncing and glowing when entering the building, now she appeared to have lost all her color and drooped as she walked.

They also noticed that Ben was walking around in the sort of frustrated way that they had always attributed to women problems in the past.

When they met in the hallway, Veronica walked straight past him and Ben slumped as if in defeat.

All of their friends watched them leave and wondered what Ben had done to incur Veronica's wrath. Once they left the building several people made bets on how long it would take Veronica to get revenge.

Cheyenne and Erica could be seen bickering over who they thought would win whatever argument Ben and Veronica were having.

Not a word was spoken all the way to Ben's house, nor were any words uttered as they walked across his front yard to the door.

They tried to muster some enthusiasm to greet the pets with, but it was a half-hearted effort.

The silence continued once they were in the house because neither one of them could come up with words for one another.

Ben went to the kitchen to start making dinner and Veronica went upstairs. While Ben was at work in the kitchen, Veronica made her way into the master bathroom and drew herself a bath.

As she lowered herself into the steaming water, Veronica tried to let go of some of the tension that had been building in her body all day. She had hoped that the warm water would help her to feel better, but all it did was clear her mind enough let it wander to the things that were bothering her.

With her eyes closed her mind began to run over Ben's tirade in the parking lot. Words could not describe how much that had hurt her. The most frustrating thing about it all was that she could not understand why it had hurt her so much. Logically, she knew that he was frustrated, but she could not let it go.

After lounging in the water for a time, Veronica dressed in her pajamas and went back down the stairs.

When she arrived in the living room she found Ben on the couch with a plate of spaghetti.

Charlotte was on the back of the couch near his head with her tail dangling down. She was tickling Ace's ear because he was on the couch next to Ben trying to steal some food off of his plate.

In spite of her wounded pride, Veronica could not help but laugh at the moment she had walked in on.

When Ben looked up to see a smile on her face, relief flooded through him. The way that she carried herself told him she was still hurt, but the smile lead him to believe there was hope that they could move past this.

"There's a plate waiting for you in the kitchen. It's probably still warm."

Veronica nodded and moved into the next room.

When she got there she found that the food had cooled down significantly while she was in the bath. She placed her plate in the microwave and went to pour herself a glass of milk.

She heard Ben enter the room, but she did not pay any attention to him until she felt his presence right behind her.

He reached around her and guided her hands to place the jug of milk and the glass down. Then he wrapped his arms around her.

She leaned back into him and drew a breath, "You told me you understood. You told me you had my back. You told me that you would never think less of me for staying away so long."

Ben rested his head on her shoulder, "I know I did. And I don't think any less of you. I'm sorry about what I said. You know I didn't mean it. I was angry and you know that I say stupid things when I'm angry."

Veronica pulled out of his arms and turned to face him. "I know that, but you wouldn't have said it if some part of you wasn't thinking it."

Ben stepped forward, "I'll admit when you first said you were coming back I wondered if you would be okay. But I don't wonder anymore. It only took a moment for me to realise that you're as good a cop now as you were then."

By this point they were standing toe to toe looking into each other's eyes. All it took was one small dip of the head and Ben's lips found hers.

For the first moment, they were both shocked by the turn of events. Ben had not planned to kiss her and Veronica had been so steadfastly ignoring the urge to kiss him that she never expected it to happen.

Ben was the first to get past his surprise. He took her shock as a bad sign and hesitantly started to pull back.

Their lips breaking contact jolted Veronica into action. Before she gave herself time to overthink it, she followed Ben and reclaimed his lips.

When she returned his kiss Ben found his arms wrapping around her waist so that he could pull her closer to him. The kiss continued until the microwave interrupted them by beeping.

Ben and Veronica awkwardly pulled apart, retrieved her dinner, and moved back into the living room.

They did not discuss their kiss that night, nor did they repeat it.

In fact, they went about their night acting like nothing at all had happened. When they went to bed there was no discussion of who would sleep where. They climbed in on the sides

that they had slept on the night before and continued to act like nothing romantic had happened between them.

DAY 6

When they woke, Veronica found they were spooning. Much like the morning before, they did not allow themselves to feel awkward when the woke up. The routine that they had established was repeated.

They were friendly with each other, but they never touched. Neither one of them knew how to react to what had happened the night before, so they silently agreed not to do anything about it until they could decide what they wanted it to mean.

When they arrived at the station they both independently decided to 'act natural.' As they entered the building, they were both acting so courteous and polite that the people who knew them best knew that there was something going on. The people who did not know them well still knew enough to try to get out of the bets they had made the night before.

They spent some time in their respective locker rooms, dodging questions and getting changed. Then they met up again in the hallway and moved over to the detective's office.

Before they could make it there, Veronica was waylaid by a small, curvy blonde that was seriously pissed off.

"Some nut job with an obsession breaks into your apartment and you don't call me! What the Hell is that?!" Natasha stood in front of her best friend with her hands on her hips, tapping her foot, waiting for her answer.

Ben looked past Natasha to see Cheyenne and Erica peering around the corner so that they could watch this conversation take place. He smiled smugly and turned to Veronica, "Someone's in trouble. I'm gonna let you deal with this."

He tried to move past Natasha but she grabbed his sleeve and yanked him to a stop. "Oh, no you don't! I have a bone to pick with you too. You have to wait your turn. Idiot best friend trumps just plain idiot!"

This time it was Veronica's turn to be smug. She stuck her tongue out at him, "At least I'm not the only one in trouble. I wonder what you did..." she mused.

Ben shoved her off balance, so she punched him in the arm after she caught herself.

Natasha eyed them suspiciously as they rough housed, but she let it slide because that was a conversation she needed to have alone with Veronica.

Natasha's gazed fell once again on Veronica, "I am waiting for my explanation!"

Veronica could not stop herself from laughing when she saw the anger flashing in her friend's eyes. She had known Natasha for so long that it was hard for Veronica to take her seriously. "Tasha, take it easy! I'm sorry I didn't call you. Things got so crazy. I got home and there was this stuff all over my living room, and we had to call it in. Then we had to deal with Blake because he was even more angry than you, if you can believe that. Then we had to go over to my old house and deal with another crime scene. We didn't get home until late and then we had to be here early to meet with Blake again. Then we spent the rest of the day working on this investigation and dealing with Blakes fabulous new rules... It was just... all so insane." Veronica looked at Natasha imploringly, hoping that she would calm down.

Natasha was silent for a moment so Veronica thought that everything was okay again, "Okay... I guess I get that. Now you have to explain to me why you didn't call me last night. If something this major had happened to me I would have called you in a second."

Veronica's shoulders slumped as she tried to come up with a reason for her radio silence. The truth was that with everything else that happened, she had not thought to call Natasha.

Fortunately, Ben tried to come to her rescue. "We were both tired when we got home last night so we ate and went to bed."

The same suspicious look that she had before appeared on Natasha's face.

Veronica knew that Natasha wanted to question her on who went to bed where, but she wanted to avoid that entire conversation. She knew that Natasha had enough tact not to bring it up with Ben in the room so she made a tactical retreat. "Well, Tasha, I would love to keep talking but if Blake thinks I'm slacking off I'll be in serious trouble. I'll leave you to attack Ben now." Veronica winked at Ben and practically skipped into the detective's office.

Cheyenne and Erica were snickering at the corner.

No sooner had the door to the office closed then Natasha turned on Ben. "So... my best friend can't or won't go home because some psycho broke into her apartment. I have a guest room in my place, and you have her sleeping on your couch. Tell me she wouldn't be better off staying with me." The challenge was evident in her eyes, but there was also a hint of something else. She was enjoying watching him squirm. Natasha was certain that neither of them were sleeping on the couch, she needed to get one of them to admit to it.

Ben glanced around the room and pulled Natasha into the less populated corridor leading to the equipment locker. He answered Natasha in a hushed but insistent voice. "Veronica is most certainly not better off staying with you. For one thing, I can protect her way better than you can. I know you're going to say that she can protect herself, but she is so much more safe living with another trained police officer. For another thing...she's not sleeping on the couch." His voice became even quieter as the humor in Natasha's eyes intensified. "I'm pretty sure you already guessed that, so the questioning is unnecessary. And before you ask...yes, we just slept. If you want anymore information than that, you are going to have to ask Veronica. I don't do girl talk, so don't even try."

Before Natasha could try to interrogate him about what other information there could be, he cut her off. "I have to go catch up with Mark and Ronnie. Goodbye, Natasha!"

Natasha laughed, saluted him, and sauntered out of the building.

Watching her go, Ben noticed her high-fiving Cheyenne and Erica on her way out.

When Ben entered the detectives' office he walked straight over to Veronica. "Thank you so much for dropping me in it back there. Yes, I returned the favor. No, I'm not gonna warn you how much you're gonna have to explain." Then he returned the wink that she gave him earlier and moved over to his desk.

He never got a chance to sit down because Mark walked into the room with news for Ben and Veronica. "Sorry to interrupt, but Blake wants to see you guys."

The pair exchanged a glance and shuffled over to Blake's office. Before they made it all the way to the door Veronica muttered, "There's no way he knows something's up."

Ben inched up closer behind her and whispered in her ear, "That's right...because nothing's up...right?" His hand grazed from the small of her back across her side as he stepped past her to open the door.

Veronica fought to keep the blush off her face as she stepped into Blake's office.

Ben fought a similar battle to keep the smirk off his face as he entered the room after her.

For the second day in a row Blake paused for a moment before he spoke. Thanks to his glass walls, Blake was able to see their entire interaction as Ben and Veronica approached his office. If he ever had any doubts that something was going on with them, he no longer did. It took him a moment to stop himself from making a comment about it. They needed a little more time left to their own devices before anyone caused too much of a fuss. He did wish that he could get involved in the bet the most of his officers had started.

Once Ben and Veronica were both sitting in front of him, Blake started talking. "I had an idea last night that I would like you two to follow up on. Before you get all offended again Ben, I was not trying to do your job for you. I just had an idea. I know you guys had a bit of a rough day yesterday, and I can't follow up on this myself, so I was hoping you would. I'm sure you would have covered this angle eventually anyways. All I'm saying is, hear me out and if you don't come up with anything else today, look into it."

Ben was in a great mood so he found it amusing that Blake was trying so hard not to insult him. "Boss, before you say anything else, I should probably apologise for yesterday. I shouldn't have reacted the way I did. You know me, my temper gets the better of me sometimes."

Blake was glad that he could get on with things. "It's good to see you've finally admitted it. Anyways, I was thinking about the period where our guy went dormant. The question I'm asking is; why he went dormant for so long? The way he's behaving now shows that he is obviously still angry, so why did he stop communicating for such a long time? We know that it doesn't have anything to do with anything new that Veronica did, so what changed?"

Veronica looked down sheepishly. "That might not be entirely true, sir." Veronica would not look Blake in the eye as she continued. "Well, you see, you can probably tell I finished the physical therapy for my leg a while ago. I was using the excuse of getting back in shape and getting my head on straight before I took the steps to start working here again. Well...the truth is...I didn't think I was ever gonna come back. That's why I started working at the museum during my leave of absence. I know I hadn't told you anything, and I'm sorry. Ben was the only person who knew I wasn't planning to come back, and I know he didn't tell anyone. So, the killer probably knew that I was running out of time on my leave of absence. This might be his sick way of welcoming me back."

Normally, he would have been frustrated with her for keeping things from him, but they did not have time for lectures at the moment. "Okay...we can talk about that later. But I don't think that will turn up much in the investigation. Anyone who was watching you as closely as this guy appears to have been, would have known you had not contacted us about coming back. I still think your best bet is to look into why he left you alone for so long after promising revenge."

Neither Ben nor Veronica was sure how they would be able to check that information, but they were willing to play off their boss' hunch.

If Veronica was being honest, she would

have had to admit that she was not sure anything they checked would be useful. With so many people watching her and her apartment 24/7 they were bound to catch him next time he decided to taunt her. She would never tell Blake or Ben, or anyone else for that matter, but she was using herself as bait.

They would get angry and throw her in a safe house for the rest of the investigation, but she was perfectly fine with the situation. She was willing to do anything that had to be done to get this guy. If that meant that she had to continue dangling herself in front of him, and deal with bodyguards all the time, she could do that. She was also willing to chase what she thought would be a dead end line of investigation until he slipped up and gave them another clue to look into.

Blake mistook Ben and Veronica's silence upon hearing his idea for shame at not thinking it up themselves. "I know. It's shocking that I came up with this all by myself, right? Like I said, I'm sure you guys would have looked into it on your own eventually."

Veronica's lips tightened into a thin line in an attempt to avoid laughing. Laughing at one's superior is a bad idea. Ben saw her struggling and thanked Blake so that they could get out of the room.

Ben and Veronica practically sprinted to the detective's office and collapsed into each other as the door closed. Their laughter filled the room and they were both grateful that there was no one else there. Once they had recovered from the laughing fit, they straightened up and looked around.

Ben became distracted by all of the faces turned in the direction of the office. "Right now I'm wishing we didn't have glass walls for all of our offices. There is no such thing as privacy in this building."

The mischievous smile that he loved so much flashed across her face. "Oh, there are plenty of places to find privacy in this building...Nick and I found all of them."

Although it was an offhand comment, Ben was blown away by it. This was the first time that Veronica had talked about Nick without an ounce of sadness on her face since he died. He thought back to the kiss they shared the night before and could not help but wonder where some of the private places were. Someday he might ask her, but for now he would keep those thoughts to himself. He could not wait to kiss her again, but he knew that she needed time to digest what happened last night. If he pushed her now she would clam up and then he would never have a chance. Ben was a bit shocked as these thoughts flew across his mind. In the past three days Veronica had gone from being his best friend to being a woman that he had to try not to touch.

"Okay, before we draw anymore attention to ourselves, we should get working."

Veronica sat down in the chair that she had moved to Ben's desk yesterday. "Fine, but you do know that if this idea pans out you and I will never hear the end of it."

Ben smiled, "Nah, it's good for Sarge to use his skills sometimes. He only took the promotion because he needed the money, otherwise he'd still be a detective. He loved it, but when his daughter got sick he needed to bring in more cash. He does this with a lot of cases. He'll call the lead detective in, give them a few suggestions. They're always good...usually lead to something. I'm not sure what happened with this one. Maybe he was desperate to give us something to do. I don't know about you, but I was running out of ideas."

The talk of Blake's daughter sobered Veronica up quickly. "How is Sarah doing? Did the chemo work?"

A genuine smile graced Ben's features as he answered her. "She's doing well. She went into remission a few months ago. Blake and his wife threw this big party for her. Half the precinct showed up. It was good to see her smiling again. She's so young to have gone through all of that."

Hearing that Sarah Blake was doing better made her happy. Sarah had always been a sweet girl and when she was diagnosed with lung cancer it had broken her heart. She knew she should have kept in touch after Nick died, but she did not do a lot of things that she should have done after Nick died. "That's great! Maybe someday soon I can go see her."

The smile continued to shine on Ben's face, "I think Sarah would love that."

Once they had both managed to focus their minds on work again they started brainstorming reasons why a psychotic, obsessed killer would put his criminal life on pause for so long only to pick it up right where he left off.

They cleared the timeline of victim's lives off of their board and started writing up any idea that came to mind. It all started out serious. The first few items on the board included "moving to a new city/state/country," "recovering from an illness," and "changing his M.O. and staying active." As the list became longer the suggestions became sillier. At one point, Veronica was spinning in her chair and periodically stopping to point at the board and yelling out suggestions. The end of the list included such things as "recovering from a sex change operation," "hiding from a vigilante," and "abduction by aliens." Once they hit "abduction by aliens," Ben knew that it was time for a break so they decided to meet up with Ryan and Cheyenne at Uncle Sam's for lunch.

When they all got there, Cheyenne and Ryan sat on one side of the booth while Ben and Veronica sat together on the other. All of them were still feeling a bit awkward about the conversation they had two nights before so they avoided the topic as they ate. Instead they chose to reminisce on old times. They spent an hour swapping stories and making fun of each other. Laughter filled the room as they all let themselves get lost in each other's company.

Neither Ryan nor Cheyenne had realized how wrong it had felt to have Veronica be gone until they were sitting at a table with her in uniform again. Neither one of them had seen much of her in the past year, but they were both on the scene when she found the new card on her windshield. They could see the dramatic difference in her countenance between then and now. She had so much more color, only a few days later. Her eyes were starting to sparkle again and they loved seeing her smile and laugh.

While Ryan and Cheyenne were watching Veronica and admiring how well she was doing under the circumstances, Ben and Veronica were having fun trying to get the other to blush. When they first sat down they made a point of making sure that their legs were not touching. As the meal progressed, they slowly relaxed more and more until the full length of their legs were resting against one another.

Veronica felt like her whole body ignited when his knee brushed against hers. At first she had a difficult time concentrating on all the stories that were being told, but by the time their legs were fully touching she had managed to regain her poker face. This was totally blown to pieces when Ben dropped his arm under the table and placed his hand well above her knee. She squirmed in place and did her best not to blush or lose track of the conversation. She knew that she needed to turn the tables on him or she was never going to hear the end of it. To do this she discreetly crossed her legs under the table effectively trapping his hand on her thigh. The subtle flinch that followed made her smile wider. It appeared that she had called his bluff and won. That is, until he shifted his hand higher up her leg. She glanced over at him and noticed that he had slightly lifted one eyebrow. Veronica was determined not to let him win so she slowly shifted her foot over to made contact with his leg and then she started rubbing her foot up and down it. She was sure that this tactic would have been more effective had she not been wearing her bulky uniform boots, but this would do for now.

For the first time in years, Veronica was actively trying to keep all thought of Nick out of her mind. Flirting with Ben, kissing Ben would be too strange if she thought about how he was her dead fiancé's best friend. The morning after Ben told her that he wouldn't be coming back to the cemetery, Veronica told herself that she was going to start doing the things that make her happy again. She knew that it was not healthy to be living the half life that she had ever since she woke up in the hospital. In all honesty, she probably would have found herself back at the station eventually. However, what she never expected was how good it would feel to get this close to another person again, especially seeing as that person was Ben. After Ben kissed her last night, she had been going over everything in her mind. It was fun, having someone to do all these things with again. No matter how strange it felt, she wanted to see where this would go.

When they finished their burgers, everyone got their things together and started heading back out to their cars.

As they were approaching the door, Cheyenne tugged on Veronica's arm and hissed in her ear. "By the way...I totally saw that. There is something going on between you two and I. Want. Details." Cheyenne smiled knowingly at her as she passed.

This is gonna be interesting.

Veronica followed Cheyenne out to the lot and climbed into Ben's truck.

He was already inside and waiting for her.

"That was so mean."

Veronica smirked at him, "A lady never starts a fight, but she can finish them."

This earned a deep-belly laugh from Ben, "Did you seriously quote 'The Aristocats'?"

Veronica laughed in turn, "Did you seriously admit to knowing that movie well enough recognize the quote?"

Ben pushed her into the door of the truck, "Hey! I have a little sister. That was one of her favorite movies growing up. She must have made me sit through it a thousand times when we were kids."

Veronica shoved him back, "Yeah, and I'll bet that you made Megan watch The Sandlot at least twice that many times."

Ben nodded his head and started the car. When they got to the station, their antics continued as they crossed to the detective's office. They were so distracted that they did not notice two people were already there. When they opened the door they both stopped in their tracks and became silent.

Blake and Mark were standing in front of their board reading it.

Blake turned around and they looked down guiltily. "Abduction by aliens...interesting." He lifted an eyebrow and left the room.

Mark had been able to hold in the laughter while Blake was there, but now that he had gone there was no reason to. Mark doubled over and almost hit the floor he was laughing so hard. "Sex change operation! I forgot how ridiculous you two could be! Although, it probably would have been better if you had erased the stupid ones before you left the building." Mark picked up an eraser and started removing all of the suggestions at the bottom of the list. "Don't worry, if anything, seeing you two goof around makes him worry about you less. I did notice that you were missing something from this board. Have you considered the possibility that this guy went to jail. If he was put away for something minor and got out, it would explain why he dropped off the face of the earth for so long."

Veronica was skeptical, "Would someone that careful get caught for something minor enough to only get him a year?"

Ben understood why she was unconvinced, but he knew that they had to look into everything. It did not matter if they doubted the theory or not. "It's worth looking into. We'll definitely add it to the list. Thanks, Mark."

They spent the next few hours working on the first theory on their list. This was long and frustrating because they were relying mostly on the goodwill of realty companies and apartment managers. There was no way for them to track who had entered the city recently so they had to come up with some creative methods.

A judge would never give them warrants for the information they needed without more evidence, so they had to try to talk people into giving it to them voluntarily. They called all of the major realtors in the city and begged them to provide access to their client lists. The plan was for them to run the records of any names they got to see if any had lived in the city a year ago. They would take all of those people and check to see if any matched the sketchy physical description they possessed.

The problem was the realty companies; they were under no obligation to provide any information to the police. In fact, many of them made it their policy not to give out any information on their clients. With every person they spoke to they had to explain who they were going after and what that person had done. A few were moved enough to agree and give them their client lists. Even though most companies refused to cooperate with them, they still got enough names to keep them busy for the rest of the day. When it was time for them to leave they had the names of about fifteen men who had recently moved back to the city after spending a year away. They were planning on giving those names to the police psychologist the next day so that she could check whether or not the men fit the psychological profile.

Before they left Ben and Veronica stopped

by Blake's office to update him on their progress for the day. He listened to them describe what they had done and what they had come up with, and then he gave them his suggestions. "You aren't going to get anywhere with the other realty companies. They knew the story and they didn't care enough to give you the information, and we would need a whole Hell of a lot more than a theory if we want to get any kind of warrant. I suggest that you move on to another theory while you wait for the shrink to get back to you on the names you already got. If you keep turning over stones then eventually we'll find the hole that this man lives in."

Blake watched Ben and Veronica as they left the building. It was obvious how close the two of them had become over the last few days. All anyone had to do was watch them walking together to see it. They moved as a unit; their steps were in sync with each other. When they came across an obstacle they would move closer together and squeeze past it rather than separating and going to either side of it. Sometimes, when they were close enough, their arms would brush one another's as they moved and if you watched carefully, you could see that their hands would momentarily hesitate before they separated. The most amusing thing was that they thought they were hiding it so well. Blake couldn't help but wonder what it was about the men of this precinct that Veronica found so appealing.

They think they are being so subtle. EVERY-ONE KNOWS! They are all being too polite to say anything, but I'm not that nice. Maybe it's time they realize that they're not very good actors.

Ben and Veronica had managed to keep things from getting too awkward during the day, but when they got back to his house that became far more difficult. When they had been at the station and at lunch they had to keep up the appearance that everything was normal. It was fun to mess with each other to see if the other could keep a straight face, but it was not serious.

When they were at home there was no one to pretend for anymore. They could do whatever they wanted; the only problem was they no idea what they wanted to do. When they got home they spent a lot of time saying hello to their pets, changing into more comfortable clothes, and avoiding all contact with each other.

Eventually, they found themselves on opposite sides of the living room without any more excuses to stay away from each other. Slowly they started making their way closer together until they were standing right in front of each other.

Ben looked down at her, "I get... if you don't want to... if you want to forget about..." He eventually stammered to a stop not knowing how he wanted to finish that sentence.

Veronica stood thinking for a moment. "I'm not sure how this is gonna work. I don't even know for sure what this is. We could stop now and say it's because we want to save our friendship, but I think we both know we would be lying. I have no idea where this came from. Until last night...I never even entertained the possibility...but now I can't stop thinking about it. I'm not saying I want us to jump in and run with this. I think we should take it slow, do the things that make us happy and go from there."

Ben moved a bit closer and twined the fingers of his left hand with her right. "I can live with that. I do seem to remember something that made us both happy last night."

Veronica smiled and tipped her head up as she rose up on her toes.

They were a moment from finally kissing when the doorbell rang.

Ben paused for a moment, "Ignore it. They'll go away."

Veronica let out a small laugh and leaned towards him again.

Once again, they were interrupted before they could get too close. This time whoever it was had started knocking on the door.

Ben tipped his head back and groaned, "I will kill them."

Veronica started laughing as the knocking became more insistent.

Ben scowled at her and stalked over to the door. He threw it open and groaned once again. He turned to Veronica, "This one is for you."

Veronica looked at him quizzically, but when Natasha sauntered through the door holding two bottles of wine she understood.

Ben grabbed his keys and headed for the door. "It looks like girl talk is imminent. I'm gonna head over to Mark's place. There's a weekly poker night that some of the guys have...guess I won't be missing it this week. Call me if anything happens, and do not go anywhere the protective detail can't get to you." With one last look he trudged out the door.

Natasha and Veronica heard the engine turn over and then there was nothing.

Natasha burst out laughing, "Did I interrupt something?"

Veronica chucked a pillow at her before starting to laugh herself. "Shut up! If we are going to have this conversation, we are going to need a lot more wine and I need to make a call."

Twenty minutes later, there was another knock on the door.

When Veronica opened it, she was surprised to see Erica grinning next to Cheyenne.

Veronica smiled good-naturedly, "I didn't know you were bringing Elsa."

Cheyenne grinned wider while Erica looked confused. "Elsa...?"

Veronica took pity on her and explained, "Ice Queen. Don't you remember the nickname Andrew gave you?"

At this, Erica gave a startled guffaw and the three started laughing together.

Erica's laugh had always had a somewhat sinister quality to it, so when she was laughing hysterically, it almost sounded like a cackle.

When Natasha began to get annoyed with being left out of the joke, they stopped and explained it to her.

When the five newbies had started at the station, Erica had been relieved, because that meant that she could pass the infuriating moniker of "rookie" on to them.

Andrew had taken an instant liking to her, but Erica had never cared for him. This resulted in some truly uncomfortable nights at the bar and Erica having to freeze out Andrew so that he would finally take the hint. This suited her fine because she had never been a particularly affectionate person in public, but it did earn her the unfortunate epithet, Ice Queen.

After becoming friends with Cheyenne, Jennifer, and Veronica, she had opened up to the group more and even scored herself a few invites to their rookies-only movie nights. However, the nickname never died.

Once they were all seated with a glass of wine each Veronica started speaking. "Okay, this is how this is gonna work. If we are gonna talk about this, it stays between the four of us."

Natasha grinned at Veronica and took a sip of her wine. "I knew there was something going on!"

Cheyenne could not contain her laughter. "You should have seen the two of them at lunch. They literally couldn't keep their hands off each other...or their feet," Cheyenne spoke in a mocking tone.

Veronica tried to hide her face behind a pillow, but Cheyenne would not allow it. She pulled the pillow back as she spoke again. "I know you two thought we couldn't see you, but you were wrong. Ryan might have been oblivious, but I saw the whole thing. Don't worry... I won't say anything."

Erica cut in, "You mean to tell me that Veronica dared to feel up Ben in front of our poor, innocent Cheyenne? Before we go on, I have to ask, is this conversation going to be Cheyenne-able? Should we have her cover her Mormon ears? We wouldn't want to shock her."

Cheyenne slapped her, but was obviously a little worried about what the answer might be.

Before Veronica could answer, Natasha cut in. "Please! We both know that she's a bit of a Jack Mormon. Note the wine glass in her hand."

Cheyenne turned even more red.

Veronica chugged down half of her glass of wine. "Fine...here it is. We kissed...once. And...that's it. That's the whole story." Then she chugged down the rest of her wine and refilled her glass. She summoned up the most innocent look she could manage and gave it to her three friends because she knew they were not buying it.

When Natasha started speaking, Veronica retrieved the pillow to hide behind, but she still peeked at them from over the top of it. "Yeah, right! That is so not the whole story! If you want to make up for not telling me about moving in here, you owe me way more details than that."

Veronica lowered the pillow and hugged it. "Okay, fine. I did tell you the truth. We have only kissed once..." Veronica took a deep breath. "It happened last night. We were talking. He was apologizing for saying something stupid. I didn't even notice how close we were until he was right there. I didn't know what to do at first. It was so weird...I mean...he was going to be Nick's Best Man. He pulled away and I thought 'screw it' and I kissed him back...Then the microwave went off, and we haven't kissed since. We didn't even talk about it until we got home earlier. We had some fun with it today. Neither one of us are jump-into-a-relationship type people, especially not with each other. So we're gonna go slow. We're gonna do what feels right. If it grows into something more...we'll deal with the weirdness of it then."

Cheyenne, Erica, and Natasha were silent for a few moments. None of them had expected to get the whole story from her. At least not without having to pump Veronica full of wine first. They got over the shock of Veronica opening up to them fairly quickly.

Cheyenne was the first to speak. She raised her glass and said, "To Ben!"

Natasha, Erica, and Veronica all burst out laughing and raised their own glasses, "To Ben!"

All four women clinked their glasses together and took a sip. They spent the rest of the night working their way through all four bottles of wine, laughing, and dancing to music.

When the clock struck midnight, Veronica poured Natasha into one cab and Cheyenne and Erica into another, and told them to come back the next day for their cars.

Cheyenne had not drunk much, but she was extremely tired and Veronica worried about her driving.

Veronica was still stumbling around downstairs when Ben made it back from his poker night.

He chuckled when he saw her struggling to walk in a straight line from the living room to the kitchen with the empty wine bottles. "You know you are gonna have to work tomorrow and yet you still get yourself stumbling drunk. You are so gonna regret that in the morning." Ben took a look around his trashed living room. "What in the world did you two do to my house?"

Veronica shuffled into the room behind him and crashed onto the couch. "Four, actually. Cheyenne and Erica came over too. There was lots of drinking...and dancing...there might have been some talk of you."

Ben continued to laugh throughout her explanation. "And what exactly did you tell them about me?"

Veronica looked down at the couch for a moment then tipped her head up again to look him in the eye. "I told them that we had only kissed once." Veronica moved with surprising accuracy to straddle his lap, "Then I told them I intended to change that."

Before Ben could speak or there could be any more interruptions, Veronica crashed their lips together. They spent the next few minutes making out on the couch like teenagers.

Eventually, Ben pushed her off him. "Don't think I'm not enjoying this, because I am, but you're drunk. As much as I would love to continue this, I think it's probably best if we follow your earlier plan and take this slow. I don't want you to wake up tomorrow and regret more than the wine you drank tonight."

Veronica looked at him for a moment and then slumped onto the couch next to him. "Fine. I might have some difficulty with the stairs tonight. I think it's best if I sleep here."

Ben thought about it for a moment and then shook his head. "I don't think so." He stood up and scooped Veronica into his arms.

She squeaked and threw her arms around his neck.

"I said we should take things slow, but I like waking up with you in the mornings. We're both adults, we can sleep in the same bed without letting things go too far."

Without a comeback, she snuggled into his chest. She lost consciousness before they even made it to his room.

DAY 7

Veronica felt like death warmed over when she woke up the next morning. It had been a long time since she had had a hangover this bad. If her brain could make a sound, she was sure it would be screaming in agony as the sun light from the window reached her now open eyes. She groaned and flipped over so her face was buried in the pillows.

When she heard Ben laughing from the bathroom she groaned again. "I hate you."

Ben started laughing louder.

"Shut up!"

Ben managed to stop laughing long enough to say, "I told you that you'd regret all that wine this morning. I left a present for you on the table." Then he continued to laugh as he went back into the bathroom to finish getting ready.

Veronica lifted her head enough to see the two aspirin capsules and bottle of gatorade on the bed-side table.

"Bless you!"

She shifted herself up to take the pills and gulped down at least half of the gatorade bottle. What with her brain being in so much pain, Veronica had forgotten that Ben had been there for some of her more intense hangovers and was well aware of her favorite cure.

Ben allowed her to stay in bed for as long as he could, but eventually he had to get her up so she could eat before they headed over to the station.

"You have to get out of bed now. There are eggs and a cup of coffee waiting for you downstairs... A shower might be a good idea too. You smell like hangover and sweat."

Veronica rolled out of bed and started to walk out of the room. "Bless you twice."

Ben chuckled as he watched her leave.

When they made it to the station she could be seen sporting a pair of dark sunglasses. Everyone knew what it meant when she did not remove them after she entered the building.

The first thing she did upon arriving at the station was to go straight to the break room to pour herself a new cup of coffee. The aspirin had kicked in, so thinking was less painful but it still felt like her brain was about two sizes too big for her head.

Once she had finished with her newest jolt

of caffeine, Veronica went over to the locker room to get changed into her uniform. While she was there, she noticed that Cheyenne was nowhere to be seen.

"I swear if she called out sick…"

Veronica pulled out her cell phone and dialed Cheyenne's number.

After the fourth ring a groggy Cheyenne answered the phone, "First of all, I hate you. Second, no, I didn't call out sick. Thirdly, if you bothered to look at the schedule, you would know that today is my day off. I'm going to hang up now because I'm tired and I want to sleep in. Goodbye, Veronica. I'll see you when I don't feel like punching you in the face for letting me drink and keeping me up so late. Oh, and slap Erica for me. I told her the two extra wine bottles was a bad idea."

When Veronica heard the click of Cheyenne hanging up she started laughing. "At least I'm not the only one in bad shape today. I wonder how Tasha's doing?"

She finished loading all of her stuff into her locker and met Ben in the hallway to have their morning meeting with Blake.

When they made it into his office, Blake was waiting for them with a smile on his face. "Veronica, I got a call from the crime lab. Looks like you can get your car back today. They didn't find anything in it."

Veronica was grateful she was going to

have her own vehicle again. She did not mind riding with Ben, but missed her independence.

Blake did not have any more news for them, so he sent them on their way.

Before they moved on to researching a new theory, they found one other thing that they wanted to look into. They looked up to see if there were any strings of unsolved murders in other areas that even somewhat matched their killer's MO.

Unfortunately, they were not able to find any traces of a serial killer with a penchant for burying people alive that had not already been caught or killed.

When they had exhausted all methods for researching this theory, they turned to their board to start looking after other ones. Both of them were tired of calling people and begging for information so they decided to work the only theory where they already had access to all the information they needed.

Veronica still found it difficult to believe that someone so meticulous would get caught for something that would only put them away for a short time, but it was a theory that needed to be looked into.

The first thing they did was run a search for all men that had been arrested around the time of the bombing at Veronica and Nick's home and were recently released. They came up with far more names than either of them wanted, but it gave them a place to start. They went through all of their files and narrowed that list down by filtering out anyone who would not have been physically able to dig the graves and carry the bodies. Many of the names that they had were repeat offenders. They checked police records to make sure the men were unaccounted for on the dates of the abductions. This narrowed down their list a little bit more, but they lived in a large city and it was full of criminals who would love pulling one over on the cops.

They were so engrossed in going through every man's file that they decided not to go out for lunch. Instead ordering Chinese food and having it delivered to the building.

It felt like old times as they leaned back in their chairs chowing down on General Tso's chicken while they continued to work through the files that their search had kicked out.

Mark and the other detectives had come and gone a few times throughout the day, but other than that they were left undisturbed.

By the end of the day they had 47 more names of potential suspects to give to the psychologist. When they stopped by her office, she thrust the pile of files from the day before back into Veronica's hands as she took the new one.

"Only a few of those matched the profile. I put their names on the note at the top. I would appreciate it if you would check out those guys before you give me any more names. I have other things to do and this stack is going to take me days to work through."

Ben and Veronica thanked her and went on their way. Stopping by Blake's office as they left, they gave him the names that the psychologist had identified.

"We've got Jerald Simpson, Andrew Marx, Rafael Castillo, Randy Sanders, and Jason Axley. Veronica and I will look at them more in depth tomorrow. Right now we have nowhere near enough information to check out their places, but we can run a more thorough background check to see if we find anything."

Blake saw nothing wrong with that course of action, so he let them go.

When they walked through the door into the parking lot, Ben and Veronica both stopped in their tracks.

Veronica was the first to speak, "You have got to be kidding me!"

As she fell back against the closed door Ben spoke, "What is it with this guy and vehicles?"

He pulled out his cell phone and dialled Blake's number. After a moment he started speaking, "Guess what Veronica and I found when we got into the parking lot...Nope, there appears to be a white note card on my windshield...No, we did not go check it out...Yup, we'll stay here and wait." Ben put his phone back into his pocket.

When he turned around and found Veronica leaning against the door he grabbed her arm and pulled her off of it. Moments later Blake and four patrol officers ran through it.

Blake spoke as the others grouped around Ben and Veronica. "I've got the bomb squad and the crime techs on the way. I want both of you back in the building right now."

They were both ready to argue; they wanted to see what was on the card. But before they could say anything, the other officers started herding them into the station.

They were escorted back to Blake's office and told to stay there until Blake came and got them. Once again, they were ready to argue or try to break out, but the entirely glass wall between the office and the rest of the station discouraged them.

They sat for ten minutes without speaking or moving before Veronica turned to Ben and finally said something. "So, what do you think was on that card?"

Ben put his arm around her shoulder and hugged her to him. "I guess we're about to find out.

Half an hour after that, Blake stormed back into the room. "Bomb squad cleared the car. The techs are going over it right now. I wanted to show you what was on the windshield before they took it with them."

Once he finished he slapped it down on the desk in front of them. "Turns out it was a photo, not a card."

They both looked down and gulped. The photo that they were looking at was of the two of them on Ben's couch last night in a compromising position. There was a note written in red ink across the top of the photo, 'YOU THOUGHT NO ONE KNEW?'

Blake sat down in the chair across the desk from them, "Is there something you'd like to tell me?" If Blake had worn half moon glasses, Veronica would have sworn he was pretending to be Dumbledore.

Ben and Veronica slumped back into their chairs and looked at each other.

She spoke first, "Deja Vu."

Ben was far more angry than anything else, "Bastard bugged my house!"

Blake cut in before either of them could continue. "That much is obvious. I've sent a team to your place to sweep for bugs and collect them all. It's gonna take a while so you two are gonna have to find another place to stay for the night."

Ben and Veronica were both still staring at the photo with identical expressions of shock and anger.

She was the first one to snap out of it. "Yeah, uh, my apartment has been cleared. I guess we could both stay there tonight. I was kind of hoping to be able to stay away from there for a while, but...desperate times, right?"

Ben looked up at Blake, "Can we stop by my place first? Charlotte and Ace are still there."

Blake sighed and nodded, "Fine, but make it quick and settle down for the night."

Ben and Veronica nodded their understanding and got up to leave.

Before they could make it out of the door, Blake stopped them. "What you two do when you leave this building is none of my business, but don't let it affect your working together. If it does I'm sending Veronica back out on the street and she won't be working with the detectives again anytime soon. There is a reason why we discourage partners from dating. I know you aren't official partners, but for the moment you might as well be. If I see any of...this...in my station, there will be no second chances."

When they made it back out into the parking lot they both realised that they didn't have a car there.

"I guess it's a good thing that my car is cleared. It's not that far a walk to the crime lab. Let's go get it."

Ben shook his head, "We need your keys first."

Veronica started digging through her seemingly bottomless purse. "If I remember correctly, I put my keys in my purse when we left my apartment last. I don't think I ever took them out... Ah ha!...Victory!"

Veronica waved her keys in the air. "Well, alrighty then! To the crime lab!"

Veronica was suddenly happy that they had finally hit October, because they had gotten past the worst of the Phoenix heat. It was almost pleasant out as they walked down the sidewalk that was interspaced with palo verde trees. Every few steps, their hands would brush together as they walked.

After about ten minutes, Veronica hesitantly grabbed his hand. She refused to look at him until he shifted his hand to intertwine their fingers. She blew out a relieved breath and smiled at him.

"So, my guess is that by tomorrow everyone is gonna know about that photo. What are we telling people?"

Ben sighed because he knew that they were eventually going to have to have this conversation. "I suppose we tell them the truth. Something happened that we weren't expecting...now we're figuring out what it means. Other than that, it's none of their business."

Veronica gazed forward while she contemplated his words. "I guess that works. It's just that...I just got back...and Nick was your best friend...this is really complicated."

Ben stopped walking and pulled her to a stop with him. "Believe me, I know exactly how complicated it is. I am well aware that if Nick hadn't died you two would be married with a child and I would probably still be enjoying a string of one night stands. You and I were never meant to feel any of this. I can't help but wonder if you are only feeling this because Nick was my best friend. I don't wanna be his substitute."

Veronica raised the hand that was not twined with his and placed it on his cheek. "I have absolutely no idea why this is happening. I wasn't planning on it either. In fact, I didn't want it. I've never wanted a substitute for Nick. All I know is that this, whatever it is, it's more than just a physical attraction. There are real feelings here. I just don't want to push them too far too fast."

Ben seemed to accept that answer because he smiled and continued on his way. "I'm glad we got that conversation out of the way. We both knew it was coming. Now we can go back to enjoying ourselves."

Veronica smiled and squeezed his hand.

About five minutes later they arrived at the crime lab.

As they entered the building, Joe, an old friend of Veronica's, hurried forward and pulled her into a hug. "It has been way too long."

Veronica nodded and hugged him back.

After they spent a few minutes catching up Ben and Veronica headed back out of the building. "You know…If Joe weren't old enough to be your father, I might be a bit jealous."

Veronica laughed as she unlocked the door to her beautiful, green SUV. "I've missed my car."

While they had settled into their seats, Ben turned on the radio. After a second, Imagine Dragon's "Radioactive" started blasting through the speakers.

Veronica jumped and moved to turn down the volume. "Sorry. When I'm alone in the car I usually like listening to it loud."

Ben shook his head, "Don't apologize. I do the same thing. Let's go get the pets."

Veronica put the car in gear and started driving. In what felt like no time at all they were at Ben's house collecting Charlotte and Ace. They were there long enough to talk to the team of men sweeping through his house searching for surveillance equipment.

So far they had only found a camera and microphone in the living room, but neither Ben nor Veronica wanted to spend anymore time in that house until it was thoroughly searched. Whoever it was that was watching them had already spied on too many private moments and conversations for their liking.

One thing that bothered both of them is that they could not figure out how he managed to get into the house. Ben was a cop. He never left his house unsecured, and there were no signs of forced entry. Either this guy was the most accomplished lock picker in the world or he some- how got his hands on a key to Ben's home. This disturbing thought had Ben calling a locksmith before they left the house.

When they got to Veronica's apartment, neither one of them wanted to go inside. They knew that the bugs were being removed from Ben's house, but they did not want to think about what could be in her apartment. With Ben carrying Charlotte and Veronica holding on to Ace's leash, they both paused at the door.

"Maybe we should wait. We could call Blake and have this place swept too. We don't want anymore pictures of us floating around. We're gonna have a hard enough time living down the last one."

Veronica wanted to agree with him so that she did not have to go into the apartment again, but there was something she had to do first. "No, he knew we would have to come here tonight. I want to see if he left anything for us this time."

Ben squared his jaw and nodded.

He passed Charlotte over to Veronica and pulled out his gun. As he moved to step in front of her, Ben caught the annoyed look on her face. "Humor me."

Veronica huffed but moved behind him.

Ben pulled out his keys and inserted the spare that Veronica had given him after she moved into the building.

Once the door was open, Veronica put Charlotte down and drew her own gun.

This time it was Ben's turn to take on a disgruntled expression.

Veronica shot it right back at him, "That's the best you are ever gonna get."

Ben pursed his lips, but nodded anyways. "Fine."

As a unit, they moved through the apartment as they cleared it. They separated momentarily while Veronica cleared her bedroom and Ben moved down the hall to clear the spare room that Veronica had turned into a library shortly after she moved in.

While Ben was in the library he heard a clatter coming from Veronica's room and then hurried footsteps. He took off, running down the hall. The few seconds that it took him to reach her room felt like the longest seconds of his life. He could feel his heart beating so fast, he was sure he would have a heart attack. The entire way down the hall he was kicking himself for not going in with her. They both knew that eventually the killer was going to try to hurt her or worse and he let her walk in on her own.

As he moved down the hall with his gun drawn, he prayed that when he got there he would find Veronica and not an empty room. He had no idea how she could have been taken so quickly, but he did not want to find out if it was possible. He never knew that so much could pass through a person's mind in such a short amount of time. He found himself making promises to God that he had never made before if only he could find her safe.

As he approached Veronica's open bed-room door, he could see her gun lying on the floor in the threshold of the room and he felt his heart leap into his throat. *Please...*

When Ben fully entered the room he was stunned to a stop by the scene before him. The entire room was covered in rose petals; literally every flat surface. He saw a card on the bed and cautiously moved forward.

'ENJOY.'

Moments after reading that he heard a sound coming from the bathroom to his left. He quickly spun on a heel as he once again raised his weapon. He could not see anything so he started walking towards the door.

Once more, a few seconds felt like a life-time as he crept towards a room that may or may not contain something he did not want to see. During that time he recognised the sound that he was hearing. It was the sound of someone retching. When he finally reached the door and turned to face the rest of the room he found Ver-onica kneeling in front of the toilet puking her guts out.

Ben let out a breath that he had not real-ized he had been holding, and holstered his gun. Once it was safely back in place he walked over to Veronica and held her hair back as she continued to vomit. When that turned into quiet sobbing he stood and walked over to the sink to retrieve a towel for her. While his back was turned he heard the toilet flush and then Veronica walked up behind him and beat him to the sink.

She turned the tap on and filled her mouth with water so that she could wash the taste away. Once she had cleaned up a bit she moved back into the living room to find her phone and call Blake to have him come run the scene at her apartment again. While the phone was ringing she looked over at Ben and said, "I'm so tired of this."

Not for the first time, Veronica was well and truly terrified. Her secret plan to use herself as bait had failed epically. The killer had gotten into the station's parking lot and her apartment without ever being seen. Deep down she knew that this was the killer telling her that he could get to her anywhere. It did not matter how many people she had watching her, he would always be there. She had never feared for her life more than she did in this moment. The only thing she could think of to give her any kind of hope was that he might not have come up with a plan to deal with the surveillance cameras in the station's parking lot and they might finally find out what he looks like. The chances were slim, but at the moment it was all she had to cling to.

Twenty minutes later, it was a familiar scene as Blake, a few patrol officers, and several crime techs combed through Veronica's apartment.

"How does he keep getting into our homes? There has never been any sign of a break in."

Blake appeared to be as annoyed as she was. He was not a fan of getting these calls every day. "I don't know! I guess that's something we're gonna have to ask the sick son of a bitch! That is of course if we can ever catch the bastard!"

Blake had always been know to be even tempered, so to see him lose his cool once again so soon after yelling at them in the exact same apartment was enough to silence everyone in the room.

Ben had found a cat carrier that he had left there once and placed an annoyed Charlotte in it. Now both she and Ace were waiting by the door.

"It's looking like Ronnie and I are gonna have to find another place to stay for the night. I have to admit, I'm starting to run out of ideas."

Natasha spoke from the doorway. "No need for that. You two are staying at my place for now."

Veronica motioned for the patrol officers to let her into the room and then hugged her.

"You know I only called you to avoid another pissed off visit at the station. You didn't have to come all the way down here."

Natasha pushed her off. "Yes, I did." She turned to Blake, "These two look like they haven't had a proper meal all day. I'm gonna go take them for food. I don't care if you want them to stay. By the sounds of things, they've been through enough today. If you want to ask them any questions it can wait until tomorrow." Then she turned and flounced out of the room.

Ben and Veronica were sure that Blake was going to take his gun out and shoot her right there in the living room, but for some reason her outburst seemed to lighten his mood a bit.

He looked over at the pair and said, "Well, you heard her."

They jumped and followed after their friend once they retrieved their pets, and found Natasha in the hallway.

"Tasha, I thought he was gonna kill you. What in the world would make you think it was a good idea to talk to him like that?"

Natasha stood sassily with her hip thrust out. "Oh, please! That man knows I could snap him like a twig."

Ben and Veronica shared the same incredulous look and waited for the real story from their friend.

She deflated a bit, "Fine! I called him when I was on my way and asked him if he needed you two tonight."

Veronica started laughing first, but Ben joined in soon after and said, "So, you asked permission before you did that! Yeah, you're super tough!"

Natasha shoved them both. "Hey, hey, hey! No laughing! Not only did I put your boss in a good mood, but I am going to be feeding you and giving you a place to sleep tonight."

Veronica did her best to put on a straight face. "Okay, no laughter...but let's get out of here now. You were right when you said we haven't eaten much. Not to mention the fact that I recently emptied out the entire contents of my stomach. I would kill for a burger right now."

Natasha promised that she would stop at Five Guys on the way back to her place so they could get settled in. By the time she made it there with three delicious smelling bags of food, Veronica had already found the extra bedding and made up the guest bed while Ben fed the pets.

The three of them spent a night watching movies on the couch while they scarfed down delicious burgers and ridiculously greasy fries.

Natasha was determined to give the two of them at least one normal night in the midst of all this insanity. The only rule was that nobody was allowed to drink any kind of alcohol. Natasha was still not fully recovered from the night before and did not think that she could survive adding any more liquor to her system.

In spite of all of the crazy things that they had been dealing with for the past few days, they did all manage to have fun. After a while it became evident that everyone in the room was in desperate need of sleep so they slipped off to their beds.

Veronica made a mental note to remember to thank Natasha for not making a big deal about the sleeping situation in the morning.

In all honesty, Natasha desperately wanted to comment on it and would have any other night. Given what had happened at Veronica's apartment though, she decided to hold off on that until there was a night when Veronica had not been terrorized by an obsessed stalker.

DAY 8

en rose with the sun because he wanted to wake up before either Veronica or Natasha. Like he did when he stayed at Veronica's apartment, he made breakfast before anyone else in the house gained consciousness. It made him laugh how both of them stumbled almost simultaneously into the kitchen as soon as the smell of bacon had made it through the whole house. In never ceased to amaze him how well developed their sense of smell was even in sleep.

When they entered the room and saw the amount of food that he had already made, they practically tackled him in gratitude. Neither one of them were morning people so having a guy around that was willing to wake up and make them food was seriously useful.

The pleasant night that they had continued into a stress free morning as Natasha fought to keep things as light as possible.

She only cracked when Ben and Veronica were finally ready to head out to the station.

Before either of them could make it to the door, Natasha launched herself at Veronica. "You be careful."

She held onto her closest friend so tightly that Veronica had a hard time breathing. Remembering a particularly funny moment in Natasha's favorite television show, Gilmore Girls, Veronica commandeered one of Rory's lines. "...Ribs...breaking...lungs...crushing..."

Natasha let go of her and attached herself to Ben. "You better take care of her."

Ben started laughing and pushed her off. "Oh, I see how it is...I don't rank higher than a bodyguard?"

This succeeded in making Natasha feel better. "You take care of yourself, too." She started laughing and pushed them out of the door.

They were both nervous as they approached the station. Between being stalked by a crazy killer and having their entire precinct find out about them, they were about the have a very long day. They sat in the SUV for at least five minutes without moving once they reached the parking lot. Leering coworkers and bad jokes were waiting for them inside. Eventually, they admitted defeat and got out of the car. When they got to the door of the station, they both hesitated.

After a moment Ben turned to Veronica, "Are you ready for this?"

Veronica shrugged, "Not much of a choice, I guess. Thanks to 'our little friend' everyone is gonna know about us."

Ben smiled and grabbed her hand, "Let's get this over with."

Together, they pulled the door open and walked through it. They both cringed as they made their way fully into the building, but for some reason nobody reacted.

The longer they were in the building, the more they expected someone to say something to them. As they made it closer and closer to Blake's office, they realized that either everyone was playing it remarkably cool or nobody had seen the picture.

Knowing their coworkers the way they did, they were well aware that most of them had no poker face. This was the kind of information that everyone would be jumping at the chance to gossip about and nobody was saying a word.

When they finally made it to Blake's office they were both full of questions. Before they could get any of those questions out, Blake cut them off.

"Before you say anything, I have sworn everyone who saw the picture or your apartment to secrecy. Aside from them, nobody will know anything that you do not want them to know."

Ben and Veronica both sagged in relief with a nearly identical "Thank you, sir!"

Blake nodded and continued, "Now that's out of the way...what's your plan for today?"

Veronica perked up at this question. "Last night gave me an idea about that. I think we should give up on the theories about why he disappeared, at least for now. Its way to wide a net to cast for the moment. We can't check every man in the city to see if he matches any of that criteria, which is what we would have to do for it to be effective. I think we should look into how this guy is getting into our homes. Mine, I almost get. Its an apartment building and they aren't exactly known for being secure. Ben's place, I don't get at all. His house is more secure than Fort Knox. The only way he's getting in there without leaving signs of a break-in is with a key. Where did he get the key come from?"

Ben chimed in at that point. "I was thinking the same thing. It's gonna be a lot easier to track down one key than its gonna be to check out all those theories thoroughly. To be honest, that would take years and we don't have that kind of time or resources."

Blake looked back down at his work, "Sounds like you have this all under control. Check any names that you come up with against the names you already found in the past couple of days. Just in case." With that, they were dismissed.

When they left Blake's office they looked around to find that nobody was paying much attention to them. Suddenly, their day was looking like it was going to be a lot better than they were expecting when they arrived. Thanks to their boss, they had not yet become fodder for the rumor mill at the precinct. They still had a crazy killer after them, but they were also closer than ever to finding him.

There were only a few keys to Ben's home in existence, all they had to do was track all of them to the people who had them and they would find him. When they made it into the detective's office they greeted Mark and started working.

He was still investigating the bombing at Nick and Veronica's old home, and it appeared he was not getting far at the moment. Ben had been working with him for years and had never seen Mark look so frustrated. When they entered the office, Mark barely acknowledged their presence even when they were talking to him.

At first, Veronica tried to ask him how things were going, but the monosyllabic responses and the annoyed glares soon had her retreating back to Ben's desk. When she got there they shared a look and went back to working.

Ben already knew where all of the keys that he had given out were, so they focussed on the ones that previous owners and realtors would have had.

As they were working Veronica heard Ben mumble, "I knew I should have changed the locks when I moved in."

Veronica knew that Ben was already kicking himself enough, so she chose not to give him too much of a hard time about it.

All day long, they kept hitting dead ends as they looked for the key that the killer somehow managed to get hold of. Across the room they could hear Mark typing furiously on his computer and knew that he was drawing a blank like they were.

They spent most of the day tracking down every key that had ever been made for Ben's house. They talked to realtors, former owners, and anyone else who ever could have had a key to the house. It took them hours, and by the end of it, they felt like smashing their heads against a wall.

When they had left Blake's office, they had been filled with confidence that they would catch the guy today. At least, they thought they would be a hell of a lot closer. Instead, it looked like they were going to finish the day with even more questions than they had when they started. They had accounted for all the keys to Ben's house and come up with nothing.

About two hours before they were set to leave the station, Ben angrily slammed the phone back into its receiver. "This is hopeless!"

Veronica looked out of their glass wall to find half of the squad room watching Ben as he continued to fume. Even Blake had noticed the shift in attention, and he was watching them from his office as well.

She knew that Ben's increasingly bad mood and outbursts were going to cause people to begin to question whether or not he was fit to continue investigating. If Ben were to be removed from the case, it would only be a matter of time before she was removed as well. After all, a patrol officer can only work with the detectives for so long. Especially when the detective that had arranged this assignment was no longer permitted to work the case.

With this thought in mind Veronica stood and pulled on Ben's arm until he came with her. "You need to take a break."

She brooked no argument as she hauled him out of the office and along the side of the squad room until she reached another hallway. She continued to pull him behind her as she made her way down this hallway and into an observation room. It was small, with little in it but a table, a few chairs, and equipment to record everything happening on the other side of the two way mirror. But watching an interview was not Ben and Veronica's object today so the mirror was ignored as she pushed Ben to sit down at the table.

Ben growled frustratedly as he was shoved down into a chair. "What the hell are we doing here?"

Veronica felt her temper flare up at the gruffness in his voice. She knew that none of it was directed at her, so she did her best to contain her anger before it boiled over. Moving around to the other side of the table, she sat in the chair across from him.

"You need to calm down. We already have enough focus on us because of this guy breaking into our homes and leaving 'presents' for us. We cannot afford to be drawing any more attention; especially negative attention. If Blake starts to think that we can't handle working this, he won't give us a chance to prove him wrong. You have to know that the only reason we are being allowed to work this case is because you, Nick, and Blake were best buddies in the Academy. If you weren't friends we would have been barred from this investigation a long time ago."

Ben glared at her from across the table.

She could see the anger and frustration seething out of him and heard it in the way his voice rose in strength and volume.

"It doesn't matter if we get kicked off the case, does it? The guy is a fucking ghost! Every time we think that we are going to get even a little bit closer to finding him...it turns into a dead end!"

Veronica delivered one swift kick to Ben's

leg as a warning before he let his frustration get the best of him. Her voice cut across his in a threatening tone before he had a chance to complain.

"I think we've already established that it's not a good idea for you to take your anger out on me."

For a moment, it felt like time stood still.

Then a wide grin spread across Ben's face. "I don't know about that...I seem to recall some interesting results after last time I yelled at you. Maybe I should yell more often."

He leered at her and it was like all of the tension left the room.

Veronica wanted to be mad at him, but she could not stop herself from laughing. She kicked him again, but this time was more playful than the last. "It's not funny! I don't want you to think you can kiss me every time you piss me off and it will all be good. That was a one time deal. From now on...you piss me off...I expect grovelling."

Ben let out one of those explosive laughs that seemed to shake the walls. "Okay, I'll keep that in mind. I haven't pissed you off yet, have I?"

Veronica leaned back in her chair, crossed her arms over her chest, and leveled him with an even stare. "Not yet...but watch yourself."

The grin on Ben's face widened as he stood up and stalked over to her chair. When he stopped in front of her Ben leaned over and and spoke a few inches from her face. "Will do..." He closed the distance between them and placed a soft and sweet kiss on her cheek.

Veronica had closed her eyes as his face got closer to hers and was disappointed when she felt the kiss to her cheek. As he pulled back she opened her eyes, "Tease."

Ben chuckled and walked back out into the hallway.

While Ben and Veronica crossed the squad room to get back to their office, everyone noticed Ben's change in mood. When Veronica had pulled him out of the room he had been brooding and tense. When he walked back, he was grinning from ear to ear and all the tension appeared to have left his body. Everyone was wondering exactly what Veronica had done to calm him down, but for the first time ever they had enough tact not to ask. They did not, however, have enough tact to stop making bets about who would catch them kissing first.

Everyone who had seen the photo yesterday diligently kept their mouths shut with a slightly worried glance in the direction of Blake's office. He was not a man to be trifled with, so when he gave a direct order nobody in their right mind questioned whether or not to follow it. That did not stop them from smirking as they listened to the conversations happening around them. They enjoyed the fact that they knew something before any of their friends did. They looked forward to the day when they got to rub it in everyone else's faces. Until then, they would have to content themselves with quietly laughing and coming up with ways that they could mess with Ben and Veronica once everything was out in the open.

When they reentered their office, they found Mark. He was clearly feeling better than he had been earlier in the day. He too was far more relaxed and was being less harsh as he typed.

In spite of their lack of results, Veronica could feel the knots in her shoulders start to loosen when there was a commotion outside of their office. She could hear the chatter pick up in volume and glanced up to see what the cause was. When she looked out, she found half of the precinct staring at their computers and the other half staring at her.

An uncomfortable feeling started to creep into her system when she heard Mark clear his throat from his desk.

"Um...I, uh...you guys might want to take a look at this..."

As uncomfortable as Veronica felt, Mark looked ten times more awkward.

Ben and Veronica straightened up, and with one last look through the glass stood up and walked over to Mark's computer. When they got there, they both stiffened and fearfully looked in the direction of Blake's office.

"This will not end well."

Veronica nodded and then shrugged her shoulders. "It could have been worse."

That was true, but this was bad enough. Filling up Mark's computer screen, and most likely everyone else's, was a photo of Ben and Veronica from yesterday. The two of them were blissfully walking hand in hand with smiles on their faces. A disembodied voice that had obviously been electronically altered emanated out of the speakers, "I thought you ought to know."

Everyone in the building visibly flinched away from their computers.

Moments later, both Ben and Veronica's phones beeped simultaneously. They cautiously walked back over to Ben's desk and picked them up. When they checked their messages, they both found a text reading, "Secret's out. You're welcome."

Veronica's head dropped to her chest as she closed her eyes and wished that she was dreaming.

For a moment, they silently debated what they should do next then they quickly left the office. While they crossed the squad room, they did their best to avoid making eye contact with anyone.

Jack crossed in front of them.

If you had asked him, he would have said that he chuckled at their panicked expressions. The truth was that the only word to describe the noise that he made was giggle. The grown man giggled and then he spun around and faced the rest of the room.

His booming voice filled the squad room, "In the immortal words of my friend here...Pay up bitches!"

There was an uproar of laughter as almost everyone in the room lined up to place bills in Jack's hand.

He glanced over at Ben, "Everyone was making bets on when you two would get together. I was the only one who bet that you already were."

The only people in the room who had conspicuously remained seated were the officers who had seen the picture and Veronica's bedroom yesterday.

Before Ben could reply to his good friend, the door to Blake's office burst open. "Everyone get back to work. I think you'll find you have control over your computers again. You two, with me."

The joviality of moments before leached out of the room as people somberly moved back to their desks. However, there were still people pulling out their phones to update their friends who were currently out on patrol, or not on duty.

Ben and Veronica slinked their way over to Blake's office whilst trying to avoid touching each other in any way. When they got inside, they moved over to their usual seats as Blake closed the door and crossed over to sit behind his desk.

"I'm probably going to be getting a call soon from my boss, rightfully asking me why you two are still partnered up. I know this wasn't your fault, but I don't think there is anything else I can do to keep this between us. It's Friday, and the day is almost over. I'm going to send you two home early because you've both been working overtime this week. When you get back...we'll see. I'm going to do everything that I can, but I can't make any promises. I'll try to keep you on the case, but they might not give me a choice."

Veronica stared at him blankly for a moment, then nodded. "I understand." With that she stood up and went to leave the office.

Before she got to the door, Blake stopped her. "Where are you going?"

She turned with a defeated look on her face. "I'm gonna go change out of my uniform and then head home. You said we were supposed to leave for the day, right?"

The guilt was evident on Blake's face, "Yeah, okay. I'll see both of you on Monday." He dismissed them and they left to go get their stuff together.

Everyone could read their faces as they crossed the squad room again, so this time there were no jokes make.

After Veronica had changed back into her

own clothes, she and Ben made their way out of the building.

Once they reached the parking lot, Ben grabbed her hand and squeezed it reassuringly.

"We'll still get him."

The defeated look from before disappeared as she nodded. "Oh, I know. And I don't care what Blake says, I'm gonna be there when we take him down."

Ben was glad to see her looking more determined again, he was beginning to think that her actions in Blake's office had been a performance to make Blake feel bad so he would fight harder for her.

Veronica unlocked her car and hopped into the front seat.

Ben chuckled and climbed into the passenger seat. "That was an excellent manipulation in there. He's not usually that susceptible to guilting."

Veronica grinned as she put the SUV in gear and started driving to Natasha's house so that they could once again pick up their pets and move back to Ben's place. Now that the locks were changed, it felt like the safest place they could be.

When they had retrieved Ace and Charlotte and loaded them into the SUV Veronica commented, "We have done this way too many times."

Ben was holding onto Charlotte, trying to

soothe her because she was never a fan of being in cars. "I totally agree."

They stopped momentarily at the locksmith's office to collect the new keys and then went straight to Ben's place. This time Ben wanted to control exactly how many keys were floating around in the world and exactly who had them, so he only had three keys made. He kept one for himself obviously, the other two were going to Veronica and his mother. There were about a thousand people at the station who used to have keys to his house, but until this psycho was behind bars he was going to wait to give them new ones.

Both of them had been expecting to work every day until they managed to close this case, so neither of them knew what to do with themselves with a weekend off. Ben had a standing Saturday night dinner set up with his mother, but that was it.

When they made it home Veronica went to Ben's kitchen and started digging through his drawers and cupboards. He leaned on the doorframe and watched her with a bemused expression for a few minutes. "What are you doing?"

Veronica continued rummaging through his kitchen without answering him.

Ben cautiously made his way farther into the room, still unsure of exactly what she was doing. "Please don't tell me you want to cook. I wouldn't like to spend the entire weekend with food poisoning."

Veronica slammed the drawer that she had been inspecting and spun around to glare at him. She grabbed the towel hanging off the oven handle, balled it up, and threw it at Ben's face.

"No, I'm not cooking. I'm looking for your stash of take out menus, since I know that you do not cook every night. And I'll have you know that I am a far better cook than anybody gives me credit for."

Ben snorted, but did not respond. Instead, he walked out into the living room and pulled a stack of menus out of a drawer in his coffee table.

Veronica shook her head and stepped forward to take them from him. She started sifting through them and silently thanked God that she lived in a large city where basically every type of food could be delivered. She pulled a menu out of the stack and handed it to him. "What do you think of this one?"

Ben looked down at the Mexican food menu and nodded, "Works for me...as long as you're the one that calls."

Veronica looked at him quizzically.

"I love the food, but it's always loud and I can't understand a word they say."

Veronica snatched the menu out of his and and muttered while she was dialing, "Jackass."

He snickered and then stood back as Veronica deftly ordered all of his favorite foods.

Forty minutes later, there were boxes of food spread across the coffee table.

They were picking at them with their forks while watching a baseball game. The Diamondbacks and the Cardinals were playing each other which led to a fun night because Ben was rooting for the Cardinals, but Veronica had always been a D-backs fan. They spent three hours yelling at the screen like the people playing could hear them.

When the game finally ended with the Diamondbacks as the winners, Veronica took it upon herself to do a victory lap around the living room.

Ben was a good sport and laughed while she danced, but he quickly changed the channel to a rerun of Bones to distract her.

Unlike most people they worked with, who avoided watching cop shows, they had always loved them in spite of their inaccuracies.

"Oh, Oh! It's the one with that guy from Firefly! I love this one!" Veronica clapped happily and then dove onto the couch next to him.

While the episode was going, Veronica decided that she needed to have something dessert-like so she once again went rooting around in Ben's kitchen. She found the makings for brownies and quickly threw them together. When they finished baking she placed the entire tray on a wooden cutting board and then put it on the coffee table along with a gallon of vanilla ice cream and a couple of spoons.

Ben looked at his coffee table in amusement. "What do you have against plates and bowls?"

Veronica shrugged, "Less dishes."

Ben thought about that and nodded. He suddenly understood why there had not been any dishes stacked up by Veronica's sink when they had stayed there.

They spent a few more hours munching on brownies and ice cream while they channel surfed. Eventually, Ben shut the TV down and started packing up the leftover food.

"We should get some sleep. Ma's coming over tomorrow night and we need to clean."

Veronica gave him a confused look as she picked up boxes of food to carry to the kitchen. "The place looks fine. Why do we need to clean?"

Ben scoffed and joined her in the kitchen with the tray of brownies and carton of ice cream.

"You've clearly never met my mother. I love her, but that woman's house is spotless. She would never say anything, but she would be silently judging the entire time she was here."

"Huh. So um...is she gonna have a problem with the whole me staying here thing? I can find somewhere else to be when she comes over. Or I can pull a Harry Potter and stay in my room, making no noise, and pretending I don't exist."

Ben had finished putting all of the food away, so he turned around and advanced on her. When he reached her, he pulled her into his arms and gave her a chaste kiss. "I don't want you to go away...but we might want to keep the PDA down to a minimum. I don't want to deal with my mother asking what my intentions are. Not only is it kind of embarrassing, but neither one of us knows what the answer to that question is."

Veronica wrapped her arms around his waist and buried her face in his chest. "Do you think this will ever not be complicated?"

Ben placed a kiss on the top of her head and tightened his arms around her. "I have no idea. I say we ignore everyone else. They'll get used to it eventually."

After a moment, they separated and went upstairs to get some rest after a long and difficult week.

DAY 9

The next day, Veronica and Ben busied themselves with cleaning every surface and organizing every object in Ben's house. Normally Veronica would have complained about the work because she was not a fan of cleaning, but today she was glad for the distraction. It felt wrong to her to be taking a day off right now, but she knew that showing up at the station would only end badly for her. By two o'clock the house was practically sparkling and they were out of things to do.

Veronica took a look around the living room and could not help but think that it looked like a page ripped out of a catalogue. "Are you telling me that you do this every Saturday?"

Ben flopped down on the couch and grinned, "Nope, but I don't usually have an extra person who has drinking nights with her girlfriends in my living room. Not to mention the dog shedding everywhere."

Veronica dropped down onto the couch next to him. "Hey, you forget that I know all of your friends. Just because poker night was at Jack's house this week doesn't mean I don't know it's usually here. Plus, Charlotte sheds at least as much as Ace does."

Ben shrugged, "Fine, I admit it. I clean every Saturday, but usually not this thoroughly."

Veronica gawked at him, "So you used me for my cleaning. I don't believe it."

Ben had a satisfied smile on his face, "Pretty much. Now, what are we going to do with ourselves until I have to start making dinner?"

They spent a few more minutes relaxing on the couch before they decided to go for a run to get rid of some of the pent up energy that they had in their systems.

"If we're gonna work out, we need to stop by my place first. All of my running stuff is there, and I'm out of clean clothes anyways."

Ben leaned back into the couch for one more second before pushing himself off of it. "Okay, we'll drive over to your place so you can change, then we can go run around that park you thought I didn't know you would always hit before the cemetery. Yes, I even knew you were going there when all you could do was limp around it with your cane. We should get back here with enough time to clean up and start cooking before Ma gets here."

He held his hand out and when she took it, he pulled her up and off the couch.

After waiting for Ben to change and finding her keys, Veronica headed out the front door to her SUV. Once they had both piled in, she started driving back to her apartment. The car was silent until Veronica spoke the question on both their minds.

"Do you think we're going to find anything there?"

Ben would normally have shrugged at this, but he was feeling so tense that it was physically painful for him to move his shoulders. "I hope not."

They both held their breath as they stood outside of her apartment, staring at the door.

"We have to open it eventually."

For a moment, Ben thought she had not heard him because her expression did not change at all.

Finally, she spoke. "I know. I was taking a moment to remember and appreciate the days when I knew that my apartment was going to be exactly as it was when I left it last."

With that, she stuck her key in the lock and turned it. After hearing the click of the tumbler she took a deep breath and pushed the door open. She let out her breath as she looked around the room and did not see anything ominous.

"One room down."

She and Ben quickly worked their way through the whole apartment and sighed with relief when they found everything exactly where it was meant to be. Veronica quickly packed some more clothes into her overnight bag and then changed to go running. As she stepped back out into the living room Ben stopped and took in her tiny black shorts and tight blue shirt.

A slow smile spread across his face. "We need to run more often."

"Stop that."

Ben opened the front door, "Fine, fine. Let's get going."

They ran over to the park near Veronica's apartment and started doing laps around it. For a few minutes, it felt strange to be running with someone other than Ace but she got used to it quickly. It was nice having someone to pace herself with.

After a couple laps they started to feel competitive and began to push their strides. By the time they were on their last lap, both of them were moving much faster than either of them would have been if they had been running alone.

As they were approaching the one and only water fountain in the park they both lengthened their strides as far as they could go and raced over to it. When Ben reached it first,

Veronica bent over double and started gasping for air.

Between gasps she rasped, "No fair...You used your old...cross country...training."

Ben straightened up after getting a drink and fixed her with a skeptical stare. "Oh, please. I haven't been on a cross country team in over two decades. That was pure talent. Admit it...I'm faster than you."

Veronica slumped over the drinking fountain and started gulping in water. When she finished, she turned around and smiled sassily. "Never!"

Ben smiled and stepped closer to her. Thinking he was going in for a kiss, Veronica raised herself up on her toes. Leaning to the side, Ben grabbed the car keys off the bracelet on her wrist and started sprinting back towards the parking lot.

He yelled over his shoulder, "First one to the car gets the first shower."

"Oh, no you don't," and she took off after him.

Ben made it to the SUV first and jumped inside then locked the doors before she could get to it. She stood at the passenger side door and started hammering on the window.

"Admit it and I'll unlock it for you."

Veronica stood stubbornly outside for a moment before she tipped her head back and growled, "Fine." Slowly, so that Ben could hear every word through the window, "I admit you run faster than me."

Ben smirked and unlocked the door.

When they made it back to Ben's house he headed upstairs to the bathroom while she moved to the kitchen. Taking a look at what was on hand, Veronica started pulling ingredients for pesto chicken out and spreading them across the counter. She also pulled some rice out of the pantry and poured it into the rice maker with chicken broth and some herbs to add flavor. She was about get started mixing the pesto when Ben arrived in the kitchen freshly washed and in clean clothes.

"Step away from the food."

Veronica looked up from her work and glared at him, "I can cook some things."

Ben walked over and crowded her away from the counter. "I'd rather not test that theory on my mother. Now, shoo."

Veronica huffed, "Did you seriously 'shoo' me? What in the world would make you think that was a good idea?"

Ben continued working on the pesto. "Go take your shower."

After a moment of staring angrily at Ben, Veronica spun and flounced out of the room. She made sure to be extra loud as she stomped up the stairs and over to the bathroom. She was so busy fuming while she was showering that she did not hear Ben enter the room for a moment and then abruptly leave again. Nor did she hear the doorbell ring, or Ben scramble around as he answered it in surprise. She did however notice when she got out of the bathroom that her overnight bag, with all of her clothes in it, was no longer sitting on Ben's bed where she had left it. Her annoyance with Ben quickly returning, she wrapped herself in a towel and started down the stairs.

"Seriously! What are we in high school? You had to steal my...Oh!"

Veronica clutched the towel tighter around her when she saw a small woman with silver hair and an amused smirk sitting on Ben's couch. Ben was sitting in the chair across from her with a guilty look on his face and her overnight bag at his feet.

"Veronica, this is my mother. She came a bit earlier than I was expecting. Ma, this is my friend Veronica. She's been staying with me for a couple days."

Still highly embarrassed, Veronica nodded and smiled at her. "It's nice to meet you Mrs. Becker. Ben, would you mind..."

She stared pointedly at her bag and he nodded.

"Sure thing."

He picked it up by the handle and tossed in over his head towards the stairs. Veronica squeaked and held onto her towel as she reached out with the other hand to snag her bag out of the air.

"Thanks."

She then turned tail and dashed back up the stairs into the relative safety of Ben's room.

Once she got the door closed she leaned against it and sighed. "I cannot believe that happened."

After taking a few moments to get over the horror of what had occurred, she tossed her bag back onto the bed and started rummaging through it.

"Okay, I just showed off way more skin than I ever wanted to, so I think it's time to go for something a bit more conservative."

She pulled on a pair of black slacks with a sapphire blue, button down shirt that had the sleeves rolled up to the elbow. Once she was dressed, she moved back into the bathroom to blow dry her hair and apply her makeup. On any normal day, she would let her hair dry naturally and forgo the makeup, but she wanted to avoid going downstairs for a few extra minutes. Not to mention the fact that Ben's mother was impeccably groomed and had seen her wearing nothing but a towel. Her first impression may not have been great, but she wanted to do everything she could to erase that image from Mrs. Becker's mind. She stopped at the door and took a few breaths to calm her nerves before she opened it and headed back down the stairs.

She heard the oven timer going off and Ben walking over to the kitchen. Knowing this meant she was going to have to be alone with his mother, Veronica slowed her steps to make the encounter as short as possible.

When Veronica finally made it into the living room, Mrs. Becker stood up to greet her. "Hello again. It's nice to see you fully clothed. I'm sorry for my son's juvenile sense of humor. You can blame his father for that."

Veronica grasped the hand extended to her and shook it. "It's fine, really. Ben's always taken great pleasure in messing with me."

Mrs. Becker smiled graciously. There was an uncomfortable silence between them until Ben reentered the room announcing that the food was ready.

Oh, thank God!

As she walked by Ben to get to the dining room she glared at him and muttered under her breath, "You will pay."

Ben nodded and followed after her to the table where he had already set up three steaming plates of pesto chicken with rice.

Mrs. Becker took her seat on one side of the table while Ben and Veronica sat on the other. Nobody knew what to say so they all sat there in silence while they ate.

After about five minutes Mrs. Becker started speaking. "So...what are you working on lately?"

Veronica coughed as she began choking on the water she had been drinking when Mrs.

Becker spoke. She glanced over at Ben to see how he would handle the question.

He did not want to worry his mother by telling her what was going on, so he decided to try to avoid the question. "Ma, you know I can't talk about an open investigation."

Mrs. Becker glanced suspiciously between a guilty looking Veronica and Ben, who was desperately trying not to meet her eye. She knew that there was more to the story than an open investigation, but she also knew that she would not be getting any information out of her son that he did not want to give. She used to be able to get anything out of him, but as he grew older he became less susceptible to her inter-rogation techniques. She liked to think he was such a good detective because he had learned from her.

Reluctantly, she decided to give up on this question for now, but she would be getting back to it once she got her son alone. For now, she was content to make her son's friend squirm some more.

She turned her eyes on the woman sitting next to her son, "So, Veronica, are you sleeping with my son, or is there something wrong with your place?"

Veronica once again choked on her drink, and Ben shifted uncomfortably in his chair.

"Mother..."

Mrs. Becker held her hand up to stop her

son. "It's a perfectly reasonable question. I remember her from a few photos of you and Nick, so I know she's not from out of town."

Veronica had regained control of her lungs and placed her hand on Ben's arm when he opened his mouth to speak again.

"You're right. I'm not from out of town. Nick was my fiance before... Anyways, I've been having some trouble with my apartment lately and Ben offered me a place to stay until it gets sorted out."

Ben and Veronica both thought that she was satisfied with that answer until her questioning gaze landed on Veronica again. "Oh, so you're sleeping on the couch then. I didn't see any extra pillows or blankets in the living room so I assumed you weren't."

Mrs. Becker began smirking again when she saw Veronica and her son shifting in their seats. They reminded her of her students when she asked them if they had done their homework. She looked over at Veronica to find her face turning an amusing shade of red. Then she glanced over at her son to find Ben glaring at her like he did as a teen when she "embarrassed" him in front of one of his girlfriends.

Having sufficiently punished her son for not answering her question earlier, she chuckled and then went back to eating her dinner.

Ben tried to get everyone talking again with small talk, he even brought up politics because that usually got Veronica in the mood for a heated discussion. Unfortunately for him, his mother did not feel the need to make the night any less uncomfortable and Veronica seemed to be fascinated by the rice on her plate.

They ate in relative silence until Ben finished and got up from the table.

"Ma, I had the locks changed at the house. I've got a copy of the new key for you."

Mrs. Becker noticed Veronica looking uncomfortable again as Ben got up to get the key, but she assumed that was because Ben was leaving her alone. She was confused when Veronica's face became even more red when Ben returned. She pulled her purse out and started digging through it.

While she was digging she was muttering, "Hate this stupid thing...too big...no side pockets...I miss the old one."

Veronica stared at her with a quirked eyebrow.

Ben found it all highly amusing and tried to keep it going. "What, did you break the old one? It wouldn't surprise me. You carry too much stuff around."

Mrs. Becker threw her purse to the ground after finding her key ring. "No, I did not break it. I was walking home from work a few weeks ago and some delinquent stole it right off of me."

Ben was so focussed on his mother that he did not see Veronica's face go suddenly white.

"Ma, why didn't you tell me? Please say that you at least called the police?"

Mrs. Becker gave him an annoyed stare. "Of course I called the police. They said it was unlikely they'd be able to find it, but that they would look into it."

"I told you to start driving to work Ma."

Mrs. Becker's anger rose, "Benjamin Becker, you may be a police officer, but I will not be lectured. I only live a few blocks away from the school. I refuse to believe that it is unsafe for me to walk to and from work."

Ben gave an exasperated sigh and leaned back into his chair. "Fine. Far be it from me to try to keep you safe."

While Ben and his mother were arguing, Veronica was busy getting her blood pressure back under control. She could not wait to get Mrs. Becker out of the house so that she could discuss her idea with Ben. If she was right, they had one more clue to follow up on when they went back to work on Monday. She looked down the table and noticed that everyone else was far closer to finishing their dinner then she was so she started wolfing it down as discreetly as she could.

It was not long before everyone had finished and all attempts at conversation had run out so Mrs. Becker was getting up to leave. She hugged her son goodbye and smiled courteously at Veronica.

Veronica tried to be as polite as possible as she said her goodbyes, but she could not help but want to shove her out the door.

The second the door closed and Veronica heard Mrs. Becker's car start up, she plopped down on the couch and dropped her head down into her hands.

Ben thought that she was feeling bad about the disastrous dinner they had with his mother, so he sat down next to her. He rubbed her back to try to comfort her, and it was then that he noticed her shoulders shaking. Thinking that she was crying, he wrapped his arm around her and held her closer.

"Oh, come on...it wasn't that bad. You should have seen some of the things that she and my dad did to my girlfriends in high school."

After a moment, Veronica lifted her head and he found that she had been laughing, not sobbing. He sighed in relief when he saw the dazzling smile spreading across her face.

She grabbed Ben's head and dragged his face down to plant an unexpected kiss on his lips.

When she pulled back Ben looked even more confused. "Not that I'm complaining, but what's going on? Most women don't react this way after an encounter with my mother."

Veronica giggled and kissed him again, "I know how he got into your house."

Before Ben could ask her what she had

meant, Veronica laughed again and pulled him in for another heart stopping kiss. He let himself melt into her and enjoy the moment.

After a few minutes, Ben extricated himself from Veronica and put some space between them. "Again...no complaints, but please explain."

Veronica began laughing again. "You know, if you had paid attention at dinner you would have figured it out already."

Ben levelled her with a glare, "I've been a bit distracted. Thank you very much. Remember how you walked down my stairs in nothing but a towel? Now, I repeat...explanation please?"

Veronica rolled her eyes, "Fine, fine...I'll tell you. Remember when your mom said that she had her purse stolen?"

Veronica gave Ben a knowing look and his face visibly brightened. She could almost see the light bulb going off above his head.

"You don't think...but that was weeks ago...the investigation was still stalled then...you weren't even staying here."

Veronica rolled her eyes again, "I think we both know that this guy is more than capable of planning ahead."

Ben sobered and nodded, "This it true. I'll give Blake a call tomorrow. He'll get the file from the precinct that handled Mom's call. They probably don't have much, but it's still worth looking into. From the sound of things, Mark's hit a bit of a wall on his side of the investigation so Blake will probably put him on it. Who knows, we might have a name by the time we get back to work on Monday."

It was Veronica's turn to calm down and nod, "As long as I am there for the take down, I don't care who runs the investigation anymore."

Ben leaned back with a skeptical face, "That's a bit of a change in tune. It wasn't that long ago that you were so hell bent on being a part of this investigation that you bullied our boss into fast-tracking your return to the force."

Veronica smiled, "Yeah, I admit that I want to be part of this investigation. It's killing me that I might not be able to anymore, but I need to be able to at least pretend to be okay with it. Give me that at least."

Veronica decided she and Ben needed to celebrate this new break they had in the case, so she jumped up from the couch and practically skipped over to the kitchen to get a couple bottles of beer. When she opened the refrigerator, she was horrified to find that it was completely devoid of alcohol.

Ben could hear her yelling at him from the kitchen.

"Oy! How dare you be out of beer on a day when your mother is coming to visit! You should have known better!"

Ben shook his head and pushed himself off of the couch to go after her. "You're right. I definitely should have predicted that my mother would inadvertently give us a break in our case, and that you would feel the need to celebrate with Guinness."

Veronica spun around and punched him in the shoulder. "No, but you should have known that I would need a drink after dealing with your mother for a night."

Ben threw his head back and groaned dramatically, "She wasn't that bad."

After saying that, he turned around and moved over to the table by the front door and picked up his keys.

As he went to leave, Veronica spoke again. "What in the world are you doing?"

Ben shook his head and turned to face her. "You're kidding, right? I'm going to the store to get you beer, so I don't have to hear about this anymore."

Veronica laughed and skipped over to him so she could kiss him on the cheek. "Bring chocolate too, please. Oh, and pistachio ice cream!"

Ben looked at her for a moment, "You are the strangest person."

Veronica gave him a quick peck on the lips. "Yeah, but you love it."

In order to avoid a potentially awkward situation, Ben simply smiled at her and walked out the door. Once he got outside, he pulled out his phone and called Blake so that he could get Mark working on their new lead.

DAY 10

*A*nd they've taken the bait!

They are too predictable for their own good. By the time they get back to work, I will have set up everything I need to make it look like someone else has been pulling the strings all along. I just need them to find my sacrificial lamb. By the time the week is out, he will be in prison and I will be free to do whatever I want.

Ben and Veronica woke up the next day to the realization that they did not have anything planned for the whole day. They were in danger of sitting around waiting for the weekend to end so they could get back to work.

Veronica knew that if she wanted to prove to Blake that they could leave their work at the station they were going to have to find a way to let off some steam and relax.

After they spent two hours sitting on their couch watching reruns of NCIS, Veronica jumped up and grabbed her keys off of the table next to the door.

"That's it. We need to get out of this house."

Ben turned the tv off and moved a disgruntled Charlotte off of his lap.

"What is it you propose we do instead?"

Veronica disappeared into the kitchen for a moment and came back with two water bottles. She spoke as she tossed one to him, "Get in the car and leave the rest to me. We are going to have fun today so we can walk into work tomorrow and make sure Blake isn't worried about us."

Ben shrugged, "Okay."

He grabbed his keys so that he could lock up and walked out the front door. When Veronica joined him outside she saw him standing by the driver side door.

"Very funny."

He chuckled and moved over to the other side of the car.

Veronica knew immediately where she wanted to take him. It seemed childish to some people, but she had always gone to the zoo when she needed to spend a day forgetting about life.

When Ben finally realized what signs they were following, he started grinning too. He hadn't been to the zoo in years, but he used to go all the time when he was growing up. His older brothers used to threaten to lock him into the monkey exhibit and leave him there.

As they crossed the bridge to get in line to buy tickets, they saw a class of children hanging over the railing, watching all the turtles in the water below them. After paying the forty dollars it took to get them both into the zoo, they spent a few minutes staring at the map and bickering over where they would go first.

Veronica had always been a huge fan of the lions and tigers, but Ben was more interested in visiting the reptiles. After spending ten minutes arguing like an old married couple they decided to pick a direction and start walking rather than going to specific exhibits.

Veronica knew the zoo better so she subtly pushed him in the direction of the big cats.

They ambled along for a while, stopping at every exhibit to see what was there and read the plaques that they found interesting.

When Ben realized that they were about to come up on the lion exhibit he turned to Veronica. "You totally planned this."

She grinned and skipped out of his reach as he moved to tickle her. He chased her all the way to the wall surrounding the lions where he grabbed her and held her to him while they stared down at the majestic animals.

Some of the parents in the area gave them accusing looks because of the slight rough housing and the public display of affection, but Veronica and Ben ignored them. Today was their day to forget about the fact that they had any kind of awkward history and the deranged killer that seemed bent on driving them crazy. Today was their mental health day and they were going to take advantage of it.

They strolled around the zoo for several hours and saw everything they cared about. When they both realized that they were absolutely starving they made their way back towards the entrance to the zoo.

As Veronica walked past all of the food places and towards the exit, Ben stopped and gave her a questioning look. Veronica turned around, "The food here is ridiculously expensive. Besides, my favorite restaurant is about ten minutes from here. I am determined to make this the perfect day."

Ben started walking again. "Well, if that's the case..."

He pulled her into him and kissed her. Veronica responded, wrapping her arms around his neck and pulling him closer. After a moment they pulled apart and turned back towards the exit. Their hands came together and held all the way through the parking lot to Veronica's car.

Veronica drove them to the corner of University and Hardy in Tempe and turned off the road at a gas station.

Ben glanced around, "Where is this 'favorite restaurant' that you were telling me about? I know you've eaten a lot of gas station food on the job, but this is a bit ridiculous."

Veronica rolled her eyes. "Look beyond the gas station, moron."

She pointed to the building past the station and Ben noticed a sign reading 'Rosita's Fine Mexican Food'.

Upon entering the building, Ben took in the child's drawings pinned up on the walls, the green vinyl booths, and the Mexican pinatas hanging from the ceiling in the bar. He gave Veronica a skeptical look, but she simply rolled her eyes again.

"Give it a chance. This place has the best Mexican food in the city."

Ben shrugged and followed her as the waitress led them to a booth.

Veronica continued talking as they sat. "I've been coming here for years now. It's nowhere near where I live, so I don't get here often, but it's well worth the drive."

The skepticism never left Ben's face. "We'll have to see about that. I grew up in this city. I'm fairly certain I already found all of the good Mexican food."

Veronica met his gaze. "I bet you the bill for lunch and dishes for the rest of the week that you like it."

Ben reached his hand across the table, "Bet accepted."

They shook hands and turned back to their menus.

After a few minutes, the waitress came by with their chips and salsa and they ordered their food. Veronica ordered a couple cheese enchiladas and Ben ordered a chimichanga. Before the waitress could leave Veronica added one last thing to their order. When Ben glanced at her, she silenced him before he could speak.

"Trust me."

"Okay."

Veronica told Ben stories from a few of the times that she had been there while they waited for their food. She was finishing telling him about the time that she had brought Nick to the restaurant and the waitress had shamelessly started hitting on him, when the food finally arrived.

Ben stared in appreciation at the huge plates filled to the brim with steaming, hot food. They both wolfed their meals down in record time because they were so hungry from skipping breakfast and spending the day walking around.

Ben had completely forgotten about the extra item that Veronica had ordered until the waitress placed the bowl of deep fried ice cream with two spoons in the middle of the table. Ben used one of the spoons to scrape off some of it and stared at it suspiciously.

While he was staring, Veronica had scooped up some for herself and placed it in her mouth. The look on her face was more than enough to confirm to him that the ice cream was good. Without further thought, he placed the spoon in his mouth, and for the first time tasted the deliciousness that is deep fried ice cream from Rositas.

He looked up to see Veronica staring at him with a triumphant look in her eyes.

"I win."

After Ben paid the bill, he and Veronica got back in the car and she drove them to Ben's house.

When she pulled into the driveway and shut the car off, Ben spoke. "That's the extent of your perfect day? The zoo and Mexican food? You're easy."

When he realized what he said he tried to backtrack.

Veronica laughed. "Nope, one more thing will do the trick...we're going to have a poker night. You call up the guys and I'll call up the girls."

Ben shared her grin and climbed out of the car. "Fine, but tell them to contribute some booze and pizza money."

Veronica laughed and pulled out her phone while Ben unlocked the door. They were once again greeted by Ace and Charlotte pacing exuberantly and meowing behind him.

Ben walked into the kitchen and pulled out his phone while Veronica dropped to her knees by the doorway to be smothered by her lovable puppy.

"You like having someone to hang out with while I'm gone, don't you?"

Charlotte chose that exact moment to pounce onto Veronica's lap and rub up against her. "And you must love having a woman in the house. I imagine I smell significantly better than Ben does."

Ben cleared his throat from the doorway of the kitchen and scowled at her.

Veronica snickered and pulled herself up off the floor so that she could make her calls.

A while later, people started arriving at Ben's place. Upon entering the house, Veronica informed them that nobody was allowed to discuss any cases unless it was a funny story. Anybody that was caught breaking this rule would be forced to take a shot of their least favorite form of alcohol.

By the time everyone arrived, there were ten people squished around Ben's dining room table. Cheyenne and Erica had shown up together again so they were sitting next to each other. Jack had come next and he had taken his traditional spot at the head of the table. They always let him sit there because he was the oldest of them and the unofficial "dad" of the group. Blake was at the other end of the table because he was their boss, so he was always given a place of honor. Veronica and Ben were sitting on opposite sides of the table on either side of Jack. Tyler had expertly positioned himself between Veronica and Erica because he had always had a thing for Erica. He usually found a way to sit next to her while they were doing group things, but she never seemed to notice. Natasha was sitting next to Ben, so she could make faces at Veronica every time she caught the two of them staring at each other. Mark had chosen to sit next to her, and the newest rookie, Sam, was sitting next to him.

They had given up on using real money long ago, because none of them made enough to be gambling all their money away. Someone had sprung for a set of poker chips and they had been happily playing with those ever since.

Once everyone was settled with their drinks and the pizza was ordered, the cards came out and the games began. They started with a few rounds of Texas Hold'em to get everyone warmed up. Then they let everyone take turns picking a different game. For hours they played Hold'em, five card draw, No Peeky, Indian Poker, and anything else that they could think of.

It was the perfect way for everyone to relax by drinking and having fun. At around midnight, Ace gave up on them and slunk off to pass out on the couch in the living room.

When Ben and Veronica were walking everyone to the door, they found Charlotte curled up on top of the oblivious dog and desperately rushed to snap a picture before the cat noticed them and left. Once they had poured the last of their makeshift family into various vehicles, including two Uber rides, they shifted the sleeping animals over and flopped down on the couch.

"How was that for a perfect day?"

Ben started chuckling. "Perfectly exhausting. If I don't get up from this couch now, I'm sleeping here."

Veronica stood up and dragged Ben up off the couch. She was leading him up the stairs to his bedroom when Ben spoke again.

"You know what would really make this a perfect day…"

Part of me loves them. The fact that they think it's wise for them to take a day off while I'm around is adorable.

When are they going to realize that I am the most dangerous person that will ever be involved in their lives?

They can't treat me like any other criminal.

I WILL NOT BE IGNORED!

Tomorrow I will make sure that they never stop thinking about me for even a moment.

DAY 11

Veronica woke in a tangle of sheets and Ben with a smile on her face. The day before may have started as a way to reassure Blake they were fine, but it had turned into a genuinely perfect day. She had not understood how much she needed a day that was not full of paranoia and investigation until she woke up feeling relaxed.

She left Ben in the bed and walked into the bathroom. She pulled a new outfit out of her travel bag and set it out, hoping that the steam from her shower would get rid of some of the wrinkles. At least, that was the excuse she was planning on giving to Ben for taking an extra long shower. She had always loved hot showers. As a child, she was constantly scolded for using all the hot water in the house. When she got out, she glanced into the bedroom and noticed the Ben had finally woken and she could hear him moving around in the kitchen.

For the first time in months, she made an effort to dress nicely and do her makeup. When she came down the stairs into the living room, she was in a pair of skinny jeans with a form fitting black top and black combat boots. She knew that she was going to be changing into her uniform the second she got to work, but she was starting to enjoy looking good again.

She used to relish the looks men would give her as she walked down the street, and never felt any shame when she was asked to use her looks to distract someone. Ever since Nick died, she had made a habit of blending into the background, but she was starting to realize the futility of that. Men had still been staring at her, but they had pity in their eyes. Pity had the tendency to piss her off, so she was done with that. Plus, the look on Ben's face when she walked into the kitchen was enough to make her blush. It might have been a bad sign that she was letting a man affect her this much, but she loved feeling admired again so she was choosing not to dwell on it.

Both Ben and Veronica had had a lazy start to the day so they had to rush through breakfast in order to make it to work on time. Blake had instituted an unofficial rule that anyone showing up to work late after a poker night would be banned from the game for at least a month.

Once they had eaten and fed the animals

they opened the front door to find yet another "present" from their mysterious friend. On the welcome matt by Ben's front door was a Phoenix Zoo pamphlet, a Rosita's menu, and a poker chip. There was also a white note card.

HOW WAS YOUR "PERFECT" DAY?

Ben saw it all and slammed the door shut. Before Veronica even had a chance to react he stepped into the living room and started kicking an ottoman.

"SON OF A BITCH!"

By the time he controlled himself again, the ottoman was in pieces and Veronica was already on the phone talking to Blake. When she hung up, she glared at Ben.

"Yeah...killing the furniture is incredibly helpful. Clean that up before Blake gets here."

Ben had tossed the remains of the ottoman into his dumpster when Blake arrived with Erica and her partner, Sam. A van from the lab was not far behind them.

While the lab techs were taking pictures and bagging the items left on the doormat, Blake went into the house and pulled Ben and Veronica aside.

"Well, at least we know he can't still get into the house. This definitely confirms that he had a key to the old lock. If he still had access to the house, he would have left it on your pillow or something. The bad news is that whoever this guy is, he still has eyes on you. Ears too, by the looks of it."

Ben and Veronica had both come to this conclusion as well. They were trying to figure out what he could have bugged that they could have missed. Veronica's car and Ben's house had already been gone over with a fine toothed comb. They had checked their keys and cell phones before Blake had gotten there, but had not found anything. They were both drawing blanks on where the killer could possibly have hidden a bug that they had not checked yet.

Mark walked in then, "Okay, now I'm confused. Didn't we just check this house and Veronica's apartment for bugs?"

Ben was the first one to respond. "That's what we were talking about. There's one thing that's bothering me. How does he know what kind of poker chips we use. None of them were missing last night, so that means that one was not from our set. Somehow, he had to have seen our poker game last night, but how?"

The four of them moved into Ben's dining room and around his table. When they got there, Blake took over the conversation.

"Okay, if he could see and hear everything in this room, then he would know everything you did yesterday and what our poker chips look like. If you were trying to spy on someone in this room, but couldn't leave an actual bug behind, how would you do it?"

Mark, Ben, and Veronica took their seats

from the night before and started looking around the room. Silence filled the dining room until their answer came from an unexpected source.

"We are all idiots."

All four of them turned around to see Erica standing in the doorway staring at the wall on the opposite side of the room. Like people watching a tennis match, all of their heads turned at once to see what she was staring at.

When Mark realized she was staring at Ben's desktop he turned a skeptical eye upon Erica. "We checked all of Ben's equipment when we swept the house for bugs. There was nothing there."

Erica nodded, but was not convinced. "Yeah, we checked for physical bugs, but did we check the software on Ben's desktop? He has a webcam. With the right skills, our guy could have used that to see this room whenever he wanted. He proved when he hacked our system at the station that he has those skills." When she stopped talking, she noticed that everyone was looking at her with mystified expressions.

Only Veronica had ever heard her say that much all at once and there was usually alcohol involved when she did.

A slight blush rose to Erica's cheeks. "What?...I had a friend in college who played a hacker in a Shadowrun campaign. She did a lot of research so she could stay in character."

More mystified expressions.

"It's a table-top role playing game. Does it surprise anyone that I was a geek in college?"

Her annoyance more than the comment itself shocked all of them back into action. Ben moved to his computer and booted it up. Once the login screen appeared, he typed his password rapidly into the answer field and waited for his profile to load.

When the computer was fully set up, Ben spun in his chair and addressed Erica. "I have no idea what I'm looking for. Did your friend give you any more details?"

Erica's eyes dropped to the floor and resumed her usual state of reserve. This answered Ben's question better than any words could have and everyone in the room let out the breath they were holding.

Blake took over again, "Okay, we'll turn Ben's computer over to the lab. See if they can come up with anything. In fact, I want everything in this house with recording capabilities turned over to be checked. That goes for your cell phones too. I want to try to cut off our guy's stream of information. Maybe he'll slip up trying to regain it. We can pick up a couple burner phones for you on the way to the station."

Ben and Veronica reluctantly turned their cell phones over. At this point, they were both cursing the fact that they had smartphones capable of being hacked and turned into a spy tool.

After taking a moment to talk to one of the lab techs, Blake turned back to the others. "Alright. Erica, take Sam and start canvassing the neighborhood. I'll send Cheyenne and Ryan to work on it too. When they get here, you can head back. Mark, Ben, Veronica, go to the station and meet me in my office."

He glanced around the room and was met with reluctant nods. Knowing that his orders would be followed, he left the house and got in his car so that he could return to the station. This case was causing a mountain of paperwork to build up and he needed to keep working on it.

Mark, Ben, and Veronica shared a brief farewell with Erica and Sam and left the room.

On the way to the station, Veronica wondered how many tense and uncomfortable car rides she was going to have to sit through before this was all over.

When they were about five minutes away, Ben finally started speaking. "He's gonna pull you off the case. You know that, right. He's gonna send you back out on patrol. At this point, he doesn't have much of a choice. We've lost momentum on this case and we can't justify having a patrol cop working with the detectives if there's nothing for them to do. Not to mention a patrol cop that has an emotional connection to the case and is currently a target. Right now, his bosses are asking him why he's letting a newly returned cop put themselves in danger by working the case. At this point, we're lucky if he doesn't stick us both in protective custody for the duration."

Veronica glared at a driver that tried to cut her off and wished that she was in a squad car at that moment. "Yeah, I figured that out when he told us to meet him in his office. I'm not gonna fight him on putting me back on the street. I don't have that kind of pull in the department. But if he so much as whispers the words 'protective custody' I'm gonna kick up such a fuss he'll wish I'd stayed at the museum. He can't technically order me into protective custody, so I'm not going. Besides, between being on patrol and staying at your place, I'm never going to be more than ten feet away from another cop until this is over. That might as well be protective custody."

Ben was silent for a moment and then suddenly grinned.

Veronica was suspicious.

"What exactly about this situation is funny?"

Ben started chuckling under his breath. "I'm sure with official protective custody you wouldn't get to have nearly as much fun at night."

Without taking her eyes off the road, Veronica reached across the car and swatted Ben on the back of the head.

"Keep your mind out of the gutter!"

Then she fought to keep the smirk off her face.

When they got to the station, they tried to act casual but nobody was buying it. If anybody in the building had doubted that Ben and Veronica were together, they no longer did. As they moved to the locker rooms, it seemed they were connected by a tether. They were never more than a couple feet apart and neither one of them could keep the smiles off their faces.

In light of what had happened that morning, everyone had expected a different attitude from the two of them.

Apparently, they both managed to find a way to get their minds back on work while they were in their separate locker rooms because they had their game faces on when the moved back across the building. They paused for a moment outside of Blake's office to steel themselves for the conversation they were about to have.

When Veronica walked into Blake's office, she found him bent over his desk typing rapidly into his computer. She could tell that this case was starting to wear on him as well. They could not do much as investigators right now, but he could do even less as an administrator. Plus, judging by the sweat circles under his arms, he was dreading the coming conversation even more than Ben and Veronica were.

Knowing Blake, he was terrified that he was going to make her break down or worse; blow up. Veronica had never been well known for the former, but these were new circumstances for everyone. The latter however; the latter was something she was famous for among her friends. They had all had a taste of the stereotypical red-head temper in the past, and they all feared having to deal with any more of it.

To be completely honest, she felt bad for Blake in that moment. She knew that it must be terrible to have to give orders to your friends. Hanging out and having fun one night, and then being the boss the next day must be exhausting.

Somehow, they had managed to beat Mark to his office so they sat down in the chairs opposite Blake's desk and waited. Blake would not look Veronica in the eye, so she knew that Ben had been right in the car. As much as Veronica valued Blake as a friend and sympathized with him, she was not going to make this moment any easier for him. If he was going to put her back out on patrol, he was going to have to face her and say the words.

For a minute, the only sound in the room was the ticking of Blake's clock on the wall. It seemed like none of them were even breathing.

Then the door swung open again and Mark stumbled into the room. "Sorry, I got stopped at every light on the way here."

Blake nodded and took a deep breath. "I'm sure you all know why you're here...Veronica, I know I told you I would keep you on this case for as long as I could. But I can't do it anymore. My decision to let you come back and work this case put us all on thin ice. With everything that has happened in the past week...there's nothing more I can do. Veronica, I'm sending you back out on patrol. You'll be riding with Erica. Sam has been here long enough now that her training is almost over. Jack's been riding alone recently, so I'm switching Sam over to him."

Veronica felt the anger start to bubble up inside of her. "You're putting me with Erica because she's a training officer, aren't you? You could have just as easily put me with Jack. I am not a rookie."

For the first time since she walked into the room, Blake looked up and stared her right in the eye. "You haven't done this job in a year. We have to anticipate a bit of...rustiness."

Blake visibly flinched when Veronica shifted in her chair.

"Fine, I'll ride with Erica."

Everyone in the room looked momentarily shocked that she backed down so easily, but none of them said anything about it. They did not want to bring any more attention to her shame at being gone for so long.

Blake spoke again. "Okay, I guess you should go catch up with your new partner. She should be back from Ben's place any time now."

Veronica nodded stiffly and then stood to leave the room. She hesitated at the door. "Can Erica and I be at the take-down."

Blake answered in the affirmative and Veronica left.

It turned out that Erica was not back yet, so Veronica stood in the squad room and tried to surreptitiously watch Blake talking to Ben and Mark. It looked like Blake was doing all the talking and Ben and Mark were doing a lot of nodding. She was desperate to know what was happening, but she did not want to push Blake. Besides, she knew that she could get any information that she wanted out of Ben later that night. He might try to hold out for a few minutes, but she had a few tricks up her sleeve.

She was in the midst of planning how she would get Ben to talk when she heard someone walk up behind her. Suddenly she heard Erica's voice in her ear.

"You have dirty in your eyes."

Veronica jumped about a foot into the air and spun to find Erica behind her with a bemused expression upon her face. Veronica arranged her face into an innocent expression.

"I don't know what you're talking about." She tried to keep her face straight, but found that impossible under Erica's intense stare.

"How are you always sneaking up on

people? Do you have any idea how unsettling it is?"

Erica chuckled darkly and walked away.

Veronica trailed after her as Erica made her way back out of the building and to her squad car.

"Blake told me the plan earlier. Don't worry. I promise not to treat you too much like a rookie."

Veronica glared at the back of her head and sarcasm dripped from her tone as she spoke. "Gee, thanks...how nice of you."

Once they were in the car, Erica began speaking again. "Unfortunately, we don't have a particularly interesting day ahead of us. We're supposed to help Jack and Sam at a speed trap"

Veronica nodded through the whole speech. "Okay. Maybe we'll get a chance to ruin some jerk's day. That's always fun."

Erica laughed as she started the car and pulled out of the parking lot. "That's the spirit!"

Once they met up with Jack and Sam, they all tossed a coin to see who would do what. Erica and Veronica wound up manning the radar gun, while Jack and Sam were set up a little ways down the road ready to pull over the people that were caught speeding.

The first half of their shift went surprisingly fast. Neither Erica nor Veronica had been all that happy about their assignment, but quickly got over their annoyance.

They had become friends shortly after Veronica had started at the precinct and had always found that they had a lot to talk about. Once, when they had first met, they had gone to a movie with a bunch of other people from the station. Veronica had given her a ride home that night and they started talking in the car. They next thing they knew, they were parked outside Erica's apartment at 5:00 in the morning still sitting there and talking.

This day was no different. They spent the first four hours of their shift discussing their families, high school, college, movies, books and music. Veronica had forgotten how much fun she could have talking to Erica. At one point, when there were no cars in sight, they had the radio in their cruiser turned up and they were dancing around the hood of the car. They were extremely grateful that Jack and Sam were far enough down the road that they could not see the dancing.

In spite of the fact that it was October and starting to cool off in Phoenix, they were overheating in the mid-day sun because of their black, polyester uniforms.

They were both relieved when Jack called and told them that it was about time for a lunch break.

Veronica considered asking Erica to drop her off at the station for a moment, but decided against it. She had been spending so much time with Ben since she came back that she had been neglecting reconnecting with some of her other friends. Going back to work had never been about being around Ben. It was about taking control of her life again and getting things back to normal. So, rather than go visit Ben, she suggested they all go to a pizza place that she used to frequent with Nick and the others before.

They balked at first considering they had all eaten pizza recently, but eventually broke down when she guilted them saying she wanted to spend some time with them. When they walked into the restaurant, the waitress grinned at their uniforms and sat them straight away. About ten minutes after they ordered their pie, the waitress brought it over with a complementary order of onion rings.

Once she left Jack started laughing. "You gotta love the uniform! It's like a free pass into any decent restaurant, and half the time you get free food with it!"

Erica playfully eyed his gut. "Maybe you should use your free pass a little less often."

Sam and Veronica both choked on their bites of pizza and tried to reign in their laughter.

Jack paled and guffawed dramatically. "I can't believe you said that!"

His voice was slightly more high pitched than normal.

"For that, we're switching places when we

get back out there. You can pull over the speeding morons and I hope someone spits on you."

Erica smiled serenely at him and snagged
an onion ring out of the basket in front of her.

Jack seemed flustered that his punishment appeared not to be affecting her. When she
pulled her cell phone out and calmly began text-
ing, he harrumphed one more time and picked
up his pizza. Only to set it back down a moment
later when his, Sam, and Veronica's cell phones
all chirped in unison.

Veronica turned a questioning eye on
Erica, but she simply shrugged innocently.

When they unlocked their phones, they
all found a text from Erica reading "Worth it."

At which point, Sam and Veronica finally
lost control and fell apart laughing.

Jack shoved his phone back into his
pocket and hostilely bit into his pizza.

Erica smiled sweetly at him and continued eating.

After a few minutes of continued grumpi-
ness from Jack, Sam began to get worried that
she was going to have to spend the rest of the day
with him in a bad mood.

Eventually, Veronica took pity on her and
scolded Jack. "Jack, stop sulking. You're freaking
out the rookie."

She turned to Sam.

"Stick around here long enough and you
will be pranked or made the butt of a joke or

two. Its how we bond."

She turned back to Jack.

"Remember the time that you signed Erica up for a booty call website and she kept getting emails from random guys on it?"

Jack tried to keep a straight face, but could not do it. He broke into a grin that would have made the Cheshire Cat proud. "Point taken."

After that, he flicked a pepperoni at Veronica.

She retaliated by sending a sausage sailing across the table and into his drink.

"That was uncalled for! I'll warn you Sam. If you value your health, never prank Ronnie. Her retaliation is always way worse than what you did."

Veronica sent at evil smile across the table at him, "Very few people prank me twice, and people always come to me for advice. I see no problem with that."

The rest of their lunch break was spent telling Sam stories about some of the shenanigans that had take place over the years.

Erica and Veronica spent the rest of their day pulling people over whenever Sam or Jack radioed them. Fortunately, they did not get spat upon. But they were lied to and flirted with left, right, and center. One guy had the gall to tell them that he was speeding because his wife was in labor. They asked him which hospital she was at, but he could not answer them. He could not even think of the name of one hospital in the city. He sputtered for a few moments and then got offended that they would even ask him. In the end, he wound up angrily snatching the ticket away from Erica and then pulling away quickly. Their day could also not have been complete without pulling over at least one lawyer who promptly demanded their badge numbers. They had to explain to him that he could not sue them for harassment because he had been going twenty miles over the speed limit, so they had cause to pull him over.

When their shift was coming to an end, they all piled into their squad cars and drove back to the station. After returning their equipment belts, Erica, Sam, and Veronica went to the women's locker room to change into their street clothes.

Cheyenne was already in the room when they got there. "Heyo! How was your first day being out on patrol again?"

Veronica shrugged in response. She knew Cheyenne was only being nice, but it felt like she was being treated like a rookie.

Trying not to let it get to her, she mustered more enthusiasm and answered Cheyenne. "It was fine. We got to piss off a lawyer. That always makes for a good day. You?"

Cheyenne smiled, "It was okay, I guess.

Ryan and I got stuck helping the drug squad serve warrants all day. You know how that can be."

As Veronica changed out of her uniform pants, she noticed Sam looking at the jagged scar on her leg. Realizing that she had been caught, Sam found some fascinating lint on her own pant leg and began picking at it. Veronica realized that Sam had probably heard about what happened a year ago and must be curious. She finished changing in silence and left the locker room.

She was greeted by the sight of Ben leaning against the wall in the hallway. "I heard you got stuck at a speed trap all day. Let's head over to the bar. I'll buy."

Veronica slumped against the wall next to him. "It wasn't as bad as I expected. But I will certainly take the beer."

Ben and Veronica made a silent agreement not to talk about what he and Mark had been doing all day. She did not want to hear anything about the case until he had a name to give her. So, on the way to the bar, she told him what had happened during her lunch break and they both had a good laugh about it. Ben had been on the receiving end of more than a few pranks and jokes since he had started at the precinct. At one point, Nick had superglued his hand to his desk phone. He had to wait for one of the women to produce a bottle of nail polish remover before he could detach himself. The prank war that had ensued was legendary.

When they walked through the door, they saw Tyler and Ryan sitting at the bar. Both were already half way through their first pints of beer. Tyler tried to play it cool as he looked up at the door, but his disappointment at seeing them was obvious.

Ryan saw him glance at the door for the fifth time in as many minutes and smacked him on the back of the head to get his attention. "You know, if you talked to her, you would know if Erica was coming tonight."

Veronica snickered while Tyler muttered something that sounded suspiciously like "Assholes" into his drink.

Tyler was saved from further embarrassment by the bartender arriving to see if Ben and Veronica wanted a round. They both ordered PBR and were mocked for about the hundredth time for not having more refined taste. They had both learned to enjoy the beer when they were college students who could not afford to drink expensively. The upside was that they got to mock all of their friends when they got their bills at the end of the night.

When Erica and Cheyenne arrived, Tyler gave a girlish giggle and stood to greet them. He then suggested that they all find a table to sit at because there were so many of them now. With all the newcomers, they would have taken up half of the bar.

They found an empty table that could fit them all, and he once again made sure to be sitting next to Erica.

As per usual, she remained completely oblivious.

Veronica felt bad for Tyler. Erica was amazing, but she was the type of person to never even consider the possibility that someone might take an interest in her. If Tyler wanted anything to happen between them, he would have to sack up and ask her out on a date. Given Erica's intimidating presence, she doubted that would happen anytime soon. For now, he was content with sitting next to her all the time, and watching her when he thought that nobody could see him. He was mistaken. The only person who had not figured out that Tyler had a thing for Erica was Erica. Veronica had been away for a year and she could still see it.

Once they were all seated around the table Ryan raised his glass. "I'd like to propose a toast. To Veronica. For her first day back on the streets doing *real* police work. We're glad to have you back."

Being the only detective in the room, Ben felt the need to flick a peanut at Ryan. But he still drank with everyone else.

Veronica felt her cheeks start to heat up with embarrassment, but she thanked Ryan and took a deep gulp of her drink. She had never been comfortable with people talking about her while she was sitting right there. Even when they were saying positive things. If fact, she found it worse when people were saying nice things about her. At least, when they were being jerks, she had every excuse to be offended and leave the room. But, when they were saying good things, she had to sit there and smile while everyone was nodding and watching her.

They spent a few hours drinking, laughing, and generally having fun. It was nice getting to wind down with friends after work.

Eventually, they all began to regret not getting food before they met at the bar. Fortunately, a few people had volunteered to be designated drivers, so they all piled into their cars and went their separate ways.

Veronica had had more to drink than Ben, so she decided to let him drive this time.

When they were in the car, Ben asked her what kind of food she wanted.

"We have eaten so much pizza and burgers lately. I feel like we should try to find something else that is not so unhealthy."

Ben sat silently for a moment and then he started the car. "I know exactly what we should do."

She tried to guess what he was planning the entire drive back to his house, but he would not tell her anything.

Once they got there, Ben sat her down on the couch and informed her that she was not to go anywhere near the kitchen. Twenty minutes later, he walked back into the living room with a platter piled high with steaming waffles. "Its breakfast for dinner night."

Veronica smiled and followed him into the kitchen to help him retrieve the toppings.

When she got to the kitchen she saw a gigantic jar of Nutella sitting on the counter with all of the other fixings.

She stared at him with a questioning look, but he simply shrugged and said, "Trust me."

He grabbed the Nutella and a few other items and walked back out of the room.

She chose a couple jars of jam and a can of whipped cream. After placing them on the coffee table, she fell back onto the couch next to Ben. He pulled a waffle off of the pile and slathered it with Nutella, dropped a dollop of strawberry jam on it and sprayed it with some whipped cream.

She had thought that it was for him, but he put it on a plate and handed it over to her. Veronica hesitantly cut off a chunk of the waffle and placed it in her mouth. She almost swooned at the explosion of melt-in-your-mouth, chocolatey, beautiful flavor that she encountered.

"Oh, my God!"

Ben laughed while he made up a waffle of

his own and said, "Told you so."

Veronica nodded and kept eating. They spent the rest of the night experimenting with the fixings on their waffles and watching episodes of Rookie Blue. When Veronica started nodding off on Ben's shoulder, he sent her up to bed. She changed into her pajamas and fell asleep almost as soon as her head hit the pillow.

DAY 12

When she woke up in the morning, Veronica instantly felt that there was something wrong. It did not take her long to realize that the problem was that she was alone in the bed. Judging by the state of Ben's pillows, she had been all night. Her heart jumped into her throat. She could not help but think that it would not be the first time her least favorite subject came at her through one of the men in her life.

Jumping up, she ran to Ben's closet where he kept his gun safe. After retrieving her gun she checked out the exercise room down the hall and then turned to search the rest of the house. She slowly crept down the stairs with her heart hammering away in her chest, terrified of what she might find. She had horrifying images running through her head as she came to the landing at the bottom of the stairs. Upon entering the living room, she almost dropped her gun in surprise and relief.

She found Ben.

Better than that. Ben was completely okay. He was fast asleep on the couch with his head thrown back and an open file on his lap.

She took the file and set it and her gun down on the coffee table. Then she plopped herself down on his lap.

He tensed and his head snapped up. Before he had a chance to comprehend what was happening, she grabbed his face and pulled him in for a kiss. He responded vigorously as he pulled her closer.

After a few minutes, Veronica pulled back for air.

"Well, that was a nice wakeup call." Ben glanced behind her and continued. "Why is there a gun on the table?"

Veronica blushed and stammered, "Um...no reason."

She extricated herself from his lap, grabbed the gun, and ran back up the stairs. When she came back down, Ben had a thoughtful expression on his face.

"Penny for your thoughts?"

He glanced up and his face cleared. "Just thinking about life."

Veronica smiled and went to the kitchen to throw some poptarts in the toaster. They were running a bit late so they did not have the time for a real breakfast. Besides, they had stuffed themselves full of waffles the night before.

It did not take long for them both to be showered, dressed, and ready to leave for work. They grabbed their keys, strapped their guns to their belts, and started heading towards the door. They were both standing in front of the door when they froze and stared at it.

Ben was the first to speak. "You don't think...not again...right?"

Veronica reached for the handle, "Only one way to find out."

She held her breath and pulled the door open. There was nothing there.

She and Ben both breathed a sigh of relief. Then they had to quickly jump into action as Ace tried to run out the open door. Ben lunged and caught hold of his collar. He dragged the dog back into the house while Veronica reached to pull the door closed again. Once they had him corralled in the living room, they quickly moved back to the front door and left the house.

They both slowed to a stop again when they reached the driveway.

"This is ridiculous!"

Veronica stomped forward and checked both of their vehicles for "gifts." Once again, there was nothing to find. She unlocked her car. "Let's get out of here already."

Ben nodded silently and joined her at the

car.

They were both feeling foolish for being paranoid, so there was not much conversation on their way to work.

Veronica desperately wanted to ask Ben what he had been working on last night. But she also did not want to know the answer to that question. She did not want to know how close they were getting to finding Nick's killer, because she was terrified to learn that they were not any closer than they had been at the beginning of the investigation. She did not want this dragging on any longer than it already had. Spending a year in limbo was more than enough.

Ben knew this, so neither one of them tried to start that conversation. The awkward silence continued until they got to the station and had to separate. Veronica needed to change into her uniform and find Erica. Ben went straight to his office to continue working.

When he got there, Ben found Mark already at his own desk doing the same thing that Ben had been doing the night before and would continue to do today.

They were checking the names of known offenders in the area that Ben's mother lived and worked. They had received the file on his mother's stolen purse, but there was not much in it. It had not given them any clear suspects, but at least they had work to do. They were checking to see if any of the people they looked at were on any of the lists that Ben and Veronica had already compiled. They were also looking at their files to see if it was even remotely possible that they could be a suspect. It was a long and slow process that would most likely not give them anything, but they were willing to do it anyway. They were hoping to catch a break, because the purse snatching was the only lead that they had.

Ben looked up from his work in time to see Erica and Veronica heading out of the building. He remembered that morning and smirked.

"She was totally worried about me."

Mark lifted his head, "Huh...What?"

Ben flushed and looked down at his desk. "Nothing."

Erica and Veronica did not have any special instructions that day, so they were riding around making traffic stops until a call came in.

They were almost two hours into their shift when they were called to a pile up on the 51. They were nearby, so it only took them a couple minutes to make it to the scene. When they arrived, they found that the accident had involved three vehicles and two of them were completely totalled. The third card had the front end crushed in a bit, but was otherwise in one piece. It looked like it had been too close to the other cars to avoid the carnage. Within seconds of their arrival, the paramedics also made it to the scene. They checked out the driver from the third vehicle to see how she was doing, and stood by while the fire department continued to work to free the other drivers.

Erica and Veronica were asked to take witness statements from all of the people who had seen the crash. Most of them were annoyed to be stuck there, but they all told their story. It looked like one car had tried to merge into the HOV lane and wound up bashing into another car. They had both lost control and smashed into the median. The car behind them had not reacted in time to stop. Fortunately, that driver seemed to be completely fine.

They spent about two hours getting statements from everyone who had seen anything. They also had to get and confirm phone numbers and addresses for everyone, in case they needed to talk to them again.

After they were done with that, they had to direct traffic away from the closed lanes so that people were not stuck there all day. They also had to supervise when the tow trucks arrived to take the mangled vehicles away. When all of that was over, they still had to wait for the street sweepers to come and clean all of the glass and oil off of the road. In the end, the only evidence that anything had happened on that spot were the fresh skid marks still visible.

When they were finally able to open up all lanes of traffic and leave the scene, it was well past time for them to eat lunch. They were both aware of the amount of paperwork that went along with accidents like this, so they decided to get something to go and eat while they worked. They hoped that they would be able to finish their paperwork that day so that they would not have to continue working on it the next day.

Erica suggested they stop at Gyro House and order as many platters of food that they could afford. She knew everyone would be picking off their plates. Plus, having a few people at the station owing her a favor was never a bad thing.

After setting themselves up in the breakroom with their food and paperwork, the pair got down to business.

Veronica texted Cheyenne and it turned out she and Ryan had been stuck at the scene of a robbery all day and had not eaten anything either. About ten minutes later, they walked into the break room with their paperwork. They each gave Erica and Veronica some money and the four of them tucked in for a long afternoon of filling out forms. This was a fairly normal occurrence, so when Blake walked in to get some coffee he merely nicked a few kibbi balls and continued on his way.

They stayed there for as long as they could, but eventually ran out of food and work that could be done without a computer. At which point, they all trudged out to their desks and continued working on trying to finish all the paperwork.

Erica and Veronica spent the rest of their day inputting data and looking people up. They also had to keep track of what was happening with the drivers in the hospital so they knew what kind of charges to lay on the one who had caused the accident.

As they got closer to the end of their shift, Veronica would occasionally glance around at the detective's office to see if Ben showed any signs of wanting to leave. But every time she looked, he was still hunched over his desk rifling through papers and typing into his computer.

So she kept working.

She at least pretended to keep working.

Mostly she sat at her desk trying not to stare a hole into the glass wall of Ben and Mark's office. The other detectives had all gone home for the day, being exhausted from working all of Ben and Mark's investigations now. They did not complain because they wanted justice for Nick and all of those women, but things were starting to pile up.

Veronica wondered how much longer Blake would be able to justify keeping this case a priority if no new leads came up. Every time she saw Blake staring at the detective's office with an uncertain and concerned expression she knew he was thinking the same thing.

Forcibly turning her mind away from that topic, Veronica started contemplating her relationship with Ben. It was new and strange, but he made her feel alive.

She had been so lost in her own thoughts that she did not notice when he stalked up next to her and perched himself on the corner of her desk.

"Penny for your thoughts?"

Veronica jumped and met his gaze. "Nothing...just thinking about life."

She gave him a meaningful look and a slow smile spread across his face.

Once he was able to wipe the sappy grin from his face, he spoke again. "Well, your shift ended two hours ago and I'm tired. Why don't you go change so we can go home?"

Veronica gave a theatrical sigh and stood up. "If we must."

She logged off her computer and said goodbye. Before she left, she made Erica promise to leave within the hour.

Ben followed her to the locker room then propped himself on his customary spot at the wall. She changed quickly and they left without another word.

While she was driving back to Ben's house,

she told him about her day. In spite of his best efforts to nod along to the story, Veronica could tell that Ben was mostly tuning her out.

She was not ready to ask what the problem was yet, so she kept talking. She continued to talk when they made it to his place and while they heated up some leftovers for dinner. She basically gave him a play-by-play of everything that had happened that day.

Eventually Veronica ran out of things to say, so silence fell over them like a dark cloud. Finally, she stood up and retrieved her wallet. She pulled a penny out of it and sat back down on the couch. Dramatically, she set the penny on the coffee table and slid it across to Ben.

"Don't tell me you're thinking about life."

Ben spoke hesitantly, "I promised Mark that I would run an idea by you, but I don't like it."

Veronica waited for him to continue but he did not. "I'm going to keep staring until you start talking."

Ben groaned and dropped his face into his hands. "He wants to use you as bait."

He lifted his head and met her blank stare.

"He wants to wire you up and send you to the dump site alone. We would be nearby of course, but if something happened it would take a while for us to get to you."

Veronica thought it over for a moment. "The dump site is too obvious. I mean, why would I ever be going there? He'll know it's a trap. I should go to the cemetery instead. That would seem more normal. Plus, we can have plainclothes cops in the park and the surveillance van could be closer."

Ben paled and stammered out, "You are actually considering doing this?"

She met his gaze levelly. "I'm more than considering it. If this works then it could all be over."

Ben sat up straight, "Or you could end up dead!"

Veronica huffed indignantly. "He hasn't killed me yet."

Ben's eyes blazed, "No, he's just played with you, and that got my best friend killed. It also almost killed you as well. I won't send you into this when we don't know what his endgame is! You are not invincible!"

It was Veronica's turn to have blazing eyes, but she replied with deadly calm. "I am aware of that. And I'm not asking your permission. If you can give me an alternative; great. But until you can give me a viable plan or lead, you don't get to shoot down this idea."

Knowing that he was in the wrong, Ben slumped back into the couch. "Please, let me try everything else first? Give me a few days before you talk to Mark. And if you go in...I'm going to be on the other end of the wire...Please."

Veronica slumped next to him. "Okay."

Ben grabbed her hand and they held onto each other in silence for a while.

Veronica turned on How I Met Your Mother in an attempt to lighten the mood.

After a while, they finally felt the tension leave the room as the relaxed.

This time, Ben was the first to start nodding off. He argued when Veronica turned the television off and began dragging him up the stairs, but she would have none of it.

"You've slept on couches three times in the last week and a half. You are not 20 years old anymore. You will kill your back if you keep doing it. Especially if you sleep sitting up again."

Ben knew that he could not win the argument, so he grudgingly followed her up the stairs and into his bedroom. Half of him desperately wanted to keep working while the other half of him knew that he would not make it through another day if he did not get some decent sleep. He could feel his exhaustion deep in his bones. It was like every cell in his body was screaming at him to lay down and close his eyes.

Once he finally admitted how tired he was, it became impossible to think about anything else. He changed into a pair of old sweats as fast as he could and then passed out seconds after making it to the bed.

DAY 13

When his alarm went off in the morning, Ben found himself curled protectively around Veronica's form. He tried to imagine what Nick would say to him in that moment. Would he be angry or sad? He wondered if what he and Veronica were doing was wrong. But the more time they spent together, the more he was convinced that there was no reason to worry. For the first time in a year, they were both on their way to being genuinely happy. When he felt Veronica stir as she too began to wake, he rolled off the bed and reached to turn his alarm off.

They had developed enough of a routine for the morning that there was little discussion as they got ready. They prepared and left the house in an almost mechanical way as they both clutched to-go mugs filled with the life giving liquid they loved so much.

When they were once again able to make

it to the station without any surprises, they began to wonder why their tormentor was giving them a break. Neither one of them were all that keen to find out what he was building up to.

They did not discuss the conversation they had had the night before, but Veronica did not seek Mark out when they arrived. Instead, she went about her usual business by changing into her uniform and following Erica as they made their way across the building and to their squad car.

That did not stop Mark from finding her before she and Erica could leave. When Veronica saw him walking towards her with an expectant look on his face, she cut him off before he could speak. She did not want anyone else at the station to hear about his plan. They would all have an opinion about whether or not it was a good idea. Most of them would side with Ben, but she did not agree with them.

She had promised Ben that she would wait, but she believed this was their best chance.

She spoke as swiftly and circumspectly as she could manage so as not to raise Erica's suspicion. "Ben talked to me last night. We're thinking about it."

Mark knew not to push too hard, so he simply nodded his head and went back to the detective's office.

When Veronica turned back to Erica, she

found her wearing a bemused expression.

"So, you're 'we' people now? That didn't take long." When she saw the confused expression on Veronica's face Erica continued. "'*We* would love to come.' '*We've* had a long day.' '*We* got you this gift.' 'We' people."

Veronica looked uncomfortable with the direction this conversation was going. "It's because of this case. And because I'm staying at his house. We're together all the time"

Erica gave her an almost pitying look. "I'm not saying it's a bad thing. I think it's great. You have been getting so close this past year that it was basically inevitable."

Veronica was getting more uncomfortable with every word that Erica spoke. She and Ben had agreed not to overthink what was happening between them, but it seemed that their friends were going to do it for them. This was one of the few downsides of being so close with your co-workers. She nodded noncommittally to Erica and made her way out of the building.

They did not have any special assignments again, so Veronica had a lot of time to think. In that time, she thought about Ben and Nick, and Mark's plan. More than anything else, she thought about the man responsible for everything that had happened. His sudden radio silence was unsettling. She wanted to believe that he had stopped because he thought they were getting close to finding him, but realistically she knew that was wishful thinking. All she had to do was look at the desperation in everyone's eyes to know they were running out of ideas. The "hail Mary" pass that Mark was proposing was another indication. Their subject had other reasons for being so quiet over the last couple days, and Veronica wished she knew what those reasons were. Maybe that was the point. Maybe he wanted to know how crazy the silence would make her. When that thought occurred to her, she became determined not to think about it or him.

Normal... Normal life. That is what this is all about. He does not get to win.

She put her stern face on and focused on the calls that were coming over the radio.

Little did she know, Ben did have another idea. It had occurred to him the night before, whilst he was racking his brain for anything that might stall Veronica becoming bait. He and Mark began checking out local pawn shops to see if any of his mother's belongings had turned up. He did not expect to find anything, but he knew that he had to try. Most pawn shop owners would answer questions easily. They wanted the cops out of their store as fast as possible so that their inventory was not looked at too closely.

Ben was starting to contemplate giving up on this idea when something caught his eye. There was a bracelet sitting in one of the cases that he recognized at first sight. His mother had been wearing it ever since her wedding day when her parents had given it to her.

When the owner gave him the receipt for it, he had a name. Jason Breckstein. For the first time in days, his shoulders started to relax. It was probably a fake name, but it was a name. He confiscated the bracelet as evidence and told the owner to call if 'Jason' came back.

He called Mark and told him to go back to the station. During the drive back, he fought to control the adrenaline coursing through his veins.

He was moving quickly to the detective's office when Blake intercepted and summoned him.

This can't be good.

He slowed and changed direction.

Across the room, Erica was leading a dirt and muck-stained Veronica towards the women's locker room while she tried not to touch anything or bump into anyone.

Ben could not help but smirk in spite of his anxiety.

Looks like someone had to do some dumpster diving today.

He chuckled internally and then continued towards Blake's office. Once there, all the anxiety from moments before returned. He had never seen Blake looking so haggard and defeated. Once he sat down, Blake started speaking.

"I've been on the phone all day. My bosses think that I've lost my mind. First, I let a patrol cop work a case as a detective. Not to mention the fact that this case killed one of our officers and almost got her killed too. Then, I let two detectives do the equivalent of twiddle their thumbs working the same case without anything to go off of or accomplishing anything. They don't understand why I'm letting other investigations pile up while you spin your wheels pretending you're getting somewhere with this case."

Ben could see where this was going so he cut in. "I found something."

Blake looked at him in shock.

"That's why I told Mark to come back. The day is almost over and I already found what we were looking for. He pawned my mother's bracelet. We have a name. Jason Breckstein."

Blake took charge again. "Have you run the name yet? Did you get any hits?"

Ben shook his head. "I haven't had the chance yet. I only just got in."

Blake immediately started typing into his computer. After a few moments he pulled back. "Nothing. Either its a fake name, or our profile for him is *very* wrong."

Ben sunk down in his chair. "Damn it."

Blake gave him a sympathetic look and leaned back in his chair. "Mark told me about his idea."

Ben visibly paled and began to shake his head.

Blake cut him off before he could argue. "The bosses like it. They want this case closed as fast as possible.They are convinced that this might work."

Color came back to Ben's face as his anger and frustration grew. "Yeah. Dangling Veronica like a worm on a hook is a brilliant idea." Sarcasm dripped from his tone as he spoke.

The withering glare he received for that comment was more than enough to shut him up. "We do not *dangle* our officers anywhere."

Blake paused and only continued his speech when Ben nodded glumly. "*If* we decide to go forward with this plan, she will be protected at all times. I know the situation is difficult, but we have to keep our heads. If you can't handle it, let me know now. I can't have you on the case if it is getting to be too much."

Ben straightened up in his chair. "I'm fine. I can handle this fine. That doesn't mean that I have to like it."

Blake seemed to be satisfied by that answer and relaxed. "Okay. You and Mark have one more day. If you don't have anything concrete by tomorrow, we're going to have to set up the sting. It's either that or they go over my head and de-prioritize this case. The step they'll take after that would be to declare the case inactive again. I don't like the idea of him getting to walk away for a second time. Especially with Veronica just getting back on her feet again."

Ben deflated some and nodded. "I guess I better get back to work then."

When Ben left Blake's office, he saw Veronica sitting at her desk doing paperwork.

She appeared to be freshly showered and in a different uniform. Spotting him, she rose out of her chair and glided over.

"Do you mind if we stop by a dry cleaner on the way home tonight?"

She tried to act casually, but he needed something to cheer him up, so he riled her up a bit.

"Sure, I noticed you changed. Is there something wrong with the other uniform?"

Ben's eyes twinkled innocently at her as she scowled.

"We were chasing a guy that tried to hold up a gas station. He tossed his gun into a dumpster and someone had to go in after it. I drew the short straw."

Ben chuckled. "Meaning, Erica pulled rank on you. Did you at least find it?"

Veronica's scowl deepened as she remembered pulling the item out of the pile of trash. "Yes. It was a freaking fake! I rooted around in a dumpster to find a fake gun! Why couldn't Jack and Sam have taken the call? That's what rookies are for!"

In spite of the bad mood the meeting with Blake had put him in, Ben started laughing. He remembered giving a similar speech to Nick back when they were both still on patrol. Veronica and her friends had shown up at the station shortly after that, and he had been thrilled. When Veronica fumbled with her radio while the other three had cowered in the background, he knew they would have fun with this new set of rookies.

"So, what did Blake have to say?" Veronica's abrupt question pulled him out of his playful moment.

"Huh? What?"

She looked him dead in the eye. "I asked what Blake wanted."

Ben focused on keeping his breathing even and tried not to flush. "He's having some political problems."

As always, Veronica saw right through him. "Meaning, he's having trouble justifying this investigation. How much time did he give you?"

Ben wanted to soften the blow, but he knew that would not help. "We have to show significant progress by the end of shift tomorrow."

Veronica took a deep breath to steady herself. She knew what would happen next, but needed Ben to confirm it. "Then they're gonna declare it inactive again, right?"

Ben shook his head. "No. First they want to try Mark's idea. I've been overruled."

Veronica tried to hide her enthusiasm for this plan, but he definitely noticed the color return to her cheeks.

"Jesus! You like this, don't you?! You were hoping I would say that!"

Veronica's eyes went cold again as she pulled back from him. "I've been hoping we would catch this guy. If a sting is the only way that will happen, I'll happily do it. We talked about this last night. I'm tired of calling him 'this guy' or 'the subject.' I want a name, a face. And I want him in jail."

Ben did not back down. "That's great! I think we would all prefer that you live to see that."

Before Veronica could unleash her full fury on Ben, they were interrupted by someone clearing their throat. They looked over to see Erica's measured gaze turned towards them.

"Maybe not the *best* time or place."

Veronica flushed and went back to her desk. She ignored Ben as he moved past her to get to his office. When she heard the door to the detective's office close, she looked up at Erica. "Still think we're 'we' people?"

Erica smiled at her. "More than I did this morning."

Veronica harrumphed and turned back to her computer.

Ben spent the rest of his day fruitlessly searching for Jason Breckstein. He looked into everyone in their system that had that name. Then he looked into their known associates. After that, he started going through the files of men they already looked at to see if they had ever used that name as an alias.

No luck.

He knew that it had been a slim hope, but he had no other ideas at this point.

Mark had long since gotten annoyed with all the pointless searching and had begun putting together the resources they would need for the sting when Ben came up empty.

The air in the detective's' office was filled with so much tension that the other detectives had all found excuses to flee the room.

Ben noticed a couple of them stop by Veronica's desk and say something to her before continuing on their way. He was determined not to think about her anymore, so he pushed his curiosity to the back of his mind. This became increasingly more difficult as he felt her gaze turned towards him more and more frequently.

He had planned on staying late again, but Veronica had other ideas. The moment that her shift ended, she rushed to the locker room and quickly changed. When she entered the detectives' office and approached Ben, anger was rolling off of him in waves. When his cold eyes met hers she grabbed his arm and pulled him out of the room.

Ben followed Veronica without a word because he did not trust himself not to start yelling again. When she led him to her SUV and opened the back door he was more that slightly confused. But he climbed into the back seat and scooted over to the other side so she could slide in after him.

Once the door was closed Veronica turned to face Ben.

"So, apparently I owe you an apology. At least, that's what everyone has been telling me. I think they're wrong. I think, if I owe you anything, it's an explanation."

She paused and met Ben's gaze.

"Feel free to begin that explanation any time you want."

Veronica huffed and continued, "I want to do this sting. But...I want you to be there the whole time. I know that if you are there, nothing will happen to me. If there is anyone in this world that I trust to keep me alive, it's you. In spite of what you seem to think I do want to live. In case you hadn't noticed, I do have a few things worth living for."

For the first time since he and Veronica

had fought, Ben allowed himself a half smile.

Taking this as encouragement, Veronica moved closer to him and took his hand. "I want to be able to move on. Until he's caught, there is always going to be a chance that he'll come after me. Once he's in jail, we never have to think about him again. We can just...live.Which was the whole point of my going back to work in the first place, right?"

Ben knew that he should not take advantage of the moment, but there were some things that they needed to talk about. As long as she was feeling forthcoming, he would keep pushing.

"The point was for your life to go back to normal. Well, things haven't exactly been normal lately."

Veronica feigned ignorance and thought for a moment. "Yeah. Riding with Erica has been a little strange, but I like it. We get on well together."

Ben scowled at her and used their connected hands to pull her closer.

She was nearly on top of him at this point.

"You know what I'm talking about."

She sobered upon seeing the pleading look in his eyes. "I do. You're talking about this." She gestured to their position as she perched in his lap.

"Erica said that we were inevitable. I'm not sure what I think of that, but I am glad that this is happening. I'm 28 years old. I'm way too young to turn into an old crone and I wouldn't' want to. I used to think it would feel wrong to be with anyone other than Nick, but it doesn't. It feels... amazing. I feel alive for the first time in a year. I know that sounds cheesy, but I don't know how else to describe it. I'm happy. And I think you are too."

Ben knew he was not going to get any more out of her so he did not try. Instead, he pulled her down into a kiss that was filled with all of his desperation to protect her and his joy at being able to kiss her. He had never been good with words, so he let his actions speak for him. He filled his kiss with all of the feelings that he did not know how to articulate.

Veronica wound her arms around his neck and melted into the kiss.

They remained happily entwined until they heard a tap on the windows.

Veronica jumped off Ben's lap and fell into the seat next to him. She spun in the direction the noise had come from and found Erica, uncomfortably shifting on her feet.

"Also not the time or place." She looked pointedly towards the building.

They saw Blake crossing the parking lot to get to his car.

Erica awkwardly shuffled off to her car while Ben and Veronica straightened their clothes before moving to the front seats.

Not another word was spoken as Veronica drove them to Ben's house. They had both been strongly considering continuing their activities from earlier, but they saw Natasha's Prius idling in front of Ben's house.

When Natasha eagerly jumped out of her vehicle, Ben shook his head before dropping into it into his hands and groaning. "You need to call her more often!"

Veronica wanted to laugh, but she was feeling as frustrated as he was.

Ben lifted his head and dropped one of his hands down to her knee. "Get rid of her," he growled out as he slid his hand up her leg.

Once she was good and flustered, he got out of the car, nodded at Natasha, and went into the house.

After regaining her composure, Veronica exited the vehicle. As she walked towards Natasha, Veronica tried to think of an excuse to get her best friend back in her car and on her way as quickly as possible. She was never able to finish planning because Natasha cut her off.

"I don't care what you're about to say. You have spent way too much time locked in this house lately, so we are going out. You may not try to get out of this. You may not complain. You will have fun. I already called Cheyenne and

Erica and they're coming too. Now, go say good-bye to Benny Boy and remind him that he will go to jail if he shoots me."

Veronica studied Natasha to see if there were any signs that she might waiver but did not find any. Without a word, she turned and walked through the front door.

Ben was on the couch eating leftover pizza and drinking beer.

"I'm being kidnapped."

Ben put his food and drink on the coffee table. "I know."

He slumped back into the couch as she approached him.

She knelt in front of him and spoke under her breath. "I promise I'll make it up to you later."

He leaned forward, "You better."

They shared a brief kiss then Veronica pulled away. She said goodbye to him and the animals and then left the house again.

Natasha was smirking at her when she got outside.

"He said he'll have to think of another way to get back at you."

Natasha took in the state of her smudged lip gloss and smirked again. "Sure he did."

Veronica blushed and walked past her to Natasha's car.

Veronica did not speak to Natasha while they were in the car.

It only took about five minutes for Natasha to comment. "You can sulk all you want right now, but promise me that you'll at least try to have fun tonight."

Veronica remained silent for a moment longer and then breathed out a single word. "Fine."

Satisfied that Veronica would not continue with the sour mood all night, Natasha focused back on the road. They made a quick stop to pick Erica and Cheyenne up.

"Will someone at least tell me where we're going?"

Natasha was the only one to respond. "Done with the silent treatment then? As your punishment for pouting you don't get to know."

Veronica slouched farther down in her seat and relapsed back into silence.

Knowing that Veronica had never been a fan of surprises, Natasha chuckled and kept driving. It was not long before she pulled them into a parking lot and Veronica found that she was smiling in spite of herself.

She had always loved The Salty Sow because of their delicious honey and rosemary fried chicken.

When Natasha caught her smiling, she broke out into a smirk of her own. "I told you that you would have fun tonight."

Veronica sent her a cheesy grin and exited the car. In truth, she was starving and willing to put off arguing with her friend until she had eaten something.

It only took a short while for them to get a table. They had all been there many times before so none of them needed to look at the menu.

While they were waiting for someone to take their order, Natasha decided that some rules were in order. "Okay, this is how it's gonna be. No talking about work unless you have a funny story. No talking about Ben in any capacity other than boy toy. No talking about crazy, stalking killer dude at all. Got it?"

Nobody had any objections to those rules so they all quickly agreed.

"Okay! Now that that's settled; Veronica, do you mind explaining why Ben was so ... frustrated when I stole you away?"

Veronica flushed a deep red and took a sip of her water.

Before Natasha had a chance to pry any further, Veronica was saved by the waitress arriving at the table. She was blonde and eager with such vividly green eyes that Veronica was sure they had to be contacts. She was smiling and cheerful in a way that can only be faked, so Veronica had a hard time liking her. She knew the girl was probably trained to be pleasant all the time for her job, but she had never trusted people like that.

They all quickly ordered their drinks and food and then sent her on her way.

Veronica saw Natasha turn towards her again and was surprised when Erica cut her off. She was relieved for a moment, but Erica's words quickly ended that.

"I think we all know why Ben wanted Ronnie to himself tonight. You should have seen the way they were going at it in the back seat of her car at the station."

Everyone else looked utterly shocked, but Erica seemed proud of herself. When she caught sight of Veronica's livid expression she did not back down for a moment. "What? For once I'm the one with dirt on someone! You didn't expect it not to come up, did you? If you didn't want to be teased you should have saved it until you got home. Although...Tasha would have already been there, so I guess you were screwed either way. Or...I guess not screwed would be the proper wording in this case."

Hearing such a speech come from Erica shocked them all so much that Veronica burst out laughing. Once she started laughing, it was not long before the others joined in.

Natasha, Cheyenne and Erica continued to tease Veronica about Ben until their food arrived. Once they had something else to focus on, they decided to give her a reprieve.

While they were eating, they talked about movies, television shows, books and celebrities. They kept the topics light and fun because they were all in need of a night with absolutely no stress in it. They laughed and drank and laughed some more. A good time was had by all, but when the check came Veronica found herself looking forward to going home to Ben.

That hope was dashed when Cheyenne stood up and exclaimed, "Check's paid! Off to our next stop!"

She caught the disappointment flash across Veronica's face and laughed. "Ronnie, would you relax? You can go spend time with your boyfriend later."

Veronica flushed and leaned down to grab her bag while she mumbled, "He's not my boyfriend."

Natasha jumped on that comment in about half a second. "Not your boyfriend? What exactly is he then?"

Veronica flushed an even deeper red. "I don't know...it's new."

Natasha could not help but laugh at that comment. "Well, Cheyenne's right. You can go spend time with your new 'not boyfriend' later."

Veronica grumbled something under her breath and walked out to the car.

The other three laughed and followed after her.

Ten minutes later they pulled into another parking lot and Veronica looked around to see where she had been taken this time. When she recognized their surroundings Veron-

TABITHA J ARMENT

ica burst out laughing.

"Wow! You guys are going for the nostalgia factor tonight, aren't you?"

Cheyenne suddenly looked innocent. "I don't know what you're talking about. I just need a new outfit."

Veronica noticed everyone else watching Cheyenne as she steadfastly stared out the window.

Veronica narrowed her eyes studying Cheyenne's purposefully blank expression.

"You're hiding something...and it's not just the kidnapping plans that you all made tonight. You have a date!"

Cheyenne started rubbing her forehead as she tried not to meet anyone's eyes. "What!? Uh...no..."

Natasha spun exuberantly around in her seat. "Save it. You've never been a good liar. YOU HAVE A DATE! Why didn't you tell us!? Now we really need to be here!"

With that, Cheyenne turned bright red and all of the women piled out of the car. They were all laughing and joking with Cheyenne as they entered 'A Second Look'.

When they got inside, Cheryl, one of the managers rushed forward. "Hi, girls! It's been so long since we've seen you! What are we looking for tonight?"

They pushed Cheyenne forward and she stammered out, "Well, uh...I have this um...date coming up. I kinda want a new outfit."

Cheryl hugged Cheyenne and they all started looking through the racks.

This was why they always waited to go to 'A Second Look' at night. The store was never busy so the employees were always more relaxed and had more time to help out. Veronica and Cheyenne had started shopping there during their first year on the force.

The rookies had been doing their first John sweep and needed costumes so they could pass as hookers. None of them had anything, or any money to spare, so they had ended up at the consignment store near Erica's old apartment. They went back every chance they could for years. Cheryl had been working there the entire time, so they all knew her. She and a few of the others had even been invited to Veronica and Nick's wedding.

While they were searching through the racks of dresses for Cheyenne, they heard the voice of someone else who had been working there on and off for years. Walking around the edge of the rack they were met by the sight of Andrea arguing with another regular customer, Melanie.

"Theater is not a fake major!"

Melanie laughed and walked away. She was a lawyer and had always mocked Andrea for what she was studying in college.

They all walked over with Cheryl.

"Is she still jealous of your life?"

Andrea snorted, "Yes, it's not my fault she didn't have the guts to go theater."

Everyone laughed while Cheyenne counted out her clothes and headed into the fitting rooms.

By the end of the night, each of them had a brand new dress and Cheyenne had several options for her date the next week.

When they left the store, Natasha asked if they wanted to go get a drink at 'Shea 32' but the others shot her down.

"Don't you have work tomorrow, too?"

Natasha laughed as she unlocked her car, "Oh please! This has nothing to do with you wanting to sleep...well maybe for Erica and Cheyenne, but we all know why you want to go home."

The knowing look she gave Veronica was all it took for the redhead to blush furiously as she climbed into the car.

While everyone else was laughing, Veronica seethed. "I hope you know that next time any one of you has a significant other, I will get payback."

They were all still laughing when they dropped her off at Ben's house.

She was muttering as she unclipped her seatbelt. "Yeah, yeah, yeah...you're all hilarious."

They laughed louder, so she flipped them

off as she was unlocking the door. When she got inside she saw the television on and Ben fast asleep on the couch.

She cuddled up next to him and started running her fingers through his hair.

He slowly woke up, "What took you so long?"

She grabbed his hand and started pulling him up. "I'll tell you about it tomorrow."

DAY 14

The next morning they woke up to find that once again they had been left in peace.

The fact that the killer appeared to be losing interest in his game was making Veronica more inclined to go along with the plan that Mark was cooking up. She wanted to catch the asshole before he went underground again.

Part of her wanted Ben to come up with nothing at work today so that they could get on with it. She would never say that to Ben because he had finally managed to get past her enthusiasm for the idea and she did not want to provoke his anger. If the other detectives had to deal with his foul mood again, they might revolt. So she kept her thoughts to herself and wished him luck with the investigation on their way out the door. When they made it to the office, she quickly separated from him and made her way to the locker room.

Once there, she was ambushed by Erica and Cheyenne.

"So, how did things go with your 'not boyfriend' after we dropped you off last night?"

Veronica glared at them and their air quotes. "Nothing happened. It was so damn late that we went to sleep."

Erica gave her an amused smirk. "Feeling a little frustrated then? Maybe we should go get some doughnuts. Those always seem to put you in a better mood."

Veronica shoved her into a locker and turned her back on them so that she could change into her uniform.

When the three of them left the locker room, they were startled to find Blake standing in the hallway waiting for them. Cheyenne split off to find Ryan, but Erica and Veronica were trapped. When the boss was waiting for you outside the locker rooms, it generally meant that you were about to have a truly crappy day.

"Okay, I need you two to spend the first half of the day at the Horizon High School career fair. After that you can come catch up on paperwork and we'll go over the prep work and game plan for tomorrow. Okay?"

Mustering all of the fake enthusiasm that they could manage they told Blake that they would be happy to and ran out the door.

Once they were in their squad car, Erica jumped on Blake's comment about prepping for the next day. "What's he talking about? What's happening tomorrow"

Veronica desperately wanted to avoid this conversation, so she tried to throw her off. "No clue. Now we get to spend our day with snobby high school kids who are gonna make fun of our uniforms. This also means we can't get doughnuts. If we show up there with doughnuts, we will never hear the end of it. Damn! I was looking forward to that!"

Sensing herself beginning to ramble, Veronica shut herself up and stared forward.

Erica continued to watch her with a calculating expression for a moment before she spoke again. "Oh, you know something! Spill! What the Hell is happening tomorrow?"

Veronica tried to maintain an innocent expression for a moment, but she could feel Erica's eyes boring into her and quickly gave it up. "Fine!" She huffed, "Mark had an idea to catch the killer and we're gonna try it tomorrow...If Ben can't come up with any leads that is." She could still feel Erica staring at her, but refused to say anything more.

"This is what you two were fighting about yesterday, right?"

Veronica still would not meet her eyes. "Yes. Ben doesn't think it's a good idea. He's afraid I'll get hurt. He's mad because I want to do it."

There was silence in the car for a few minutes as they continued driving.

Veronica was relieved at first, but then Erica spoke again. "Mark and Blake want to use you as bait, don't they?"

She spun in her seat to face Erica. "How in the world did you guess that?"

Erica almost laughed, but held it in. "It wasn't that hard. You said it was a plan to get the killer that Ben doesn't like and required prep work. What else would it be?"

Veronica silently cursed. *I wish she wasn't that smart. Let the lecture begin.*

"Can I get in on it?"

Veronica gaped at her in surprise. "You're not gonna try to talk me out of it?"

This time Erica did laugh. "Yeah, that would go over well. Objectively speaking, it's a good idea. I don't like that it's you, but I get it. I'll feel better if I can be there." She shut her mouth with a snap and faced forward again.

"I guess, talk to Blake. I'm sure he would let you in. Why wouldn't he? Although, he might not want too many people that are emotionally involved to be part of it. Ben's already gonna be there."

Erica gave her a pitying look at the ridiculousness of her statement. "There isn't a cop in the city that can claim to be objective in this case. Blake is gonna have to learn to live with that."

Veronica was staring out her window again. "Right, we'll talk to Blake when we get back."

When they made it to the high school, Erica let out a sigh. "The cars in the student lot are more expensive than the cars in the faculty lot. I already don't like it here."

Veronica nodded as they walked towards the office. "I told you...snobby high schoolers."

The woman in the front office told them to go to the auditorium with everybody else and wait for the event to start. Neither one of them was sure what to make of that. They had never done a career day in an auditorium. Most schools had tables set up for everyone in their cafeterias. This would be interesting.

When they made it to the auditorium and saw the podium set up in the middle of the stage they both halted and stared incredulously.

"I'm going to kill Blake," Erica seethed under her breath.

Thinking quickly, Veronica turned to Erica and began speaking. "As the most senior officer here, I believe it is your duty to do all the talking on this one."

Erica turned the tables on her just as quickly. "Oh no you don't! I think, as the senior officer here I'm going to pull rank and make you do all the talking."

Veronica was getting desperate. She hated public speaking. "But you did that yesterday with the dumpster diving!"

When Erica's triumphant expression did not change, Veronica kept talking. "Please don't make me pull the 'I have a psycho killer after me' card."

Once again, Erica said nothing.

Veronica brightened up as she thought of her trump card. "Fine. How about this? You kept me from guaranteed sex last night. You owe me!"

Erica's face faltered. She knew that all of Veronica's points were accurate, but she didn't want to be the one to speak. Eventually she gave up. "FINE! But we are SO even after this."

Erica and Veronica waited for their turn backstage, getting more and more uncomfortable by the minute. When it was finally their turn at the microphone, they both tried to pretend to be confident as they walked out on stage.

Erica tried to think of something to say, but was honestly coming up blank. "Okay, you want to know the truth about what it's like to be a police officer? Our boss didn't tell us we would be doing this today until our shift started this morning, and that kind of stuff happens all that time. It's one of the cool parts of our job. We never know what our day is going to be like. On any given day we could be serving warrants, directing traffic, working with detectives, or riding in our cruisers waiting for calls to come in. If you are looking for a normal 9 to 5 job, this is not something you want to pursue. But, if you want something a little less predictable, and want to spend your career helping people, this is definitely something you should look into."

When Erica was done talking, she asked if any of them had any questions they wanted to ask. She gave Veronica a significant look telling her that she would at least be helping with the questions.

The first question came from a boy that looked to be about 16 years old and thought he was really cool. "So, do your uniforms rip off?"

Erica and Veronica both glared at him as he was pulled away by a teacher.

"Are there any serious questions?"

Another boy, looking to be about 18 stepped forwards. "What's the worst injury you've ever had?"

Erica paled as she glanced over at Veronica. She seemed to be fine, but Erica couldn't tell for sure.

Before Erica could answer, Veronica stepped forwards and started to speak. "I was outside of a building that exploded and I had a piece of glass slice through my leg. I lost a lot of blood and I spent that last year in physical therapy trying to be able to walk without a limp."

Most of the students' expressions were blank, but a few looked almost impressed.

The boy sat down and a 16 year old

girl with a serious face stepped forward next. "What's that craziest case you have ever worked on?"

Once again, Erica felt her heart stop as she turned to Veronica to see if she was okay.

Veronica completely stunned her by keeping her cool and answering the question. "I don't know if any of you remember the serial killer a year ago who was abducting and burying women. Well, my partner and I worked with the detectives on that case."

The girl thought for a moment and then her face lit up. "Oh, yeah! I remember that one. I read in the newspaper that you guys never caught him. He disappeared after blowing up-....Oh." She awkwardly went back to her seat.

Veronica squared her jaw. "Yeah, that's what happened. Anyways...any other questions?"

An uncomfortable silence settled on the room.

"No? Okay then. Thanks for having us here today. Officer Mathers here will be back on stage at the end of this to hand out her card and answer any other questions you can come up with." With that, she turned and quickly left the stage.

Erica caught up with her a minute later. "Are you okay?"

Veronica hated that question. "I'm fine. I just don't want to go out there again. When they call everyone out for students to talk to individually, I'm going to stay back here."

Erica nodded enthusiastically. "Yeah, that's fine. Whatever you need."

They had to sit around and wait while all of the other people that had been roped into speaking that day had had their chance.

It took far longer than it should have.

Finally, they called everyone back out so they could mingle with any students that were interested in talking to them. Veronica found a quiet place backstage to sit and wait for Erica to finish up.

After another hour of being bombarded by students who wanted this to last as long as possible so they did not have to do anything for the rest of the day, Erica was finally able to pull herself away. She found Veronica in one of the dressing rooms and they left the school without another word.

When they were about half way back to the station, Veronica finally spoke. "Well... That was fun."

Erica could not help herself. She started laughing and it did not take long for Veronica to join in. They were still laughing when they pulled into the parking lot at the station.

The pair sobered up upon entering the building because they remembered what the rest of the day had in store for them.

Blake was on the phone in his office, so

they went to their desks and started working on paperwork until he was ready to talk.

About ten minutes into this, Veronica glanced into Ben's office to see how he was doing and felt her heart stop for a moment.

There, sitting at his desk, was his mother.

Oh, dear God! What is she doing here?!

Veronica desperately tried to control her breathing and continue to work, but she was failing miserably.

She could not look away from his office. It was one of those rare moments where she wished she was hallucinating. She was never more relieved than when she saw Blake beckoning her to his office. She practically sprinted across the room so that she could avoid Mrs. Becker seeing her.

Neither Erica nor Blake could explain why she was suddenly so excited to be in the bosses office. That was until, Blake looked towards Ben in the hope that he had seen her and would have some explanation. When he saw Ben's mother calmly flipping through a binder, he let out a deep chuckle before following Erica through his door.

Erica was only in Blake's office for long enough to request a position on the team. She was approved to be in the surveillance van.

After that, Veronica was stuck in Blake's office convincing him that she was going to be okay. Blake had to be sure that she was emotionally in a place where she could handle using her-self as bait. This was going to be a difficult and stressful day for everyone involved, and Blake needed to know that nobody was going to crack under the pressure.

Once they had gotten past that, they were able to work on going over the plan Mark had been putting together.

It was not terribly intricate. Mark in-formed them that he had an old college buddy who had become an on air reporter for ABC 15. He had managed to convince his friend to do a short interview with Veronica that would be aired during the news the next morning. The hope was that Veronica would be able to say something that would set the killer off and put him on the offensive. Then she would be fitted with a microphone, an earwig, and a GPS locator. She would stage a fight with Blake in the parking lot and turn over her badge. Then she would go to the cemetery and wait at Nick's grave. There would be a few plain-clothes cops scattered about and Ben, Mark, and Erica would be waiting in the van. Hopefully, the killer would make a move sometime that day so that they would not have to continue this charade.

Blake had remained silent while Mark talked, but it became increasingly more obvi-ous that he was not impressed with this plan. In the end, he made his thoughts clear. "So, our plan involves a playground taunt and then sitting around waiting for our guy to get bored?"

Rather than make excuses Mark simply asked,"Has anyone come forward with a better idea?"

Blake deflated as he admitted that no one had. "Where's your guy?"

Mark looked down at his phone. "He should be here in about half an hour."

Blake nodded his head and turned to Veronica. "You should stay in uniform for the interview. It will have more of an impact that way."

Veronica nodded her agreement and asked if she could take the next half hour to get ready.

Blake released both her and Mark so that he could return to his paperwork.

Veronica spent the next half hour freshening up in the locker room and chatting with anyone else who happened to be in the station. She even pulled her phone out and texted Natasha for a while as she tried to keep her mind off of the interview she was about to do.

Eventually, she saw Mark head out into the parking lot and return with Greg Harmon and his camera crew in tow. She took a calming breath and followed them to the briefing room. The next thing she knew the lights had been set up, a small microphone had been clipped to her vest, and a cameraman was telling them that the camera was rolling.

"I sit here today with Veronica Taylor following up on a story a year in the making."

While Greg was introducing her and the story, Veronica found herself studying the man in front of her rather than listening to what he was saying. He had wavy black hair that was a bit too quaffed for her taste and wore way too much makeup. His teeth were too straight and white to have gotten that way naturally and his skin wreaked of spray tan. All in all, Veronica came to the conclusion that this man spent more time on his appearance than even Natasha did.

In comparison, she sat before him in her uniform, with her hair up in a ponytail, and wearing very little makeup.

She zoned back into the conversation when she realized that he had finally asked her something.

This is already going so well.

He repeated his question. "I was saying, we all followed this story last year as many local women were abducted. Should we be worried that this serial killer is going to start taking women again?"

She laughed.

"Absolutely not. He may have started leaving me notes again, but so far he hasn't even threatened to start actively killing."

Greg smiled what Veronica was sure he believed was a warm and inviting smile, but all she could think of was a Ken doll.

"Okay, if this man is as harmless as you say

he is, why such a push to find him all of a sudden? After all, this case has been inactive for months now."

"Well Greg, although it seems he's lost his drive to kill, we would all very much like to see him behind bars for his previous crimes. For the first time since his last kill, he's giving us something to work with. Now that we have new evidence, I'm confident we'll find him."

Veronica started sweating as she prayed no one could tell how much she was bluffing.

If Greg noticed, he gave no sign of it. "You said he seems to have lost his drive to kill. For a man who was so...prolific in the past, what do you think happened to change things for him?"

Veronica let out another laugh that she hoped nobody noticed was fake.

"Truthfully speaking, I think he's scared. We almost found him last time. Basically, what the killer is doing right now is the equivalent to a child throwing a tantrum because he didn't get his way. The only reason that he is so fixated on me is because I helped to find his dumping ground last year."

Greg nodded. "What exactly is he doing these days."

Veronica plastered on another fake smile as she saw Mark urging her on in the background. "Oh, he takes pictures of me and leaves me little notes and presents. Your basic stalker stuff."

Greg nodded and spoke again. "You sound

pretty laid back about all of this. Are you not afraid at all?"

Veronica knew this was the best thing Greg could have asked. Without any hesitation she responded, "Not even a little bit."

At this comment, Mark was sure that they had enough to thoroughly piss off their subject. He moved around behind Veronica and signalled Greg to wrap it up. Greg took the hint and thanked Veronica for taking the time to talk to him. He filmed a quick outro and they all said their goodbyes.

They went back to Blake's office together to let him know that the interview was over.

Mark was giddy about how well it had gone. "You should have seen her talking to Greg. She never hesitated. She was smiling and laughing. Oh, and some of the things she said...I will be genuinely shocked if our guy doesn't show himself tomorrow."

Neither Blake nor Veronica were nearly as exuberant as Mark was, but they were both glad it went well. They quickly went over what the plan was for the next day and worked out what Blake and Veronica would say to each other in the parking lot. Once that was done, Blake dismissed them again and with a haggard expression went back to filling out paperwork.

Feeling drained by the difficult day she had had, Veronica could think of nothing better than to strip out of her uniform and go home. She went to the locker room and quickly changed into her normal clothes. Then she went over to the detective's office to beg Ben to leave on time so that she could get out of there.

Erica had already stopped by to let him know what happened, so he made sure he was ready to go once he saw the interview was over. They made a quick and silent trip back to Ben's house.

Neither one of them was up to doing anything or talking much that night so they heated up leftovers and hung out watching TV in the living room with their pets.

Knowing the next day was going to be long and stressful for both of them, they agreed to have an early night. At around 9 PM, they dragged themselves up the stairs to Ben's room. Curled up together in bed, they both drifted off as they tried not to think about the various ways that tomorrow could end.

They think they're so clever. Well...it won't be long before they realize that I've been running this the whole time. I'll let them think they've had their victory and then it will begin.

DAY 15

The next morning, Ben and Veronica broke their normal routine to watch the interview as it aired. Veronica studied Ben's face to gauge how likely they were to get in a fight before leaving for work. She did not take it as a good sign that his face was totally unreadable.

As the recording of her on the screen laughed and made light of the whole situation, Veronica cringed and waited for Ben to explode.

Finally, he spoke. "Well...looks like you did well."

Veronica was dumbfounded at his light-hearted response.

Ben turned to her wearing a serious expression. "I'm trying really hard not to be an overprotective jackass today. We've also talked about this enough that I know that's not how you actually feel."

With the least stressful part of their day

over, Ben and Veronica prepared themselves for what was to come.

Veronica took extra time saying goodbye to Ace and Charlotte as they were going out the door. Ace seemed confused by the extra hugs and kisses while Charlotte took on the air of a cat who was mildly affronted by the extra attention it was not looking for.

Ben and Veronica drove to the station in an awkward silence.

When they finally parked, Veronica took a deep breath and turned to Ben. "I know that you're not happy about what's happening today. I want to thank you for supporting me."

Ben leaned towards her and brushed some hair behind her ear. "I know I've been extremely vocal about not liking this plan, but none of that matters now. All that matters is making sure that we keep you safe."

Veronica glanced around the parking lot and then leant forward to catch him in a light kiss. When they broke apart, her lips were still close enough that they brushed his as she spoke. "Let's go finish this."

Ben grinned and resisted the urge to continue the kiss. "Absolutely."

Veronica sent a text to Blake to let him know they were headed in.

As agreed upon the day before, Blake exited the building as soon as he received her text and began the argument. "Veronica. I'm glad

I caught you. Com see me in my office before you change into uniform."

Veronica pretended to be confused, "What's this about, Howard?"

Blake hesitated and put on a guarded expression. "It would be best if we spoke in my office."

Veronica passed her uniform and bag to Ben who was awkwardly standing to the side.

"Do you mind taking these in for me?"

Ben glanced between her and Blake who was looking more uncomfortable by the second and nodded.

Once he was inside, Veronica turned back to Blake. "If you don't mind, I'd prefer to do this out here. Your office has glass walls and I have a feeling I'm not gonna want anyone watching this."

Blake was silent for a moment as he pretended to consider the best way to break the news to her. "I got a call from my superiors this morning. They think I was a bit hasty letting you return to work. They've decided, with everything that has happened, you are to be placed on leave again. You will remain on leave pending a full psychiatric evaluation."

Veronica pretended to argue with him. "How can they do this? I've jumped through every hoop necessary. I've been doing my job well. Did they see the interview? I'm fine!"

Blake's cautions demeanor fell and his

frustration began to show. "Frankly speaking, that interview only hurt your case. You volunteered for an interview that would be broadcast on the news without speaking to our PR liaison. And to top it off, you acted like this whole thing's a game. People have died and you were laughing!"

Veronica began shouting back at him. "I know people have died! He blew up my home with Nick still inside! I lost my child!"

Blake backed off, knowing they were reaching dangerous ground and not wanting to actually hurt her. "And in light of all of that, my superiors do not believe that you are currently fit for duty."

Veronica fished her badge out of her pocket. "You think I'm not fit for duty? Fine! I'm through trying to prove myself to you people!" She threw her badge at Blake and returned to her vehicle. Then sped out of the lot and away from the station.

Veronica drove on autopilot to the cemetery. At every red light, she prepared for the rest of her day. She pulled a case out of her glove compartment and removed the equipment. First, she slipped the small GPS tracking device under a strap in the leather cuff that was always on her wrist. Once it was secure and not visible, she moved on. At a light that was notorious for being particularly long, she unravelled the cord to the microphone and reached under her shirt to put it in place. Fortunately, she had remembered to wear a loosely fitting top that draped low over her backside to hide the bulk of the cord and battery pack. Once that was taken care of, all she had to do was turn on her ear wig and place it during her next stop.

Almost the moment that the wig was in her ear, she heard Blake on the line. "Well done Veronica. The PCs are already in place. Ben took the back way out while we were talking. He made it to the surveillance van a moment ago and joined Mark and Erica. They've all got your back and your badge is waiting for you when this is over."

Veronica smiled, "Thanks boss."

It did not take her much longer to reach the cemetery and find a parking space. She knew not to look for the van or acknowledge the other people milling about. Instead, she went straight to Nick's grave and lowered herself to the ground in front of it.

Let the waiting game begin.

Throughout the day, she pretended to have a heartfelt conversation with the headstone in front of her. Had anyone been close enough to hear her, they would have been utterly confused as she was actually chatting with the people listening to the feed from her microphone. She had Ben, Mark, and Erica in the surveillance van and Blake at the station. Even Jack,

Tyler, and Ryan commented every once and awhile as they drifted in and out of the station. It became a game to see if any of them could make her laugh. Veronica was proud of herself for never letting her amusement with their antics show outwardly. The various plainclothes cops in the cemetery were listening to the conversation as well, but mostly remained silent.

Several hours later, Veronica was beginning to think that they were wasting their time. She was about to voice this opinion when she heard Mark come over the line.

"We've got an unknown male making his way towards you."

Veronica did not let this get her excited as they'd had a few other people pass through the area with no results already. Two minutes later, she could hear the crunch of his shoes on the grass as the man came closer to her. After a moment, she saw a thin asian man with several tattoos come around the side of Nick's grave.

When he stopped and looked right at her, Veronica held her breath. The unknown man glared down at her as she discreetly shifted her weight preparing to defend herself.

Already, she could hear Mark urging the PC officers to start moving in closer. She could imagine Ben's stiff posture and Erica's shifty gaze move towards the door of the van as they contemplated diving out of it.

Finally, the stranger in front of her spoke.

"You think you're so smart."

As he reached into his pocket, Veronica lunged and tackled him to the ground. She could see the knife that he had retrieved from his pocket and worked to get it away from him.

In the scuffle that ensued, her earwig fell out, but she could still hear Ben's tiny voice yelling for everyone to move in. Before she knew it, She was surrounded by officers with their guns drawn.

The man looked around and froze; confusion clear on his face.

Confusion was quickly replaced by terror as he counted the amount of guns currently trained on his skull. He was wrenched away from Veronica and placed into handcuffs. The man was raving that there must have been some kind of a mistake and it was all a joke.

Veronica stopped listening as she watched him being dragged to a cruiser that had pulled into the lot during the fight. Because she was entirely uninterested in how he would attempt to talk his way out of this. She wanted nothing more than to have Ben hold her as she came down from her adrenalin rush, but knew that was not possible.

Neither he, Mark, or Erica would be able to leave the surveillance van until it had been driven to a secure location. That way the department would be able to continue using it during their undercover operations.

Veronica searched for her earpiece hoping to at least be able to hear his voice. After a few minutes of looking through the slightly over-grown grass, she found the remnants of it which had obviously been trampled during the com-motion. Rather than borrow a radio from one of the many officers around her, she asked the near-est one to radio in that she was heading back to the station and she ran to her car. She was defin-itely not following the speed limit as she drove.

When Veronica entered the building, she found that everyone was celebrating.

Jack was grinning and dancing around with Cheyenne. Blake was happily laughing from the doorway of his office. Across the room, she could see the glass wall of the detective's office. They were all clapping and cheering, but she could not see Ben or Mark among them.

She was beginning to think that she must have beaten them there, when she saw Tyler swinging Erica around in a bear hug. When Tyler let go and Erica turned to face her, Veronica lifted her eyebrows in an attempt to recreate Erica's mocking expression. Erica simply gave it back to her and then shifted her gaze in the dir-ection of the interrogation rooms.

Veronica knew what Erica was referring to. Before anyone could pull her into their celebration, she darted around the edges of the room. Rather than the actual interrogation room, she slipped into the first observation room, remembering that she had taken Ben there recently.

The moment that the door was closed, Veronica found herself pushed up against it. She could feel Ben dragging his hands across her body.

It took her a moment to realize that this was not passion; he was checking her for injuries. She quickly grabbed his hands and held them between their bodies.

"Hey. I'm fine. He didn't even get a swing in."

Ben leaned into her and caught her lips in a searing kiss. She returned the kiss and soon found his hands running down her sides and sweeping low to cup her butt. There was no mistaking his intentions this time. Ben pulled away momentarily and looked like he was going to say something, but Veronica tangled her hands in the hair and the nape of his neck and tugged him back down to her.

For several minutes, the only sound in the room was then breathing and the rasping of their clothes rubbing together. Ben was supporting all of Veronica's weight as they leaned against the wall so she brought her legs up and wrapped them around his waist. As shirts were yanked up and buttons were loosened, they realized how close they were to having sex in the office and simultaneously broke the kiss.

Veronica removed her hands from Benn's zipper and dropped her legs. Ben lowered her to the ground and stepped back. They both took a moment to straighten their clothes and hair.

Ben was the first to speak, "Well...it appears we should not celebrate alone while we're here."

Veronica nodded as she regained control of her breathing. "Maybe we should join the festivities outside."

They gave each other a quick once over to make sure they looked normal and then exited the room.

The moment Cheyenne saw her, Veronica found herself in a rib crushing hug. She let it last as long as she could bare and then extricated herself.

Mark appeared at her side and they fist bumped.

Blake allowed the rejoicing in his squad room to continue for nearly an hour before he reminded everyone that the day was not yet over and they all had jobs to do.

Jack announced that they would be celebrating at the bar after shift for anyone who wanted to join.

It was decided that Ben could not be involved in the suspect's interrogation, so he went back to his desk to dig into the man's past. So far, he had not even given his name, so Ben had a long night of flipping through mug shots ahead on him until the suspect talked.

Veronica retrieved her badge from Blake and they agreed that there was not enough time in her shift left to make it worth changing into uniform and going out.

As boring as she found it, she volunteered to finally catch up on all of her paperwork. For the next three hours, Veronica pretended to be focusing on her job as she tried not to stare at the interrogation room door.

She was desperate to know if Mark had gotten him to talk yet. At the very least, she wanted to know his name. So far, it did not look like Mark was having any luck. Every time she looked into the detective's office, she saw Ben wearing a glazed over expression as he leafed through a binder.

Before her shift ended, Veronica heard Ben shout. She looked up to see him practically skipping to the interrogation room and knocking on the door.

Mark opened it and took a piece of paper that Ben handed him. Mark scanned it and smiled as he closed the door again.

With that, all pretence of being on task evaporated.

Knowing that her shift was nearly over anyways, Veronica stopped by her locker to pick up her things and then joined Ben in the detective's office.

"So, care to explain the excitement?"

Ben spun in his chair to face her and let loose a smile that made the whole room glow. "I finally found him! His name is Eric Hannaman. He finished up a year long stint for criminal negligence with a weapon last month."

Ben's enthusiasm was contagious.

Veronica grabbed Eric's file and started bouncing as she skimmed through it. "We finally have a name!"

Her bouncing came to an immediate halt as she kept reading. "He was arrested for firing his gun into the air? That's just...stupid. It even says here that a cop witnessed it. Are you telling me that the guy we've been chasing for over a year now was dumb enough to fire off his weapon in front of a cop?"

Ben took the file back from her and sat down. "Yeah. I know. It's a bit silly, but everyone screws up sometime. This guy went away right after the killer went inactive and got out not long before he left the note on your card. Then he showed up at the cemetery and attacked you after we had you taunt the killer. Why else would he have done that?"

Veronica knew that he was right, but she could not shake the feeling that this guy was not smart enough to pull off the crimes their killer had committed.

Sensing her misgivings, Ben wrapped his arm around her shoulder. "Blake is working on getting a warrant to search his place. He hasn't been out of jail for long so he's currently staying at a halfway house. The day is pretty much over, so we won't be able to get in until tomorrow. We'll know more after that. In the meantime, let's head out."

Within half an hour, they were at the bar ordering their first drinks of the night.

One by one, each of their friends arrived celebrate with them. Even Blake stopped by for a short time before heading home to catch up on some much needed sleep. The drinks were flowing right up until last call.

While Veronica was drinking and making merry with everyone, she found herself watching her friends as they let off steam. They had not all been together without the cloud of this investigation hanging over them for a long time.

She saw Mark and Jack jaw boning off to the side with an awkward Sam trying to join the conversation. She may only be a rookie, but she was determined to push her way into this group of veterans.

Natasha had been called to join them and she was currently huddled with Cheyenne looking at something on her phone. No doubt they were Facebook stalking her date and judging their values.

The most interesting thing to catch her eye was a clearly still sober Erica and Tyler furtively slipping out of the bar together while everyone else was distracted.

After seeing this, Veronica finished her drink and turned to find Ben watching her from the bar stool that he had deposited himself on.

Happy that they would not be the first to leave, they made the rounds to say goodbye to everyone and left the bar.

When they arrived home again, they hurried to greet Charlotte and Ace to soothe their neglect. Once the animals were happily curled up and sleeping again, they wasted no time in moving upstairs and into Ben's room.

They both knew, based on what time it was and what time they would be expected back at the station, they should go to sleep. Neither one of them functioned well without it, but they had both been dwelling on their moment in the observation room ever since it happened. Sex in the station with all of their friends on the other side of the door would have been an awful idea, but the lack of it had left them frustrated and unsatisfied. The fact that they had managed to wait so long before leaving the bar was a testament to their self control.

That control was no longer needed.

They were alone, locked safely in a house, away from their work and their friends. They fell happily into bed together, content in the knowledge that this whole ordeal would be over soon.

Once it was, they would be able to further explore what was happening between them and what it could mean for their future.

DAY 16

T hey were both incredibly groggy when they woke the next morning.

Between the alcohol and the late night, neither one of them felt up to doing much of anything that day. Knowing that was not an option, they made eggs and drank a lot of coffee.

There was no conversation; in fact they barely acknowledged each other at all.

By the time they were ready to leave for work, they were both still hung over but feeling slightly more human than when they woke up.

In spite of the pain radiating through their skulls, they both felt their excitement rising as they left.

Today was the day that the warrant to search their suspect's house would come through. While he waited in a holding cell, they would be searching through his belongings and they were sure they would find something tying him to their case.

By the time they reached the station, they could barely contain themselves.

Veronica went to the locker room and Ben went straight to Blake's office for an update on the warrant.

When Veronica was half way through changing into her uniform she watched a dishevelled Erica rush into the room.

Veronica gave her a look, but Erica averted her eyes and said nothing. Knowing that she would have plenty of time to get details later on, Veronica decided to let it slide for now.

When she left the locker room, she saw Ben slam out of Blake's office and stomp into his own. Not sure what could have caused such a foul mood, Veronica followed him.

She did not say anything, knowing that would only lead to yelling. She simply stood next to him and waited for him to feel ready to talk.

Eventually, he took a cleansing breath and spoke. "It seems that the powers-that-be have decided no one in our precinct can be trusted to handle this investigation objectively. Now that a suspect has been found, the investigation is being handed over to another department. They came in and transferred Eric Hannaman out of here earlier this morning. They aren't even gonna let us search his apartment."

Veronica felt white hot fury rise within

her, but fought to keep it under control.

She took a few minutes to digest the information then dropped heavily into a chair. "Well, to be honest, there was little to no chance they were ever going to let me have any more involvement in the case. I'm glad I was in on the take down. And if you think about it, this is a good thing. We stand our best shot at getting a conviction if we avoid the appearance of bias."

Ben's shoulders slumped. "I'm aware of that. I just wanted to see this through to the end. At least they're gonna keep us informed."

Ben and Veronica sat for a few moments longer in silent commiseration.

He was the first to speak. "At least we have him in custody now. We don't have to worry about finding anymore of his 'gifts.'"

Veronica straightened in her chair. "That's right. I guess it's safe to go back to my apartment."

They shared a sly look and smiled.

"Well, I do have a lot of stuff at your place and Ace is happy with Charlotte. I suppose it wouldn't hurt for me to stay one more night. That is of course if you are okay with it."

Ben looked away, "I'm sure I could be convinced."

Veronica felt herself leaning towards him, then remembered the glass walls of his office.

She leaned back and cleared her throat. "Well, that's good to know. We should definitely continue this later, but for now I should go find Erica and get to work."

Veronica made sure not to look back as she exited the office. She checked on Erica and found she had finally managed to get fully into uniform. They retrieved their assignment for the day and then headed out to their car. They spent an incredibly boring day writing tickets and listening to their radio.

During her lunch break, Veronica made a call to Ben to see if he had heard anything about the case. When Ben answered, she heard the happiness in his voice.

Before she could ask what had happened, Ben cut her off. "You are never gonna believe this. They searched through Eric Hannaman's room and found my mother's purse. He even still had my old house key! Slam dunk! We have our man!"

A tightness in her chest that she had been carrying around for over a year now suddenly released as she heard those words. Truthfully, she had been harboring doubts about Hannaman, but Mrs. Becker's purse being in his room was too much of a coincidence.

He had to be their killer.

"Have they managed to pull a confession out of him?"

"Technically, I don't officially know anything about the interrogation. They've been a bit closed mouthed about it. But I've got an old friend who's in on the new investigation, and he's been filling me in. I don't think I've ever heard a weaker story. He's trying to convince them that he thought the whole thing at the cemetery was a prank. He claims that he was paid to give you a bit of a scare. He also supposedly has absolutely no idea what the guy who paid him looks like."

Veronica was giddy as she listened.

That was a ridiculous story.

"This is really happening. We've really got him."

"That's right baby, we got him."

Veronica scrunched her face with a look of revulsion."Ew, don't ever call me that again."

She heard him chuckling on the other end, "Yeah, it felt wrong the second I said it. Well, I have to try to catch up on some of the cases I've been neglecting so I will see you when you get back."

After a brief goodbye, they both disconnected.

When Veronica turned back to finish her food, she found Erica smirking at her.

"Oh no! Don't give me that look. Not unless you want to explain where you and Tyler went off to last night!"

Erica turned away and went back to her own food without another word.

"That's what I thought."

Veronica shared Ben's information with Erica.

The good mood that it brought on managed to get them through the rest of their dull day.

Without their serial killer case to work on and no special assignments, they found the final hours of their shift dragging on.

The most exciting part had been finding a drunk man stumbling down the sidewalk and yelling at pedestrians. He had tried to run away when they pulled up next to him, but only succeeded in tripping over his own feet and face planting on the pavement before they could even get out of the car. They had the joy of taking him to the emergency room to get his face stitched up before they could bring him back to the station to book him.

Even with all the paperwork that came with taking someone to the hospital, Veronica was glad they had such an uneventful day. It reminded her of what the vast majority of her days had been like before everything had happened.

When Veronica and Erica got back to the station at the end of their shift, they all decided none of them could handle a second night at the bar. But they would get together for another poker night over the weekend.

Veronica had also informed Erica that they would be spending some time together over the weekend and she would be getting Erica to talk about Tyler.

Erica was not looking forward to that conversation, but after what they had put Veronica through with Ben, she could not argue against it.

Once Veronica was back in her civilian clothes, she made her way over to Ben's desk to see if he was ready to head home for the day.

What she found was a bedraggled man sifting through a pile of paperwork looking miserable.

"Remind me next time I know I'm going to be coming to work to a massive stack of pending cases, not to stay up all night the day before."

Veronica smiled and teased him. "Don't tell me that you regret last night."

Looking up from his paperwork, Ben met her gaze."Regret is not the word I would choose, but it has been a very long day."

Veronica relaxed against the doorframe. "For you and me both. I say we head back to your place, order takeout again, and have a quiet night that ends early."

Ben cleaned up his desk as he spoke. "I won't argue with that."

For the first time in two weeks, neither of them felt any apprehension as they approached her car, or Ben's front door. They were completely positive there would be nothing to find.

Even the animals seemed to sense their re-lief and greeted them with extra vigor.

As they decided on a place to order food from and what to watch, Veronica suddenly real-ized that they were being normal. A serenity she had not felt in a long time washed over her as she remembered that the man who had been terror-izing her was off the streets and could no longer hurt anyone.

They are so damn stupid.

Do they really think I'd be dumb enough to fall for that silly little gag they ran?

I'll let them revel in their "success" for the weekend. Then I'll show them exactly what I'm cap-able of.

'Basic stalker stuff.'

I will make that bitch rue the day she ever be-came a cop.

DAY 17

Veronica woke up knowing that this was going to be a far less stressful Saturday than the last one.

She and Ben still needed to clean up his house, but this time they were not preparing for a dinner with his terrifying mother. Ben had called her the night before and asked for a raincheck on their weekly dinner because his friends were coming over for another poker night. Mrs. Becker had not been happy about that, but agreed to have the dinner on Sunday night instead.

Veronica was sure that Mrs. Becker was going to blame her for the change in plans, but she could not make herself care. She could deal with Mrs. Becker's ire later on.

They spent much of the day using cleaning to avoid talking, but eventually they ran out of things to do.

After several awkward moments of silence, Veronica was the first to speak. "Okay...so...I'm thinking that I should probably start sleeping at my own place. You know, since they've got Hannaman in custody now. We did say yesterday that I would only stay one more night."

Ben had remained silent while she talked, but started speaking when she finished. "You're trying to get out of being here when my mother comes over tomorrow night. Come on! You and I both know that you're not gonna be in any shape to drive after tonight. Stay one more night and then go back home tomorrow."

Veronica watched as Ben gave her his best dimpled smile and crumbled. "Fine! One more night! I mean it this time. I'm going home tomorrow. This whole normal life thing only works if I can go back to my own apartment."

Ben's smile only grew as she spoke. "Okay. That works. And...uh...in the name of normalcy...would you maybe want to go to dinner or something after shift on Monday? You know, like a first date."

Veronica tried to keep a straight face as she tamped down her enthusiasm. "I think that would probably be a good idea. You know, for the sake of normalcy."

They both stopped talking and grinned at each other.

Eventually Ben cleared his throat and they both got up.

They spent the rest of their day picking up supplies at the grocery store and hanging out as they waited for their friends to arrive.

Jack was the first, closely followed by Blake. They were chatting in the living room when Tyler arrived with Cheyenne and Erica in tow. Veronica raised her eyebrows at Erica, but did not say anything in front of the others. Mark made it moments before Natasha. Once everyone was there, They ordered pizza and discussed what movie to watch while they ate.

The women were trying to convince the men that *Love Actually* was not a chick flick, but were ultimately unsuccessful. The men were rooting for *Lethal Weapon*, but Natasha and Cheyenne would not agree. They only landed on watching *Twister* moments before the doorbell rang and the pizza arrived.

With everyone either scrunched into the couches or on chairs from the dining room, they dug into their food and watched the movie. This was a favorite for their group and everyone was quoting lines with the actors.

Even though they had originally planned on this being a poker night, none of them were in the mood for it. They had had an incredibly stressful two weeks and wanted to relax.

After *Twister* ended, they made a deal. If

Natasha and Cheyenne would agree to watch *Lethal Weapon*, the men would agree to watch *Love Actually* afterwards.

Throughout all of this, the alcohol had been flowing. They even made a drinking game out of *Lethal Weapon*. Every time that Murtaugh referred to his age or retirement, they had to take a drink. Normally, it would have been a shot, but they all wanted to survive the night.

By the time the movie ended, everyone was feeling pretty loose. Veronica was pushed up against Ben on the couch. Tyler and Erica had moved to the floor and she was sitting in his lap. Again, Veronica was tempted to say something, but she had enough control left to hold her tongue. She caught Natasha giving them a look, but made sure to cut her off every time that she opened her mouth. Eventually, Natasha caught the hint but she did lean over and whisper something to Cheyenne. Cheyenne nodded back to her eagerly and they continued to gossip in the corner.

When they turned on *Love Actually*, the men were buzzed enough to admit that they were enjoying it. During the scene where Hugh Grant made a fool of himself by dancing around the Prime Minister's mansion, Ryan got up and started dancing as well. Tyler pulled out his phone and recorded it to use as blackmail later on.

At the end of the night, there was only one

person that was not too exhausted or buzzed to drive. Blake had decided to stop drinking early on so he was fine to drive home and he offered to take as many people as he could. Mark, Ryan, and Tyler opted to go with him and come back for their cars the next day.

Natasha, Cheyenne, and Erica decided to hang out at Ben's place until they sobered up so that they could drive home. None of them had drank much during the last movie, so they did not think that it would take too long.

Veronica made a pot of coffee for them and they all feasted themselves on chips to try to soak up some of the alcohol in their stomachs.

Ben watched them all sharing significant glances and nudging each other so he knew there was a conversation coming that he did not want to be a part of. Telling them that he was dead on his feet, Ben retreated upstairs so that they could talk without him being in the way.

The moment they heard Ben's bedroom door close, Natasha and Veronica simultaneously turned on Erica.

"Spill!"

Erica wore an intentionally blank face as she said, "I don't know what you are referring to."

Once again in unison Natasha and Veronica responded,"Yes, you do!"

Cheyenne was giggling off to the side. "You

two have spent way too much time together."

Erica muttered her agreement and tried not to look any of them in the eye.

The alcohol was making it difficult to control their impatience so Cheyenne hit her with a pillow. "You know that this is gonna go a lot easier for you if you tell them."

Erica glared at her and Cheyenne dove to the floor to avoid the pillow that went flying towards her face. Erica turned back to Natasha and Veronica only to find that they were also armed with pillows.

Knowing that she was not going to get out of having the conversation, Erica relented. "Fine! I'll tell you! But I swear to God, the first time someone starts humming 'Summer Lovin' I'm leaving. I don't care if I have to walk all the way back to my apartment."

Veronica, Natasha, and Cheyenne agreed to those terms, and sat cross legged on the floor in front of her with their pillows in their laps.

Erica looked down at them from her place on the couch and started laughing. "You look like a bunch of first graders waiting for story time."

Natasha pulled her pillow up and swiped at her with it. "No more stalling."

Erica glared at her fleetingly then took a deep breath. "Okay, so...Tyler and I were hanging out at the bar with everyone the other night and we were having a good time. Everyone was so relieved and happy and we were too. We were both a little tipsy and Tyler asked if I wanted to get some air. Next thing I know, we're outside and talking and then...I kissed him."

Erica cringed knowing what was coming.

The three women sitting before her squealed with excitement. They heard movement behind them and watched a groggy Ben stumble halfway down the stairs.

"Do you mind keeping it down with the girl talk? I'm trying to pretend I can't hear you."

The women were still giggling as he trudged back up the stairs and closed his door again.

Veronica was the first to gain her composure and speak. "I can't believe that you made the first move! Tyler's been drooling after you forever. I was sure it would be him."

Erica bashed her in the head with her own pillow, and continued. "He has not been drooling after me! Anyways, we kissed outside for a while, then we went and got some coffee. We decided that it might be worth going on a date to see what this is between us. We haven't had a chance yet. We were thinking maybe Monday."

Veronica began laughing and everyone looked at her like she was crazy.

Erica looked offended, "It is not that funny."

Veronica managed to stop laughing so that she could explain herself. "I know. That part isn't funny. It's just, Ben and I decided today that we would have our first date on Monday. Looks like we're both gonna be having interesting nights."

All four of the women were snickering at that when they heard Ben yelling from upstairs.

"You all suck at being quiet!"

They laughed and chatted for a while longer until Natasha, Cheyenne, and Erica were okay to go home. Then, Veronica dragged herself up the stairs and curled up with Ben.

DAY 18

The next morning Ben and Veronica had to clean his house yet again.

Much like the day before, they found themselves sitting uncomfortably on the couch after everything was done.

Once again, Veronica was the first one to speak. "Well, now that's taken care of, I guess I should get my stuff together. Time to move back to my apartment."

Ben nodded and took her hand. "Yeah. We shouldn't keep putting it off. Besides, if you go back home, we can start dating like normal people."

She squeezed his hand, then stood up. "I'm gonna go get my stuff. Do you mind grabbing Ace's leash for me?"

Ben nodded and she made her way up the stairs. By the time she went back down, Ben was standing by the door with Ace on his leash.

"I'll walk you out to your car."

Veronica stopped by Charlotte, who was reclined across the back of the couch, to say goodbye to her. Afterwards, she hiked the strap to her duffle bag higher on her shoulder and walked out the front door.

Veronica was actually looking forward to being on her own for a while. It was going to feel great to be living in her apartment again. As much as she enjoyed her time with Ben, she missed her bed.

She could tell that even Ace was excited to be going home because he started whining and dancing in the back seat as she pulled into her parking lot. He was dragging her as she moved across the lot and up the stairs to her floor. It was difficult to hold him still while she got her front door unlocked. When she finally got the door open, Veronica remembered that her apartment had been picked over by her colleagues twice in as many weeks.

Her whole apartment was a mess.

She knew that it was going to take the better part of the day to put it back to rights.

Before she did anything else, she wanted to check out her bedroom and make sure that there was no trace of Hannaman left behind. She stopped in the kitchen to pick up some cleaning supplies then went to work. It took a couple hours, but eventually she was able to scrub every surface and tidy everything in her room.

Then she pulled the sheets and comforter off of her bed and threw them into the washer.

For the next four hours, Veronica cleaned her entire apartment and washed every scrap of fabric that would fit in her washing machine.

When she was done with that, Veronica grabbed a trash bag and moved into her closet. She pulled out all of the soulless and drab clothing that she had been wearing and threw it in the bag to be donated later.

For the last year, she had been trying to make sure that she went unnoticed by everyone. She had wanted to be overlooked, invisible. She was done with that. Now that the killer she had been afraid of was caught, she had no reason to hide. Ever since she moved and got her new job at the art museum, she had claimed she was protecting herself. The truth was she had been hiding. Thinking that she could ever make the museum job permanent was silly. She was born to be a police officer. It was what she was made for.

Once she was done cleansing everything in her apartment and throwing out half of her wardrobe, Veronica was completely out of energy.

She heated up a bowl of soup, changed into her pajamas and curled up on the couch. Her tv show of the night was *Rookie Blue* because it was one of her favorites and it always made her laugh. So many of the characters reminded her of her colleagues at the station, and she always chuckled in the first episode when the main character wore her radio on the wrong side.

When she could no longer keep her eyes open, she shut it off and bundled up under her freshly washed covers.

DAY 19

L *et the games begin...*

◆ ◆ ◆

Veronica woke up early on Monday morning feeling more refreshed than she had in a long time.

She showered and moved to her closet. Evaluating what was left of her wardrobe, she dressed to kill in black skinny jeans with boots and a bright purple top. She also grabbed a black dress and strappy silver heels to wear in case Ben decided to take her somewhere fancy.

Putting enough food in Ace's bowl to last until the next day, Veronica was very happy she could trust her dog not to eat it all at once.

In her excitement, Veronica had gotten ready in record time and could actually make a real breakfast before going to work. She quickly scrambled some eggs and ate them with toast and coffee. After checking she had everything that could possibly be useful to get ready for her date, she made her way out the door.

When Veronica made it to the station, she practically skipped through the door.

She checked out Ben's office on the way to the locker room, hoping to see his reaction to her outfit.

Like he could feel her gaze on him, Ben glanced up and locked eyes with her. They shared a lingering look until Jack snuck up behind her and grabbed her in a weak choke hold.

"What if I were a suspect? What would you do?"

Veronica laughed and jammed her elbow into his ribs. "Really! You're testing me again?"

Jack pulled back, "Well, you've been gone for awhile. Just want to make sure that you're back up to speed."

Veronica shoved Jack into a wall. "I am fine! Don't start treating me like a rookie again." Without giving him a chance to respond, she left him behind.

When she got into the locker room, she found Erica stuffing a dress bag into her locker.

"Is that your outfit for the big date?"

Erica glared for drawing attention to her as all the other women in the locker room swarmed.

"It's not a big date, it's just a first date."

Veronica gave an apologetic smile and moved to her locker before Erica could ask her about her own date for tonight.

Erica made a fast retreat from the room to avoid more probing questions from their colleagues.

Veronica changed quickly into her uniform and met Erica in the briefing room. They were all given their assignments for the day and moved out to their squad cars.

Right out of the gate, Erica and Veronica were called to a home invasion. By the time they arrived on the scene, the front door was hanging wide open. They exited their vehicle as fast as they could and drew their weapons as they entered the house. They quickly cleared the first floor of the house and them moved up the stairs in tandem. When they started to clear the second floor they came across a locked door. After a few seconds, they heard a woman crying on the other side. They identified themselves as police officers and the door flew open. A young woman collapsed into Erica's arms and sobbed out her thanks.

Uncomfortable with the physical contact, Erica patted her back and tried to calm her down so that they could figure out what had happened.

While Erica was taking care of the woman, Veronica took the opportunity to search the rest of the house.

The two of them helped the woman down the stairs and into the kitchen.

Veronica got her a glass of water and the three of them sat at her kitchen table. They took notes as she described the man that knocked on her door and forced his way in when she opened it. She had smashed a nearby lamp into his head and fled upstairs to lock herself into the bathroom.

They waited at the house for the crime techs to arrive and then brought the woman to the station so the detectives could get her full statement and take a look at mug shots of suspects for similar crimes in the area.

Veronica and Ben shared another moment of giddy grinning through the glass walls of his office as she walked by.

She was tempted to leave their victim with Erica to visit him, but she grabbed Veronica by the arm and dragged her along with them.

Erica muttered at her quietly so that only she could hear. "Keep it in your pants until after shift."

Glaring at her, Veronica casually stuck her leg out and tripped Erica.

Under her breath Veronica responded, "Bitch."

Erica smirked at her. "Slacker."

Veronica cut her gaze over to Erica. "Ice Queen."

Erica punched her in the arm, but regained her composure quickly when their victim turned back to look at them.

They shared a sheepish glance and then meekly directed her to the interview room.

The detective assigned to the case was already waiting for them when they arrived.

Erica and Veronica excused themselves so that the detective could conduct his interview and they could write up the paperwork required for the call.

After grabbing some lunch, they headed back out on the road.

They had been out for another hour when they received a call from dispatch that got their hearts racing.

A 9-1-1 call had come in reporting smoke coming from the Phoenix Memorial Park and Mortuary.

Veronica knew that it was silly as they had their killer in custody, but the fact that there was smoke coming from Nick's cemetery made her nervous. She could tell Erica was feeling the same way because her voice shook a little bit as she informed dispatch that they were on their way.

With the lights and sirens blaring, they sped to the cemetery as fast as they could. They could see the smoke rising into the sky as they pulled up and Veronica could tell that it was coming from the same area as Nick's grave.

Throwing herself out of the car, Veronica sprinted across the park with Erica close on her heels. She could hear Erica shouting into her radio for the fire department to come so that they could put the fire out.

Within minutes, Veronica was standing aghast in front of Nick's grave.

She could not think.

What she was looking at simply did not make sense to her.

There was a pile of paper and photographs burning in front of Nick's grave with a large sign next to it. Once again there was a message written on it in dripping red paint.

"DID YOU THINK IT WOULD BE THAT EASY?"

Veronica's head was spinning and she could not get enough air into her lungs.

Erica pulled up next to her and after a moment of silently staring, they turned to look around trying to spot whoever had left this for them.

Erica was reaching to her radio when there was a loud crack.

A fine spray of blood filled the air and coated the side of Veronica's face.

Veronica turned to see Erica's body on the ground next to her.

There was a small hole in the upper right side of her forehead where the bullet had gone in and a large chunk of her skull missing from where it had come out.

Lifeless eyes stared up at her.

Veronica went numb when she understood the implications of what she was seeing. There was nothing she could do. Nothing left to save. In the space of a second, one of her best friends had been ripped out of the world and she knew it was her fault.

Before she could reach for her own radio or even look up three more cracks disturbed the silence.

Veronica felt three excruciating kicks to her chest and abdomen as the bullets embedded into her vest. The force of them hitting her threw her back onto the ground behind her.

Veronica heard the sound of the fire department's sirens and approaching footsteps before she passed out.

By the time that the fire department arrived, all that was left was the remnants of the burning documents, the sign, and Erica's body.

The moment the call of a downed officer went out over the radio. Everyone in the precinct was speeding towards the cemetery.

By the time Ben made it to the cemetery, he could hardly breath.

As he got closer to Nick's grave, he could feel his stomach tying itself into knots and his chest tightening. He could see Ryan trying to console Cheyenne as his sobbing partner sank to the ground. Tyler was sitting nearby wearing a vacant expression with his knees pulled up and Jack was next to him placing a comforting arm on his shoulder. Mark was standing a little to the side talking to Blake over the phone. The only downside to Blake's promotion above them was that he had to coordinate from the station rather than be here with them.

Ben could feel himself slowing down as he drew nearer trying to pull himself together before he looked at the body on the ground.

When he finally looked, he stopped walking entirely.

Conflicting emotions were ripping him apart.

Ben was pained and saddened by the knowledge that he would never hear Erica's unintentionally evil laugh or received one of her handmade gifts.

He was also relieved to find that he was not looking at Veronica's body on the ground.

Guilt flooded through him because Erica had been his friend and he found himself glad that she had died in Veronica's place.

He felt the air leave his lungs and his knees

hit the ground as he remembered that Erica and Veronica had been partnered up and Veronica was nowhere to be seen. He frantically searched the crowd around them,but could not find her.

With her partner lying dead on the ground as part of an obvious message, it became clear who had her; and it was not Eric Hannaman. He was still safely ensconced in lockup.

They had been played.

When Mark got off the phone with Blake, he passed on Blake's order that they all return to the station.

Once the medical examiner arrived and started looking at Erica's body, they all made their way out of the cemetery. None of them were all that interested in watching their friend being treated as evidence.

They piled into their vehicles and made a forlorn procession back to the station.

Everyone congregated in the briefing room as they awaited orders from Blake. Some were sitting at tables with vacant stares, and some could still be seen with tears on their cheeks. Others were pacing around the room like lions at the edge of their pens. When Blake finally entered, everyone focused their attention on him.

Blake made it to the podium at the front of

the room and looked out at his officers.

The others needed to see him confident and in control. He had spent the last ten minutes trying to figure out exactly what to say, but no words had come to mind.

The senseless murder of one of his officers and the abduction of another had left him feeling untethered. He was doubting whether or not his leadership would be enough to see them through this new crisis. Blake cleared his throat to give himself a moment to bury his insecurities and pain.

"We lost an officer today. Many of you, myself included, were good friends with Officer Mathers. If any of you are not going to be able to get back out on the road today, I need to know right now. Another one of our own is missing and in grave danger so I cannot afford to be sending distracted officers out looking for her."

At this, he looked at each one of the men and women in the room, pausing longest on Cheyenne and Tyler.

In spite of everything they were feeling, everyone met his gaze with steady determination. None of them wanted to be left out of the loop in the search to come.

"Okay. Word is already out about what happened today. We've got off duty officers from other shifts and all of our volunteers from the reserve division coming in. All of the precincts have been notified and we are approved for as much overtime as required to find Veronica. The detectives are going to be going over everything we have again and all of the patrol officers in the city are going to be on the lookout for anything that could be significant. This whole city is going to be crawling with cops until we bring Veronica home. I want all of you to pull yourselves together and get out there. Do your jobs and do them well, but if you are not actively on a call, I want you working this case. Talk to all of your CIs, look everywhere you can think of, but most importantly; stay on your radios. We need to know where everyone is at all times. If you are on a call and anything feels wrong, call for backup immediately. We lost and officer today. We are not losing a second."

With nods and rousing shouts from all, people began pouring out of the room and back out into the parking lot.

Blake grabbed Sam's arm as she left the room.

"I'm keeping you on desk duty for now."

She opened her mouth to protest, but Blake cut her off.

"You are a rookie. I know you want to help, but I need you to stick to your original assignment and let your training officer focus on the job."

Rather than go to his office, Blake left the building and walked through the lot. He nodded to Jack who was in the process of getting into his squad car and walked around to the back of the building.

He heard the crashing before he saw anything.

By the time he reached the source of the noise, Ben had almost exhausted himself from attaching the dumpster.

"You okay?"

Ben glared at him and refused to speak.

"I received an order from my superiors before everyone got here. I'm meant to put you in protective custody and move you to a safe house until this is all over."

There was more banging as Ben continued to vent his aggression.

"It would not be the first time that our killer tried to hurt Veronica through the men in her life."

Ben finally plopped to the ground with his knees drawn up and his back to the dumpster. "I'm not going into hiding."

Blake looked around to make sure that no one else could see or hear them. "I know that. Which is why I plan on telling them that you left the briefing room first, and by the time I got out, you had already left the precinct. You are going to go home and work off of all those files you've been compiling for the last year. Look at everything again. Find something. Call me when you do."

Ben fished his keys out of his pocket and left without a word.

Blake went back to his office and pulled up Erica's file in his computer. He had to call her family now.

Everyone worked the rest of the day and all through the night, trying to find anything. They were all sustained on energy drinks and meals bought at gas stations.

The evening news reported on what had happened and they were soon flooded by calls from concerned citizens with "tips" for them.

They all worked all night... and no one found anything.

This is better than I ever could have dreamed.

Imagine what they would say if they knew the entire time they had been desperately searching the cemetery for their precious Veronica, she was bound and gagged in the trunk of my car.

The entire time they were having their meeting in the briefing room, she was still in the trunk of my car.

They all know that Hannaman was a scapegoat now, but still they have not even considered the possibility that the killer they are hunting is one of their 'brothers in blue.'

Idiots.

I've got that bitch trussed up in my own damn garage and they are still never gonna find her.

If any of them had two brain cells to rub together, they would have figured it out already.

DAY 20

Veronica returned to consciousness slowly.

She tried to move and found that her wrists were bound to the arms of the chair she was sitting on and her ankles were bound to the legs.

She struggled and felt pain radiating through her entire body.

Having seen fellow officers take bullets in the vest before, she knew there was a bruise spreading across her chest and abdomen. It would not surprise her if she had broken ribs.

She could feel something caked onto the side of her face and she realized it was Erica's blood.

It had dried onto her skin and she knew she had inhaled some of it. She did not think she would ever be able to forget the sickeningly sweet scent of it as it coated her nostrils.

She noted with interest that she was not gagged, but understood all that meant was that her abductor was not worried that anyone would hear her if she called for help.

She let her eyes adjust to the darkness and looked around the room.

She saw that there was a video camera set up on a tripod in front of her, and there was another chair pushed against a metal wall. That was it.

She could tell that she was in a freestanding garage, but there were no other hints as to her location. The sound of the outside world could not penetrate the metal walls around her, so she was left to contemplate what was coming in dark, eerie silence.

Veronica could feel the panic attack creeping up on her.

Between watching Erica die and the situation she was currently in, she could feel herself starting to drown in her pain and fear. She began to hyperventilate and knew that if her limbs had not been secured to the chair, she would have slid uncontrollably to the floor long ago. Her vision had narrowed down to a pinprick and she was sure that she was going to pass out.

Then she heard something that froze the blood in her veins.

The only sound in the room beyond her own wheezing breaths was the unmistakable sound of a key being inserted into a lock.

She was about to meet the man that had been tormenting her this entire time.

Mustering all of the will power she had in her, Veronica managed to slow her breathing.

She did not want to give whoever was about to walk through the door the satisfaction of seeing her panicking.

Although it could only have been seconds, the wait between the lock clicking and the door opening seemed excruciatingly long.

When the door finally did open, Veronica was forced to turn away as the brightness from the light outside seared her retinas. With watering eyes, she looked back, but she could still only see the silhouette of the man approaching her.

She watched and waited for her eyes to adjust as he moved across the space to retrieve the other chair and settled it in front of her.

He sat and stared her right in the face, clearly enjoying her confusion.

Veronica was paralyzed by the torrent of emotion ripping through her.

She could not think.

She could not move.

She could not even breath.

She knew this man; this man was her friend. Had anyone asked her thirty seconds before this moment, she would have told them that she trusted this man with her life. In fact, she had put her life in his hands on more than one occasion throughout her career.

Conflicting facts and emotions swirled in her mind and she could not make them connect.

The face before her could not be the face of a murderer. Certainly not the face of Nick's murderer.

When she looked into their eyes, she could see murderous intent but she could not make herself believe it.

Part of her mind was screaming that there must be some mistake, while the other part was slowly piecing together the facts of the case and wondering how she had missed it.

Of course the killer she was chasing was a police officer. Of course the man tormenting her was connected to her personally. How else would he know so much about them and the investigation?

No words were spoken between the two until the puzzle had fully taken form in her mind.

The part of her that was rebelling against this knowledge was forced to concede that there were no other possibilities.

She had been fooled.

And she was going to die because of it.

That was quite possibly the most beautiful

thing I have ever seen.

For a moment, she had almost looked happy to see me. Like maybe I was there to save her.

The horror on her face when she finally figured it out...gorgeous.

I gave her every hint that she needed and she still didn't see it until I was literally sitting right in front of her.

If I ever needed confirmation that she had not suspected, that was it. I am going to relive this moment every day for the rest of my life.

She's crying now.

How cute.

"Veronica. Look at me. You understand now, don't you? You never had a chance. None of them ever had a chance."

Ben felt like he was going crazy.

He had been going through all the information he had on this case ever since he got home and he had not come up with anything new.

Not one insight or idea.

He had not even stopped to sleep because every time he closed his eyes he saw Erica's body on the ground or imagined what could be happening to Veronica right now. He was living his nightmare, so he did not want to know what his actual dreams would be like.

He had been getting occasional text messages from his friends and colleagues asking if he was okay, but he would send them a terse response to shut them up and then put the phone down.

Nothing was adding up.

Looking closer at Eric Hannaman's file showed that Veronica's first suspicion was correct. He did not have the skills or intelligence to pull off all of these murders.

But it was way too much of a coincidence that his mother's purse with Ben's house key was in Hannaman's apartment. It had become clear that the purse had been planted there, but what was the point?

Why set someone else up to take the fall when you were going to get them cleared by attacking again a couple days later?

Was it to see how the police would react?

Was it a test to see if they would buy it? If so, they had all failed miserably.

Their failure had killed Erica and might kill Veronica.

There had to be something they were overlooking that would explain all of this and help.

He had stopped by Veronica's apartment to pick up Ace. It seemed that he knew how serious the situation was. He had been subdued ever since Ben had brought him home. Currently, he was curled up with Charlotte sleeping on the couch. He perked up for a moment when Ben's phone started buzzing.

He let it go unanswered.

He did not care who was calling.

The phone went silent for a moment, then it started buzzing again. He thought about answering it, but decided against it. Blake would call if they had anything, and he did not care if it was anyone else.

Once again, the phone started buzzing moments after the call went to voicemail.

Annoyed at being bothered, Ben picked up the phone without looking to see who was calling.

"Who are you and what do you want?"

There was a moment of silence while the caller reacted to his tone.

"Speak now, or I'm hanging up!"

At this, the caller jumped in. "Ben! Don't hang up. It's Joe, from the lab."

Ben was intrigued, but not enough to get over his annoyance. "Why are you calling me, Joe? I'm busy."

Ben could see Joe's exuberant nodding in his head.

"Yeah, I know. It's just...they finished up with your computer. You know, we were checking for spyware."

Ben remembered Erica making the suggestion and felt his throat close up.

"You should call Blake with the results.

I'm not officially part of this anymore."

Joe paused. "I can't."

Ben gripped his phone tighter. "Why?"

Joe huffed on his end of the phone. "I can't tell Blake because we didn't find anything. There is no spyware on that computer or anyone's phone who was there that night."

Ben felt like this should mean something to him, but he was so frazzled that he could not find the significance in his mind. "Why does that mean you can't tell Blake?"

Joe huffed again at Ben's lack of understanding. "Think about it, Ben. There was no spyware. The house had already been swept for bugs. We swept it again to see if we had missed anything the first time, and we didn't find anything. There is no way that your guy had eyes and ears into that poker night, unless..."

Ben finally put it together and felt sick. "Unless he was there."

Ben did not hear anything else that Joe said.

He hung up the phone and dropped his head down to the kitchen table in front of him. He let a sob escaped from his lips before he could swallow it down.

Not only had he been hunting a fellow officer this whole time, but that officer was his friend.

He should be relieved.

The suspect pool had dropped from thousands of people to five. Unfortunately, those five people were his closest friends in the world.

He did not even know where to start to investigate them. He also did not know who he could trust to help him. He figured he could bring Cheyenne into to work with him, but she just lost Erica. It would also put Ryan on alert if Ben called her away.

Thoughts were racing around his head at a mile a minute as he considered various possibilities and quickly dismissed them.

Eventually, he came to the conclusion that he needed help from someone on the outside. Someone who did not know his friends and had never been a part of this investigation.

Minutes later, Ben was out the door.

He drove to his least favorite place in the city to talk to one of his least favorite people.

It did not take him long to get a meeting with Internal Affairs Detective Liam Hoster.

It was not often that cops came in asking for their friends to be investigated. Ben felt queasy just standing in the building, but he knew it was his best chance.

Hoster had investigated Ben three years ago when he had been forced to shoot someone on the job. Ben hated him, but knew that Hoster would stop at nothing to get to the bottom of this. He also knew that Hoster still felt bad about being so hard on Ben, so Hoster would be the only IA detective in the city willing to take on the case and keep Ben involved.

It took about an hour for Ben to walk Hoster through everything that he knew. When he described the call with Joe and the implications, he watched as the color left Hoster's face. By the time Ben stopped talking, Hoster's face was almost the same color as his graying hair. The wrinkles around his mouth and eyes deepened to make him look even older that his 53 years.

Hoster took a moment to digest the information that Ben had provided before he spoke. "So, you're asking me to find out which of your friends is a killer?"

Ben gulped and nodded. "I'm asking you to help me complete this investigation. I've been thinking about it, and I think I know what the first step should be. We need to get our hands on the service logs from the past couple weeks and during the investigation last year. That will tell us who was working or riding alone on all of the days that women were taken. As a detective in IA, you have the authority to request that information from Blake without having to explain why you need it."

Hoster nodded along with his speech, clearly agreeing with Ben's assessment. "Okay. I'll get on that. It will take time for those files to be sent to us and even longer to go through them. I know you probably want to keep this quiet, but it would go much faster if you would let me bring some of my colleagues in on this."

Ben hesitated.

Even speaking with Hoster had gone against the grain for him, letting even more IA detectives into this was not something he wanted to do.

Hoster could tell what he was thinking. "Despite popular opinion, not all IA detectives are rats looking to jam up good cops. Some of us can be trusted."

Ben's voice was tight as he responded. "Fine. But only people you are absolutely certain of."

Hoster stood and started moving towards his door. "Okay. You wait here. I'm gonna head over to your precinct and talk to your sergeant. I'll light a fire under him to get those records as fast as possible."

Once Ben was alone in the room, he could feel his exhaustion taking taking its toll. Within five minutes, Ben was fast asleep sitting up in his chair.

Natasha felt like her world was crumbling around her.

Not only was Erica dead, but Veronica was missing and possibly dead as well.

Natasha sat at her kitchen table with a

bottle of wine, lost in thought. She took another swig straight from the bottle and felt more tears slide down her cheeks.

She had been crying uncontrollably ever since she found out what happened at the cemetery.

She knew that everyone was out looking for Veronica, but after everything that had already happened, she was afraid they would not find her in time. For the first time in her life, Natasha wished that she had followed Veronica into the police force rather than getting a degree in art history and working at a museum. She felt completely useless as she sat in her kitchen waiting for her phone to ring.

It sat silently in the center of her kitchen table and she willed it to indicate an incoming call. The longer she waited, the more deeply she drank.

She had just drained it when she heard someone knocking on her front door.

Terrified that someone felt the need to bring her news in person, Natasha felt her heart jump into her throat. Acid filled her stomach as she walked slowly to the door.

Without even glancing through the peephole, Natasha opened her front door to find one of her friends standing outside. She threw herself into his arms and sobbed. When she had finally calmed down enough to speak, she pushed away from his chest and looked at his face.

"What are you doing here? Has something happened? Have they found her?"

Natasha thought she caught a look of amusement in his eyes, but dismissed it when she took a closer look at him and could only find concern and fatigue.

He placed a hand on her shoulder. "No. We haven't been able to find her yet. I was sent here to get you and bring you back to the station. We've been thinking about the killer's previous patterns and some of us have been concerned with your safety. We wouldn't want anything to happen to you on top of everything else."

Natasha paled as he spoke.

She had never considered the possibility that she was also in danger.

Natasha knew that accompanying him to the station was the best option, so she did not argue. Besides, if no one was worrying about protecting her, more people could be out looking for Veronica.

She turned from him to collect her purse.

She would never be able to say what triggered her suspicions, but at that moment she felt alarm bells going off in her head.

She was not given a chance to respond to this alarm as an arm wrapped around her with the hand settling on her face. A strong smell was emanating from the cloth in that hand and she fought for freedom.

Disbelief and betrayal rose up in her as she desperately tried to break his hold. But it was no use. She could already feel herself starting to become dizzy and she remembered that the killer Veronica had been hunting used to abduct women by knocking them out with chloroform.

She could hear him starting to hum behind her and tried to bring her elbow back into his ribs. Clearly she did not strike with enough force because she did not even feel him flinch.

As a last ditch effort, Natasha brought her hand up to the face to scratch at his eye. Before she could even get her hand all the way up, she felt the dizziness intensify and darkness descended upon her.

She slumped back into him and felt herself being moved out of the house and deposited into his car. She fully lost consciousness before the engine even started.

It was official. Ben had lost his mind.

That was the only thing that could explain what he was seeing.

He had to be hallucinating.

Unfortunately, if he was hallucinating, so were five detectives from IA.

They had all worked together for hours to go over the service logs for Blake, Mark, Jack, Ryan, and Tyler trying to find out who had the opportunity to pull off all of the murders and take Veronica.

Ben had gone into this knowing that they were going to find out one of his best friends was a murderer, but he still had not been prepared for the reality of it.

Hoster could tell that Ben was having trouble digesting the information. He placed a hand on Ben's shoulder to offer his support.

"He's the only one that fits. He was either off shift or working alone every time that there was action from the killer. Obviously, we're going to need more evidence to get a conviction, but you and I both know this is our guy."

Ben nodded mutely and then stood up. Heading towards the office door, Ben mumbled on the way out. "I need a minute."

The IA detectives all nodded in understanding as Ben fell through the door and into the hallway. None of them could imagine what they would do if they found out their friend had murdered so many people.

Ben did not make it far.

He leaned into the wall a few feet from the door and slid down it. He collapsed onto the ground and hung his head between his legs. A few heart wrenching sobs escaped him as he tried to gain control of his emotions. Knowing that Veronica was still in danger, Ben only allowed himself the luxury of a few seconds to mourn the loss of someone he had thought was a dear friend. Once that was over, he pulled himself up off the floor, squared his shoulders, and walked back into Hoster's office.

When he returned, Hoster and the other detectives remained silent.

Ben walked to Hoster's desk and braced himself on it. With his fury barely in control, he knew that he could not be trusted to make decisions from here on out.

He would rather have his own team in charge, but there was no time to convince them of what had been found. As much as it went against everything he had always believed, he knew that the best chance of this ending well was to let Hoster and his IA colleagues handle it from here.

He hoped that they would allow him to remain involved. In an effort to show that he planned on cooperating with whatever they decided, Ben spoke.

"Okay. We don't know how much time we have. Veronica could already be dead... And we have no idea what he's going to do next. What's your plan?"

They all shifted uncomfortably in their chairs. They knew what Ben was trying to do, but they had not come up with a plan yet. They all would have felt better with Ben taking a step back if they could tell him they had a strategy.

A young detective named Sue Jenkins was the first one to speak. "Do we know where he is right now?"

Hoster answered, "No. Like everyone else, he's been out 'searching' for Officer Taylor. He's alone, so we can't be sure where he is."

Jenkins nodded. "Alright. I think our first move should be to call a meeting at your precinct, so we know where he is. We can set it up so the superintendent visits them to give a speech or something. Not only will that pull him away from whatever he's doing right now, but it will give us a chance to follow him once he leaves. Once we find where he's keeping her and can assess the situation, we can decide what to do from there."

It was not exactly a foolproof plan, but nobody else offered a better option.

After a moment of silence, Hoster picked up his phone to start setting up the meeting at the precinct.

Jenkins turned back to Ben. "Five IA detectives showing up at your precinct will not go unnoticed. We need you to be our eyes and ears there. If you could plant a tracking device on him as well, it would help."

Ben did not argue with this plan. "Supply me with the device and I'll get it on him."

One of the other detectives left for a few minutes and then returned carrying a small box. Once the box was passed to Ben, he opened it to do a quick inventory, then left without another word.

◆ ◆ ◆

Veronica heard the click of the lock again.

Holding her breath, she tried to prepare herself.

Once again, she was momentarily blinded by the light from outside.

She could hear his thumping footsteps and something dragging behind him, but was afraid to look at it.

When she could focus her eyes and had built up her courage, Veronica looked down at the body before her. A small sob escaped when she did.

She did not need to push the hair off of their face to recognize Natasha on the ground. Some of the hair puffed out and Veronica sobbed again as she realized that her oldest friend was still breathing.

Their captor leaned down and levered Natasha up so that he could deposit her into the chair sitting across from Veronica.

Natasha was unconsciously splayed back in the seat and he quickly bound her the same way that he had bound Veronica.

Veronica strained against her chair, but between the bindings and the pain of the three bullets she had taken in the vest, she knew that she would never be able to get loose. With venom in her voice, she spoke to their captor.

"What have you done to her?"

He responded casually, as if they were talking about work. "Chloroform. I couldn't have her making a scene when she realized I wasn't taking her to keep her safe. This way, it looked like she was overcome with the news about you and I was helping her."

Veronica stared at him as she started to understand the calculating, murderous nature that he had been hiding for so long.

When he was finished tying up Natasha, he turned to Veronica.

"We're going to wait for her to wake up, and then I'm gonna have some fun. You are going to watch. Once I'm done with her, I'll go get another one of your friends. I'm going to save you for last."

Veronica's horror grew with every word he said.

She could not understand how she had not seen his insanity before.

She heard the familiar ring of his cell phone and was shocked when he pulled it out of his pocket.

Before answering, he pulled out his gun and aimed it at Natasha's head. His meaning was clear; if Veronica made a sound, he would kill Natasha.

Not willing to give up the small hope Veronica had of someone finding them before Natasha died, she kept her mouth shut as he chatted with whoever was on the other end of the call. Watching him seamlessly switch into his police officer and friend persona, Veronica began to understand how everyone could have been fooled by him for so long.

He was the best actor she had ever seen.

When the call ended, he turned to Veronica. "Looks like you're in luck. You and your friend here are going to get a short reprieve. I've been called back to the precinct. But don't get your hopes up. Whatever they're doing, it hasn't bought Tasha much time."

With those words, he holstered his gun and left the building.

Veronica sat in silence again, watching her best friend breathe, praying that someone would find them before it was too late.

Ben felt rage boiling under his skin as he sat in the briefing room at the station.

He only hoped that anyone looking at him would mistake his anger for annoyance at everyone being called into a pointless meeting while Veronica was still missing.

Ben fingered the tracking device in his pocket and attempted to regain his poker face. For this to work, his target could not have any idea that Ben knew what he was.

Ben was not listening as the police superintendent spoke at the podium. It did not matter what she was saying.

Instead, he studied the people in the room around him.

He spotted Cheyenne looking grim and desiccated by grief. Her ponytail had loosened to the point that she might as well have pulled it out, and her uniform looked so wrinkled that it was clear she had been wearing it ever since she put in on when she dressed Monday morning. She rested her elbows on the table and her chin in her hands. Here eyes were red rimmed and she chewed on her bottom lip as she took the opportunity to tune out the world and relax for a few moments.

Her partner, Ryan, was sitting next to her and would glance at her every thirty seconds or so to see how she was doing. He looked as tired as Cheyenne did. It was obvious that he was trying to pay attention to what was going on around him, but with his head bobbing up and down it was clear that he was having a hard time staying awake.

Ben wondered when the last time either one of them had slept.

He let his gaze drift and landed on Jack. Like the rest of them, Jack looked as if he had not sat since the call of an officer down came over their radios. The bone deep weariness on his face made him seem older than he was. At forty-three years old, he was still many years away from retirement, but he looked ready to walk out today if it meant that he could get some sleep.

Jack was sitting next to Tyler, who looked as heart-broken as Cheyenne had. Ben remembered that he and Erica had been hours away from their first date when she was murdered and felt his eyes start to smart with tears. Tyler's eyes were drooping as he crossed his arms on the table to use as a pillow.

Ben shifted and looked at the man standing next to him. Mark was leaning against the back wall with his arms crossed over his chest. There were dark gray circles spreading out below his eyes and his normally crisp dress shirt was partially unbuttoned with the sleeves rolled up to his elbows.

Mark caught his glance and nodded towards the podium.

Ben was meant to be listening to this.

Pretending to pay attention, Ben observed Blake as he stood next to the superintendent. Even when his daughter was in the middle of cancer treatments, Ben had not seen him this bedraggled. He knew that Blake had taken some browbeating from his superiors over this case, but he never imagined it was this bad. Blake looked so fed up that he was on the verge of demoting himself so someone else could be in charge for once.

The overwhelming emotion that he saw on the faces of everyone in the room was pain.

Ben knew now who was responsible for their pain.

It made his skin crawl to be in the same room with him and act like nothing had changed. The only thing he wanted to do was grab him and beat Veronica's location out of him.

He could not do that, but he did entertain himself by imagining it a few times.

His only comfort was knowing that they would be able to follow him and find Veronica. After that, they would prosecute him so that he would spend the rest of his days in prison.

Ben could not imagine he would have many days. Even disgraced, murderous cops did not last long in prison.

Ben would personally make sure that he wound up in general population. He might even let a couple of his snitches know who he was so word spread fast.

Ben had not been paying any attention to the superintendent's words, so it came as a shock to him when he realized she had finished speaking. People were standing and starting to stretch their muscles.

Ben quickly made his way around the room and either hugged or shook the hands of all of his friends. When he reached the killer, he used all of the skills he had acquired in his time on the force and slipped the tracking device into his pocket.

Confident the killer had not felt anything, Ben pulled away and continued around the room.

When he finished with everyone, he was pulled aside by Blake. "I'm sorry Ben. With you being here and the superintendent seeing you, I have to take you into protective custody this time."

Ben shook off the hand that was holding onto his arm. "Actually, I got a call before I got here. IA wants to talk to me about the independent investigation I ran while the case was inactive. I have to report to them now."

Blake had never wanted to take Ben in, so he let him go with no further explanation.

When Ben reached his car, he pulled out his phone and sent a text to Hoster to let him know that the tracking device was in place. He then drove back to the building where IA was housed so he could be there while the detectives were watching the monitors to see where Veronica was being held.

What was the point of that? Such a waste of time!

Nobody was listening to anything that was said in that room. I actually caught a couple people napping in there.

It's no wonder they haven't even come close to

catching me. Even if any of them were smart enough to find me, they would get stuck following the orders of people like the superintendent.

Why in God's name did they think it was a good idea to pull everyone off the streets to give a speech when there was an officer missing?

I suppose I shouldn't be complaining. Them doing shit like that confirms that I have nothing to worry about.

I have two women trussed up in my garage, but they're still never gonna catch me.

Ben was only watching the screen for about twenty minutes before he jumped up and started yelling.

"That arrogant, fucking son of a bitch!"

The men and women around him all flinched away at his outburst.

"I know exactly where he's keeping her! The fucking bastard!"

Hoster forced him to sit and calm himself. "I need you to explain what you're talking about."

Ben breathed deeply for a few seconds and then spoke again; thinly veiled fury lacing his words. "He took her home. He's at his own goddamn house!"

Hoster looked uncomfortable for a moment. "Are you sure? If we get this wrong we'll lose our best chance at finding Veronica."

Ben nodded confidently. "This is the same man who used to email us videos of him abducting and burying women alive. He obviously thinks he's smarter than us and we've given him no reason to believe otherwise. Besides, he's still on shift. Why else would he go home if he wasn't keeping her there?"

All of the detectives concurred with this statement and Jenkins pulled out her cell phone. "We were planning while you were gone. I've still got a few people on the force who will talk to me even though I joined IA. One of them is in SWAT. I'm gonna call him and get his team to meet us over there. I had a feeling we were going to need their help. I already let him know what was going on while we were waiting for you to plant the tracker. He's with us for whatever we need. I just have to give him the location."

She spoke to her friend for a moment, giving him the address and then hung up.

They collectively took a second to settle their minds and consider what they could find in that garage. Simultaneously, they stood and moved towards the door.

Veronica had been silently crying for an hour when Natasha woke up from her chloroform induced sleep. She watched as her best friend tried desperately to break free of the zip ties holding her to her chair and eventually gave up.

Guilt washed over Veronica as she realized that Natasha would be safe now if they had not been friends.

She was in the middle of sobbing out an apology to her when Natasha cut her off.

"Oh, shut up, Ronnie! You and I both know this was not your fault. Nobody could have predicted any of this happening. Besides, imagine how much both of our lives would have sucked if we weren't' friends."

In spite of the situation they were in, Veronica started laughing. "I swear, if you start singing that Kelly Clarkson song, I'll start screaming!"

This got Natasha laughing as well. "You know you love that song!"

Veronica was going to respond, but they heard the door unlocking again. All laughter died instantly.

Looking at each other, they knew what was about to come.

Natasha tensed in her seat, then looked at Veronica. "You know I love you, right? No matter what."

Veronica nodded and started crying. "I love you, too."

The door swung open and they heard the slow, purposeful steps of their captor. When he came into view, they both took a deep breath to steady themselves. He ignored both of them as he walked to the camera that had been lying forgotten in the corner. He set it up on the tripod and pointed it at Veronica.

Veronica shuddered, but did not say anything. His insanity did not surprise her anymore. She felt more tears fill her eyes again as she watched him pull a knife out of his back pocket.

Without a word, he systematically cut away Natasha's shirt and pants so she was left in just her underwear.

Natasha had cringed every time the knife came near her, but there was nothing she could do to get away.

When he was done, he set the knife down next to her and pulled out his gun. He set it next to the knife and then pulled a lighter out of another pocket.

When the items were lined up on the floor next to Natasha, he turned to Veronica.

"So, where should I start? You have three options. I will either use the knife to scar up her face, use the gun to take out her ball and socket joints, or the lighter to burn her arms. Your choice."

Veronica stared at him aghast as she understood the implications of what he was saying. "What happens if I refuse to pick?"

He grinned evilly and moved closer to her. He put his face right in front of hers and spoke so softly she could barely hear him. "There are much worse things that I can do to her, and I promise you that I will do them all if you do not chose. Then I'll do the same terrible things to everyone else that I bring in here. I've been a cop for a long time. I've seen some terrible things and I will do them all to your friends if you don't play nice."

He watched the color drain from her face and then stepped back. "So...choose. Where do I start?"

Veronica's mouth hung open as she tried to make herself chose.

Her mind was screaming that this whole situation was wrong and she had to be dreaming. She wished like hell that she could wake up, but it was no use.

In an authoritative voice, he spoke again. "You have ten second to decide."

Veronica wanted to scream.

Natasha caught her eye and then spoke for the first time since the door had opened. "It's okay. Choose. I don't want to know what will happen if you don't."

The possibilities flew through Veronica's mind. She wanted to find the option that would inflict the least amount of lasting damage and take the longest to perform.

With two seconds left to the deadline, Veronica finally spoke. "The lighter. Use the lighter."

He smiled at her like he was proud. "Okay."

Veronica could feel acid burning in her throat as he leaned down and picked up the lighter.

He turned and looked at her. "Are you sure?"

She could not make herself speak again so she nodded and stared at the floor. She heard the flick of the lighter and squeezed her eyes shut.

Instantly, she could feel him in her face again.

In the same low, quiet voice he had used before, he spoke again. "That's cheating. You can't close your eyes. You have to watch."

She reluctantly opened her eyes again and looked past him to Natasha.

"I'm sorry."

Natasha looked afraid, but she was not going to break. Not in front of him.

Kneeling down, he turned to Natasha and brought the lighter up again. He flicked it on and the flame bloomed to life.

It was nowhere near her but Natasha had already broken out in sweat. Silent tears started to fall down her face as the lighter moved closer to her left hand. When it was within an inch of her pinky finger, Natasha began to shake.

Veronica could not take it anymore and began to speak. "Why are you doing this? She never did anything to you. I'm the one you hate.

Hurt me instead."

He lowered the lighter and faced her again. "Don't you get it yet? This is hurting you. This is hurting you more than any physical violence I could do to you. Now. No more interrupting. We're just getting to the good part."

He spun back to Natasha and slowly brought the lighter to her left hand.

Within seconds Natasha was screaming in pain.

Veronica nearly threw up as the scent of burning flesh mixed with the smell of the dried blood in her nostrils.

It felt like the screaming lasted for hours.

He would bring the lighter to her hand and burn a piece of it. Then he would take the lighter away and wait for Natasha to stop. Once she had quieted down, he would start burning her again.

Natasha's entire left hand and arm leading up to her elbow was covered in angry red welts now and the whole room smelled of charred skin.

Satisfied with the work that he had done on Natasha's left side, he stood up and moved to the knife and gun that were still on the floor.

"Time for another choice."

Veronica could not stand the idea of putting Natasha through any more pain.

Knowing it was not likely to work, Veronica threw all of her weight to her right side.

When she felt the left side of the chair leave the ground she twisted violently to pick up the third leg. At that point, all of her weight was balanced on one leg of the chair.

The joints around that leg of the chair gave way and she felt herself falling face first towards the ground.

At the last second, Veronica realized that the chair had broken enough that she could now move her right arm. She used it to stop her fall and shove herself onto her back.

She quickly forced her left leg straight while lifting her arms above her head. This succeeded in freeing all of her limbs.

Vicious triumph surged through her as she scissor kicked to a standing position.

Suddenly, the garage was filled with sunlight as the large garage door was ripped away. The smaller door to the side exploded open at the exact same time.

Knowing police procedure and recognizing the SWAT uniforms of the men and women pouring through the doors, he knew that he would be lucky to get off one shot.

He had better make it count.

As fast as he could, he snatched up the gun still lying on the floor next to him and lifted it. The safety was already off, so all he had to do was aim and fire.

He knew that the moment the gun was pointed at either of his victims, he would be shot, so he did not have enough time to aim properly.

Officer Jack Monroe pointed his gun at Veronica and pulled the trigger.

Less than a second later, a member of the SWAT team opened fire on him.

It only took another second for Jack to hit the ground, already dead from a shot to the head.

Natasha was screaming loudly, but Veronica was deadly quiet.

There was blood pooling under her and a large stain of it spreading across her torso. As she was no longer wearing her bullet proof vest, this shot had hit its mark.

Two police officers ran forward to catch Veronica as she fell. They gently laid her on the ground, while another cut Natasha free from her chair.

Within minutes, two sets of paramedics entered the garage. The first went to Veronica and wasted no time loading her onto a stretcher. The other went to Natasha and moved more slowly and gently in an attempt to keep her calm.

She was on the verge of insisting that she

be allowed to ride in Veronica's ambulance, but they quashed that idea before she could even voice it.

No one would be allowed to ride in that ambulance. They were going to need all of the room they could get in order to take care of Veronica.

In the end, she meekly allowed them to help her onto their stretcher and wheel her out of the garage. When she got outside, she could see Ben fighting with two men she had never seen before.

He was trying to get to Veronica, but was being held back from running to her.

Natasha yelled to him, "Ben! Ride in mine. You can find her at the hospital once we get there."

She glared at the paramedics before they could protest.

When Ben heard her yell, he spun and stared at her in surprise. Clearly, he had not been expecting to see her there.

In any other situation, she might have laughed at the look on his face. As it was, she gave him a grim smile and waved him over.

Ben hurried to them and launched himself into the ambulance seconds after she had been loaded into it.

The ride to the hospital was tense as the paramedics started to treat Natasha's arm and Ben tried to reign in his panic.

When they reached the hospital, Ben made sure Natasha was going to be alright before he tried to search for Veronica.

No amount of cajoling on his part would make the hospital staff let him into her room. She was being stabilized and prepped for surgery. Her doctors could not afford to be distracted by a loved one, even if that loved one was a police officer.

Ben was left to sit in the waiting room while they worked on her.

Eventually, word got out that Natasha and Veronica were there and officers from all over the city started to arrive to lend their support and wait for word.

Ben and his friends from the station formed a small knot in the corner as he explained to them what Jack had done and how they had found him. No one wanted to believe any of it, but the fact that Jack had shot Veronica when the SWAT team had found him was irrefutable evidence.

Once Ben had told the whole story, the group disbanded and spread out in the room as they continued to wait for news and tried to come to terms with what had happened.

EPILOGUE

For the second time in her life, Veronica woke to the sound of a beeping heart monitor.

This time, she recognized the sound straight away. She felt a panic attack threatening to roll over her as she realized where she was.

She tried to sit up in bed, but screaming pain ripped through her so she let herself drop back down.

She tried to remember how she got there, but everything after the door to the garage opening was fuzzy. Questions were swirling around in her head, but she was afraid of the answers to most of them.

When she had gained control of herself again, she noticed a weight on her left leg. She looked down and found Ben sitting in a chair next to her. His upper body was supported on the bed and his head was resting on her leg.

Fast asleep, he looked so relaxed.

She wondered how long she had been here and if Ben had been by her side the whole time. Before she could stop herself, Veronica reached down and ran her fingers through his hair.

He tensed and woke up with a start. Ben's head shot up so quickly that she was afraid he might tip out of his chair.

When he realized that she was awake, Ben threw himself at Veronica.

Normally, Veronica would enjoy the force with which he was kissing her, but with the pain currently radiating through her she had to make him stop. She gently pushed him away and he seemed to get the hint.

Once she could finally get Ben to stop staring at her and expressing his excitement at her waking up, she finally got to speak.

"Is Natasha okay? How is her arm? What happened to Jack?"

Ben had known these would be the first questions she asked.

"Natasha's doing fine. Probably gonna need a lot of therapy, but she's going to be okay. The doctors say that she's going to have a lot of scarring on her hand and arm, but there shouldn't be any permanent damage to her dexterity. And...uh...Jack is dead."

Veronica sucked in a breath and met his eyes. "Tell me you did not kill him."

Ben wanted to be offended, but he understood why she would jump to that conclusion. "No. They wouldn't even let me near the building. The SWAT team leader took one look at me at the scene and told me I could stay, but if I tried to enter with his team, he would lock me in a squad car."

Veronica giggled at that. "I like this guy already."

Ben lightly punched her shoulder.

Veronica feigned more pain than she felt and spoke dramatically. "That's right! Punch the injured girl! Speaking of which, what happened to me?"

Ben looked down at her torso. "When SWAT breached the building, Jack had time to shoot once. Fortunately, he didn't have time to aim. He didn't hit anything massively important, but you still needed to have surgery to repair the damage. Looks like you're gonna be going on another medical leave of absence. At least this time it won't be a year long."

Veronica hummed noncommittally.

For the next two hours, She asked questions and Ben told her all about how they had figured out Jack was the killer and what they had done to get her back.

When Ben told her that he had willingly walked into the office of an IA detective, she burst out laughing.

Ben understood her response; he had never exactly been supportive of them in the past.

"I know, I know. It was a bit out of character for me. But these guys were good. I might have to be nice to them in the future."

When Ben finished his story, Veronica told him what had happened to her in the garage.

Eventually, they both finished their stories, but Veronica had more questions.

"How is everyone else doing? How did they take the news."

Ben looked grim. "They're doing about as well as can be expected. Blake resigned. What with him being Jack's superior officer, the PR asshats were probably gonna throw him under the bus anyways. He doesn't mind so much. Says that he gets to spend more time with his daughter now. Cheyenne and Tyler are in rough shape. Chey's gonna have to find a new roommate because she can't afford the apartment by herself. I think Tyler is considering moving in with her, but only if they move to a new apartment. The whole idea of sleeping in Erica's old room doesn't sit well with him. Ryan is as stoic as always. He's been good at supporting Cheyenne through all of this. There's a rumor going around that he might be tapped for the new staff sergeant position now that Blake is leaving. Oh, and that rookie, Sam. She transferred to a new precinct. I think she was afraid of being judged because she's been riding with Jack a lot lately. Mark is alright. He's been staying at my place to take care of Charlotte and Ace while I was here. Before you protest; you know that he is good with the animals and he does not mind. I think he likes my house better than his own."

Veronica had remained silent as he told her about everyone.

Ben was staring down at his lap and playing with the edge of her blanket.

Veronica grabbed his chin and made him look up at her. "And how are you doing?"

Ben took a deep breath. "I'm...fine. I'm glad this is all over and we don't have to deal with a trial now. The families of all of his victims know what happened. We caught Erica's murderer before she was even buried, and we got to you and Tasha before Jack killed either one of you. I'm glad you're awake, and the doctors say that you are going to be fine. I'm looking forward to getting back to work. Although, it might be awhile before that happens."

At Veronica's quizzical look, he had to explain his last comment.

"They've assigned a shrink to come in and give a thorough evaluation of everyone that was close with Jack. They aren't looking for more psychopaths or anything; they just want to make sure everyone is in the right frame of mind before they carry a gun again. Because I was not only friends with Jack, but dating one of his victims, they are taking an especially close look at me. They're probably gonna put you through the ringer too. That is...if you want to come back, of course."

Veronica flashed him a radiant smile. " Oh, you can count on it. I'm coming back."

ACKNOWLEDGE-MENT

This book would never have been written without the invaluable assistance of Cheyenne Bramwell. Not only did she encourage me to start writing; she always helped me when I wrote myself into a corner, and stepped in as my editor when I could not do it myself.

ABOUT THE AUTHOR

Tabitha J Arment has been a story addict her whole life and is excited to be sharing her own stories with the world. She lives in Arizona with her surprisingly affectionate cat, Simon, and her endlessly energetic puppy, Ella. Yes, they are both named after characters. Guess which. Tabitha is an unapologetic nerd who enjoys doing choreographed fights with lightsabers (or any weapons, really), playing DnD with her friends, and travelling around taking tons of pictures. She has a bucket list as long as this story full of places she wants to see. Thank you for helping her with that by purchasing this book.

Contact her on-
Twitter: @tjaauthor
Gmail: tjaauthor@gmail.com
Website: tabithajarment.com

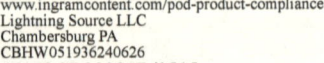